Broken Scrimshaw

One man's search for God and family
A Novel

Lane Metcalf

Work of Fiction

This is a work of fiction. Historical events, dates, places, and names of persons are either imaginary or are used fictitiously. Any resemblance to actual persons, living or dead, or events is purely coincidental.

Broken Scrimshaw

A story of one man's search for God and family.

All rights reserved

Copyright © 2024 Lane Metcalf

No part of this publication may be reproduced, stored in a retrieval system, or transmitted in any way by any means—electronic, mechanical, photocopy, recording, or otherwise—without the prior permission of the copyright holder, except as provided by USA copyright law.

Unless otherwise noted, all Scriptures are taken from the Holy Bible, New International Version, Copyright © 1973, 1978, 1984 by the International Bible Society. Used by permission of Zondervan Publishing House. The "NIV" and "New International Version" trademarks are registered in the United States Patent and Trademark Office by the International Bible Society.

BOOKS BY LANE METCALF

To Set a Prisoner Free
A story of rescue and betrayal at sea, and
God's love for all His imperfect children.
Book one of the Liberer series.

A light for the Tower
(previously entitled) The Jungle and The Tower
A gripping story of danger, devotion,
and dependence on the power of God.
Book two of the Liberer series.

Broken Scrimshaw
A story of one man's search
for God and family
in early America.

Table Of Content

Dedication i
Acknowledgments iii
Prologue v
Chapter 1 1
Chapter 2 22
Chapter 3 36
Chapter 4 49
Chapter 5 68
Chapter 6 87
Chapter 7 102
Chapter 8 121
Chapter 9 134
Chapter 10 152
Chapter 11 169
Chapter 12 186
Chapter 13 202
Chapter 14 220
Chapter 15 236
Epilogue 246
Historical Note 249

DEDICATION

This book is dedicated to my great-grandchildren. Elijah, who shares optimism and love with every smile; Ella Kate, who loves life enough to try anything and to fight against all odds for what's right; Emery, who plays hard and loves family even harder. And Everly, our toddler, whose sidelong glances unveil her wonder about me but whose fleeting smiles tell me she'll share her love when she's ready.

ACKNOWLEDGMENTS

I thank Kim Schlatter and Rebecca High for reviewing my drafts of this novel and for their suggestions and editorial assistance. Much of the polishing of this work is due to their patience with me and their commitment to excellence, traits in which they both excel. Morgan Schlatter provided insightful guidance during the early development of the storyline and especially on composing the prologue. She helped finetune my theme and the ultimate direction of this story. Betty Metcalf's reading and editing greatly improved both the tale and the telling of it.

I also thank the staff at Writers Publishing Lab, Lucas, Ben, and Parkar, for their help, patience, and skills and for sharing their creativity. This story is partly a work of all of them.

I offer a special thanks to Mark Simpson, a former pastor of mine, who years ago delivered a sermon based on Psalm 51:12, which I have never forgotten and which planted the seed in my mind for this tale I am about to tell.

PROLOGUE

Lasswade Parish, Scotland, 1811.

In the flickering light of his candle lamp, Badin Grahame used pickax and chisel to pry another chunk of the inky-black mineral loose from the wall in front of him. Squirming backward on his belly in the shallow passage, he raked his harvest toward his feet as far as he could reach. Muriel gathered the results of his labors into her creel as he slithered back to work the coal seam again. When the rock above him groaned, he glanced back at his wife, but she had lugged her burden and lamp out of sight, leaving inky blackness in her wake.

Badin had heard the earth grumble too often during his twenty-six years in the pits. It terrified him his first day underground—one day after his tenth birthday. He'd never been able to ignore it since. Most colliers working the faces of the black seams paid no attention or made every effort not to let it show, as Badin learned to do.

The coal bearers new to the job, like his fourteen-year-old daughter, Bridget, were not so ashamed to show fear. Even Muriel, along with many of the other grown women, expressed dislike of the occasional complaints from the tons of earth and rock over their heads. He often wondered what his father heard before the earth buried him in one of the Duddingston Parish pits ten years ago.

Even though Muriel had worked in the pits as a coal bearer for her own father since she turned eleven years of age, she cried when he told her he needed Bridget to help him make his allotment. She knew it must be so if the family were to survive on the meager pay of a collier. Any collier with family needed them to help, and if a man had no family, he had to hire his own coal bearers, further reducing his own earnings by a substantial sum.

When Muriel was not gathering Badin's harvest, she worked in the stair pit, carrying full creels, or baskets of coal, up stout ladders six days every week. After Badin's injury last year, and before he could return to the pit, she carried coal twelve non-stop hours every day for other colliers. Her back and legs cried in agony every minute of those three weeks, but not as badly as her heart now ached for her daughter.

Bridget was smart; the master at the school often asked her to help teach the younger children their numbers and letters. She even had her one sibling, Lansdale, reading and writing well for his age. Badin himself depended on his wife and daughter to do what little reading and numbering he needed.

Muriel hoped and prayed their daughter's education, meager as it was, could help her avoid the coal pits. But as with many a hopeful mother, the bitter reality and disappointment of life in the Scottish coal fields came all too soon.

Lansdale, or Lanny, as Bridget called her precocious younger brother, would soon be eight years of age. McDowell had already done what the other pit owners often did for the children of their bonded colliers. He had given Badin an *arles*, a new pair of shoes for Lanny, to persuade the lad to work for him when he became strong enough to endure pit labor.

The *arles* was not a legal contract but was as good as a written guarantee a job awaited the lad when he entered into a bondage agreement. During the bond period, fixed by the Scottish National Coal Labor Law at a maximum of seven years, the owner could use the worker as he saw fit or hire him out to other mine owners. The worker was bound for the duration unless the owner voided the contract. It had been that way in the Scottish coalfields since the law of 1799 freed colliers from permanent bondage. Badin accepted it as just. Such traditions, augmented by law, shaped the lives of thousands of families throughout the coalfields of Scotland.

Muriel was one of the growing factions who whispered among themselves about the evil of the law. They felt a man should be able to work the pits if he wanted but also to be free to walk away when he chose. Badin would not allow any such talk in his house—that was not the way of the past. Even his father and grandfathers had accepted bondage as a way of life—it provided livelihood. His position didn't change Muriel's opinion—she didn't see it that way. She thought it was as good as legalized slavery. But, neither did she see any way out of it nor any other way to feed and clothe her family.

Another series of pops heralded another groan—louder and longer than Badin had ever heard. He stopped working the coalface and turned an ear to the cries of earth overhead. When the rock around him started crackling, he dropped his tools, grabbed his candle lamp, and wormed his way backward on his belly.

By the time he reached the place where the passage became wide enough for him to turn around, he knew it was bad. He scrambled on hands and knees until the passage heightened, and he could run in a crouch. He had to make the stair pit and warn Bridget and Muriel. If his fears were true, their only chance would be to drop their creels and clamber up the ladders as fast as possible.

Badin's passage intersected with a larger drift, or passage, at the edge of a stoop, a column of unmined coal the colliers had left in place to support the pit roof. One of the two men running out of the drift collided with Badin. The man went sprawling, dropping his own lamp, and sending Badin's crashing against the drift wall. Both candle flames snuffed out. In the near darkness, Badin grabbed the stoop candle. Guided by its faint light, he reached for the other man's hand.

"Grab, McChord; grab and run, man!"

McChord scrambled to his knees, reached for Badin's outstretched hand but tripped over his own feet and flew headfirst to the coal dust and debris-laden floor.

"Oh God, Badin, help me."

Badin delayed his own flight long enough to grab McChord's arm and jerk him to his feet. Both men fled the increasing complaints of the mass of rock over their heads.

"Firedamp! Firedamp!"

Badin's blood chilled at the terror in those voices and at the words every collier dreaded. He turned wide eyes toward the men fleeing the depths of the pit in time to see an eerie glow fill the entire passage. A split-second later, the gas and coal dust explosion blasted him into the black walls of McDowell Pit Number 2. He never felt the tons of rock break loose over his head.

CHAPTER 1

Henrysville, Indian Territory of the United States, 1850

I awoke to severe pain in my chest and back. Each breath brought such hurt that I might suffocate rather than endure the agony. Even if I had the ability to stop breathing and ease the pain, I knew I'd never do it. I'd fight to my very last breath. A relentless will had kept me alive this long. My driven spirit would never let me surrender—not yet anyway—for I had not yet finished what I had to do.

My surroundings puzzled me. A small room, not unlike some of the rooming houses I had seen in Saint Louis and farther east, looked to be my current quarters, though I had no memory of how I came to be here. The light in the room came from a wide, short window near the ceiling. It was such that no one could see in, and no one could see out. It gave a sinister feeling to the place, too much like a New Orleans jail cell for my tastes.

A narrow chest of drawers, covered with a white cloth with two stacks of smaller folded cloths on top, stood against the wall beyond the foot of my bed. On my right, a straight-backed chair and a small desk crowded into the space between the bed and the wall. Two coal oil lamps with polished brass reflectors sat on the desk. Their presence filled me with dread. They reminded me of vultures, perching side by side, biding their time for an impending feast of dead flesh. I had seen similar lamps in ships of war and army field hospitals. I suspected them to be a part of every medical facility.

A low washstand with an enormous basin sunken into its top stood against the other wall. More of the white cloths hung across its towel rack. There was no pitcher for water on the washstand, but there was a small, flat-bottomed bowl with a curved handle on one side. Its size would allow a person to hold and move it about with one hand. I had seen similar bowls fashioned of pottery. This one was of pewter, not common in army field hospitals. Its owner would no doubt be a practitioner of its intended diabolical use. On the chest of drawers, a small pitcher as used for beverages, a drinking cup, and two stoppered brown glass bottles, which I assumed to be for some patent medicine or nostrum, stood next to another stack of cloths.

What I could see assured me this was not a rooming house. I was certain I lay in a hospital of some kind or a doctor's house, with all sorts of barbaric surgical and other tools lurking in the drawers of that odd chest. I was far too acquainted with warfare and its bloody companion—the butchery practiced by surgeons aboard warships at sea and in army field hospitals as they fought their own desperate battles to save the lives of wounded men.

This was the last place I would have chosen to be.

I lay still for a moment to take account of my faculties and limbs and to assess the damage to my body that would cause so much pain. Try as I might, I could not remember what I had done to cause me to be in this place. I found if I moved my shoulders and arms slowly, the pain did not increase. In fact, as I moved to improve my awkward position, the pain lessened. In a few moments, with some gentle movements and probing with my left hand, I concluded I had sustained nothing more damaging than several cracked ribs. My awkward position aggravated the injury and precipitated most of the pain in my chest.

Relentless throbbing permeated throughout my entire body from the peculiar numbing ache in my right leg. The hurt felt deep. It might be a severe bruise, but I dared not sit up to check for fear of bringing back the stabbing pains in my ribs.

I had suffered and lived through worse. And this place, it boded me no good. I resolved to get out of here. First, I had to find what had happened to my clothes; I could see no sign of them, nor was there a trunk or armoire wherein they might be stored, such as I'd seen in the better rooming houses of St. Louis. I had no idea where to begin searching.

With a start of fear, I clutched at my throat, sending new daggers of pain through my chest, but pain was of no concern at this moment. Relief overwhelmed me as my fingers found the buffalo-hide strap securing the deerskin pouch around my neck. Practiced touch assured me my broken piece of whale tooth was still inside the pouch.

Whoever removed my clothing and put this ridiculous nightshirt on me must have assumed I had adopted the practice, common to plains Indians, of wearing a medicine bag. Whatever the reason, they had the good sense not to remove the one thing I cherished as much as life itself.

My moment of relief soon died. My reason for living might well have been taken from me years ago, yet this fragment of carved tooth, once a weapon in the mouth of a great sperm whale, had led me on a search of many years and thousands of miles—even to kill a man for it. Uncertainty of my eternal destiny because of that indiscretion discomfited me. But for now, I had to live to again see the face and touch the hand of the one who had given me the tooth.

I had to find her—both her and our son, whom I had never seen.

Ignoring the pain in my chest, I pushed the blanket down to my waist. Any movement brought new discomfort, but I was determined. I flipped the blanket farther toward the foot of the bed and started to swing my legs from under it.

At the first movement of my right leg, I yelped. Excruciating pain almost caused me to black out. I threw my head back on the pillow and grimaced to regain control of myself. My leg felt as if an eight-head team of mules was trampling white-hot coals into it.

"What is it?" A woman's muffled cry caused me to jerk my head off the pillow and open my eyes as the door to my room swung open.

Her examination darted from my head to my feet. I stared back. Though I tried, I could not speak a word. I began to wonder if the pain had driven me mad, for there stood my Keevah.

I lay back, gasping for air and trying to stop the pain wracking my body. But my physical pain was not the worst. In an instant, I knew I had been mistaken. Her few words revealed she was not Keevah, for she spoke strongly, like an American frontier woman. Her speech offered no hint of the delicate and enchanting Irish lilt I had longed to hear for many years.

"What are you doing? Don't get up!"

Her voice softened. "You shouldn't even try to move; you've been severely injured." She moved the chair close to my bed and sat.

By now, I recovered from the shock and turned my head toward her. Compassion evidenced itself in her face. But the pain in my heart would not lessen, for even as close as she was, she still reminded me of Keevah—the same red hair that chose its own time to behave or to be wild and emerald eyes as I'd seen in no woman but Keevah. Her delicate lips and those tiny freckles on her nose could have been Keevah's, but this woman was younger than Keevah by at least twenty years. After a few moments, my breadth of vision grew to take in other details about her. She was about the same height, though more robust than Keevah, and had seen much sun and weather—as had almost every frontier woman.

She was also very pregnant.

"What is your name?" She spoke softly, as if to ease my pain.

"Grayhawk," I said. "Where am I?"

"You are in our doctor's home, Mr. Grayhawk. This is his treatment room."

"Why am I here?"

"You don't know?" Her expression mirrored none of the skepticism I saw flicker across her green eyes. She studied me for a quiet moment.

Any recent memory evaded me. I shook my head.

"Do you remember the lumber wagon?"

"I remember seeing one after I left the hotel dining room. The driver wasn't paying attention—his load was shifting."

"Ah, that is a start. And do you remember the boys chasing the wagon? They were holding sticks against the wheel spokes to make noise. Do you remember that?"

"The next thing I remember is right now—in this room."

"You pushed a little Indian boy out of the way when the lumber started sliding off the wagon; you saved his life; a lot of lumber fell on you. That's how you were injured. You've become quite a hero in our little town, Mr. Grayhawk."

I watched her take a small notebook and pencil from a pocket in her dress, the design of which struck me as utilitarian with a hint of elegance. I thought the refinement unusual for the frontier.

"What are you doing?"

"I want to make some notes so I get everything correct."

"You work for the doctor? Where is he?"

"My heavens, no! I prefer to avoid the sight of blood. My name is Ciara Franklin. I write for The Kansas Herald, our newspaper for this area. In fact, the only non-Indian published newspaper in this part of the Indian Territory. Jack the barber, and Sergeant Kirby carried you in here."

"Sergeant?"

"Yes, Sergeant Kirby of the U.S. Army. Anyway, when I heard what happened, I ran over to get the story, at least as fast as a woman in my condition could run. I could have taken my time. You certainly know how to keep a lady waiting; you've either been unconscious or sleeping since yesterday."

"I'm no hero, and there'll be no stories about me in any newspaper. I'm getting out of here. Where are my clothes?"

"Mr. Grayhawk, you are badly hurt. You can't leave; you shouldn't even try moving. That is a serious injury to your leg. Jack feels certain a bone is broken, perhaps crushed, and you may have some broken ribs too. You've also lost a lot of blood from that scalp wound. You're in no shape to go anywhere."

At her mention of it, I noticed the pressure on my head, pinching like a shrunken hatband. With care, to avoid further aggravating the pain in my chest, I raised my left arm to feel for myself. A large bandage encircled my head. I could feel considerable discomfort as I fingered the thick pad extending from above my right eye to halfway above my right ear.

"Who did this? I asked, pointing to the bandage.

"Jack the barber. He stopped the bleeding, stitched the wound, and bandaged it for you. He was the closest thing we had to a doctor until Doctor Kendrick came to us. The doctor is currently taking care of business relating to his previous practice. He'll return in a few days."

"Return? From where?"

"Our town brought him here from St. Louis. We provided him with this house, equipped just the way he wanted it. It cost us a lot of money, but it's the most modern in the entire Indian Territory. It will be worth it. We are a growing community in an area fast on its way to becoming a United States Territory. It will be only a matter of time before we become the state of Kansas. We need a doctor. Dr. Kendrick was educated back east—in Philadelphia if I remember correctly."

I eyed the pewter bowl. "He wasn't an army field doctor." I turned my attention to her and demanded, "Was he?"

"Why no, not that I am aware. Why do you ask?"

"I've seen too much of doctors' handiwork. Small bowls like that are used for bloodletting."

"I understand that's a common medical practice to rid the body of bad blood and toxins so it can heal faster. Almost all the better-educated doctors do it as a matter of treatment."

"Not all doctors, at least not those who've treated men wounded in battle—they've seen too many men bleed to death. Why take blood from someone who needs it to stay alive?"

"Well, I can't answer that question, Mr. Grayhawk. I'm not a doctor, but I'm sure they know what is best for their patients."

"Not when I'm the patient; no one is taking my blood unless I say so. And no one is sawing my leg off, either. I've seen too many wounded men lose arms and legs for no good reason."

My resolve strengthened; I was leaving, even if I had to search and find my clothes myself. Ignoring the pain in my ribs and the young woman's protests, I raised myself on my elbows and slid the upper part of my body toward the edge of the bed away from her. My injured leg hurt, but the pain was bearable by exercising more care than I had before. Convinced I could leave on my own, I continued easing myself to the edge of the bed.

Bearing my weight with my left arm caused less pain in my chest. I raised myself to a sitting position near the edge of the bed and slid my left leg, the good one, over the edge of the stuffed mattress. My injured leg protested. I chose to ignore it and pushed higher to swing both legs off the edge of the bed.

A bolt of pain ripped through my body like a cannonshot. My left hand slipped from under me as I felt myself toppling over the edge of the mattress. It felt as though my right leg was being ripped off. My gut twisted in agony. My vision began to narrow as if I were looking into an ever-tightening tunnel. Everything at the end of the tunnel brightened until I couldn't make out anything in the room. I remember falling and reaching for the vanishing image of the woman's outstretched hand. I do not know if I grabbed it, but I vaguely recall a woman screaming.

I do not remember hitting the floor.

***

A distant-sounding female voice, one I had not heard before, seeped through the fog in my brain.

"He's waking, Ciara."

I hurt all over. My body recoiled with every throb, starting in my leg and spreading from there. Amidst my confusion and pain, it was all I could do to keep from retching. After a few moments, I realized I was in bed. I opened my eyes to see the red-haired woman looking down at me. I tried to return her gaze but had to squeeze my eyes shut from pain. When I opened my eyes again, she was sitting in the chair on my right.

Another woman stood beside the bed on my left. About the same age as the red-haired woman, she wore a full apron over a simple print dress, much like any American frontier woman would wear. Her slender body and erect posture may have made her seem taller than she was. Squared shoulders gave her an almost angular appearance. Though her expression showed concern, there was nothing about her to clue me as to her tribe. But she was clearly a full-blooded Indian.

She held out a small glass to me and moved a hand under my pillow to help lift my head.

"Would you care for a drink?"

Her pronunciation was perfect.

Pushing my head deeper into the pillow and tucking my chin, I tried to focus on the glass in her hand.

"It is water," she said.

With her help, I lifted my head and tasted the water. It was good. I took the glass in my own hand and drained it. The coolness of the water lessened the throb in my leg, or at least made it tolerable.

"Thank you."

She nodded silent acceptance. I turned to the red-haired woman. "Mrs. Franklin—"

"Ciara. Everyone calls me Ciara."

"Ciara. I must confess; you win. I'm obviously unable to leave on my own right now."

"I'm not trying to win anything, Mr. Grayhawk. We are all trying to help you. Let me introduce Hesed." She gestured to the Indian woman. "She works for me; she is my friend and companion."

I looked at Hesed, then back to Ciara. "Did you two put me back in bed? I remember starting to fall."

"You did fall. We had to get Jack to help lift you. His barbershop is a few buildings down the street." She pulled her chair close to the bed, leaned over, and put a hand on my shoulder. "Mr. Grayhawk, please understand. You are seriously injured. We are simply trying to help you the best we know how."

I nodded. I could do little else under the circumstances.

"Are you hungry? You haven't eaten since yesterday, assuming you ate at the hotel."

I shook my head.

"You need rest. We'll leave you alone." She rose and stepped toward the open door. Then stopped and looked back. "I'll check on you later. Hesed will bring food when you're ready." She turned to leave.

"Wait. Understand this, Mrs. Franklin, or Ciara, or whatever you want to be called. I do not, I repeat, do not want any doctor butchering on me. I have seen what they do."

Her brow began to furrow as her eyes studied me. After several silent moments, she spoke. "We can talk after you've rested and eaten."

Her words were gentle but resolute, much like Keevah's would have been. I could not ignore the resemblance. Then she spun on her heel and left. I saw the stiffening of her back before she vanished from sight. Her companion followed, closing the door behind her.

The Indian woman puzzled me. Where did she learn to speak English better than most men in this country? And how did an Indian woman ever come by that name, Hesed? I had not heard the word for years, yet from the depths of memories and aspirations long lost to me, my mind had dredged up its ancient meaning.

I pressed my head back into the pillow and gritted my teeth. Numbness soon spread throughout my body, and I wondered about the Indian woman's water. My mind found no peace from it. How could I have gotten myself into such a bind? And this red-haired woman who reminded me so much of my Keevah, and who wanted to write about me, all the while attempting to convince me she was merely trying to help. I didn't want a doctor; couldn't she understand? And how could she help by resurrecting those tortured memories that had haunted me for so many years?

The Indian woman's water began to accomplish its purpose. Drowsiness began overtaking me, but this was not the time to sleep. I had much to think about and plans to make. I closed my eyes for a few moments of rest. Before many minutes, I became aware of a gentle ship-like motion of my bed. I soon became accustomed to the lifting and falling of the entire room, a sensation of primal rhythm I had once embraced—of strong swells in open seas.

I was young then, very young, but I have not forgotten. I willingly tuned my mind and body to the peace it offered. A few moments of rest would be good.

Even as I drifted toward sleep, I could feel it coming. It would be bittersweet. The memory and pain would linger for days. Yet, I had never been able to stop it, probably because even in my waking moments, I refused to let go of the cause.

Whenever it happened, it was always the same, every detail exactly as I remembered, and it always took me back to ten days after I turned thirteen years old. I hated struggling through every particular of the dream, yet I loved the memory that prompted it— without it, I would have no reason to live.

Glasgow, Scotland, 1816

The dream always started with me standing on the quay at Glasgow, shivering as the early morning mist penetrated my clothing. At Master McDowell's word, his two daughters and I followed him aboard the packet boat that would take us down the River Clyde to Greenock. There, we would board an ocean-going ship to cross the Atlantic. My shivering turned to trembling, not because of the chill in the air, but from sentiments deep within me. I stuffed my hands into my pants pockets to hide their shaking.

It was five years to the day after my parents and sister died in the collapse of McDowell Pit Number 2. My entire family lay in Scotland, still buried under tons of rock and earth, and I was on my way to the other side of the world. The dread of this moment had agonized me for weeks, ever since Master McDowell told his daughters and me he had sold his coal pits and property. We were leaving Scotland for a new beginning in America.

Against my will and hopes, I was leaving the home and country of my family and forefathers. By Scottish law, orphaned and indentured children, such as I, remained under bond until age 21. I had no right to resist. My deepest regret came from the realization that I had no real family and was breaking the only thread to the one I once knew. I felt a dread in my bones, a sense I would never return—never again see the familiar countryside or visit my family's eternal resting place.

Pa and Mum's faces were fading from memory. The only time I saw them, except on Sundays, they were grimy with coal dust and so tired all they could do was eat, do what chores were needed, and go to bed. In the mornings, when I roused, they were already up and gone.

Sunday was a day for worship and solemn respite. We and other families moved our worship meetings from home to home, even though the large Parish Church was within walking distance. Pa agreed with the ministers who made their rounds to preach to the groups like us that the big church's rule permitting only landowners to select ministers was both wrong and unscriptural. I didn't understand then, but I did sense truth in my Pa's position.

After our Sunday meetings, Pa would have something special for me while Mum and my sister spent time together. Sometimes we strolled through meadows or woods, and he would teach me the names of birds and animals. During the winter months, he would sing with my sister and me or play his battered but cherished fiddle, passed down to him from his pa, who in turn received it from his pa. It was a treasure to our peasant neighbors and to us for miles around. No one could remember how it came to be in the Grahame family.

My favorite times were Sunday evenings when, set free of worldly bounds and cares, we shared in heroic adventures through Pa's bedtime stories. I loved those times with him, short as they were. But I was too young; I never fully knew the man he was. There simply wasn't time.

I do remember everything about Bridget. My older sister was my life. She played with me, teased and laughed with me, and made life fun and exciting. Bridget taught me everything, including how to read and write. Not one boy in school, even the older ones, could do better than me. I loved Bridget. She made my every day exciting with her unpredictable and sometimes crazy ideas. I awoke each morning with wonderment and anticipation of what the day would hold for us. I could see it pleased her to make me laugh, learn, and grow. She was my sister, my friend, and my hero. When the day came for her to leave me and work the pit with Pa and Mum, I felt as if my world caved in.

Not many weeks later, it did.

After the accident, Master McDowell's wife insisted they take me into their home rather than allow the local magistrate to send me to the orphanage at Edinburgh. I later learned Master McDowell encountered no argument from the magistrate in documenting me as his indentured household servant.

Orphanages throughout the region were allowed and expected to hire out their charges to work in the numerous Glasgow textile mills. It was reputedly backbreaking work, from which many children suffered severe injuries—or did not survive at all. As an inmate of an orphanage, I would have been eligible for hire. It seems neither the McDowells nor the magistrate felt I deserved such a fate. I am certain Master McDowell's conscience led him to assign me to his home rather than his one remaining coal pit.

Mrs. McDowell's intentions to replace the mother I lost in the coal pit collapse were futile. Her frenetic efforts to affect the style and privilege of a wealthy landowner's wife were too wearying and compulsory to allow compassion, tenderness, or love to interfere. The all-important role of preserving the image of the lady of such a grand manor demanded her full attention. Her duties precluded her from being a mother, even to Blaire and Mairi, her own daughters, and least of all to an eight-year-old orphan son of one of her husband's former colliers. That young boy was now living in her house and proving to be more of a bother than a servant.

Master McDowell insisted I be schooled, but not at the government school as were children of the peasantry. Instead, I found myself studying under the rigorous curriculum of Professor Muir, the private tutor he hired for his daughters. That turned out to be a blessing to me. I thrived under the demanding tutelage of the old man, a retired professor at the University of Glasgow.

He quickly perceived my thirst to learn. More than once, he told me he was astonished and pleased that a peasant, such as I, could excel beyond the wealthy and privileged students he previously taught at the University. I knew I was his favorite, and though he took pains to conceal it, I sensed the two girls knew it too. I was thankful beyond measure I did not have to attend lessons in the polite accomplishments as did the girls. Spinster Finella Abercrombie taught these lessons. She disliked me as much as did the girls.

These events led twelve-year-old Blaire to gain a new purpose in life—to make certain I knew who I was—an orphan and a servant, and no more. In the presence of visitors, her parents treated me as if I were family and expected their daughters to do the same. Blair knew better. Her resolve to keep me in mind of my proper place was firm.

Mairi, nine years old, a year older than I was, feared I would steal more of what little attention her mother could give her. In her mind, an orphaned servant had no right to any of her mother's affection. In the following months, the girl developed a deep hatred for me. To prevent open conflict, I avoided her as much as possible. Though her hatred was deep, she never came to match her older sister in the skills of subtle treachery.

Relationships within the McDowell family worsened with the costly and unsuccessful efforts to reopen McDowell Pit Number 2. More than once, I heard Master and Mrs. McDowell argue about money—much as I'd heard my own Pa and Mums do. I do not know if her distress was the cause of Mrs. McDowell's ever-increasing infirmity. She died when I was twelve.

Six months later, eleven days after I turned thirteen years of age, and after the packet boat trip down from Glasgow and an overnight stay at a busy inn, I found myself dressed in the unfamiliar attire of a well-to-do businessman's son, standing with Master McDowell and his two daughters on the pier at Greenock.

They were not the family I would have chosen, but they were the closest to a family that I knew. Besides, I had no living relatives and no place else to go. It would be useless to look back, so following the others, I boarded the sailing ship, *Muireann*. Within the hour, we cast off for America.

As the hills of my beloved Scotland receded into the morning mist, and when I could do so discreetly, I whispered my final goodbye to my family and homeland. With a veiled motion, I wiped the single tear from my eye lest it give me away. The fiddle had disappeared from our house shortly after the accident. There was nothing else there I wanted.

***

Henrysville, Indian Territory of the United States, 1850

Creaking hinges, betraying a stealthy opening of the door to my room, intruded into my sleep. I awoke and judged the door wide open by the time the creaking stopped. Even with my eyes closed and feigning sleep, I was certain the Indian woman came in. She tried to be silent, but even the subdued rustle of her dress and starched apron could not hide the muted whisper of doeskin moccasins across the wood plank floor. It was the Indian woman. Ciara Franklin's hard-soled shoes would have branded her in an instant.

I kept my eyes closed and tried to continue my breathing depth and pace to not give myself away. She stood close by the head of my bed, studying me for several long moments. Before long, the rustle of clothing and creaking of the chair told me she sat. Try as I might, I could not hear her breathing. She clearly intended for me not to know she was checking on me.

Her closeness brought clues about her. She smelled of soap and freshly baked bread. Though faint, my nose picked up the smell of newly tanned doeskin—those very moccasins that had betrayed her presence. Other smells stood out, ones I could not identify until I remembered she helped Ciara with the newspaper—printer's ink and new paper. It all reminded me of the multi-faceted life she led.

There were other smells, or perhaps a sense akin to cleanliness and kindness, that touched me most. It was the sense of a woman who cared what happened to me, a sense I had experienced before, long ago. In a moment, she rose and started her furtive retreat. The door creaked before closing with a gentle click. She took her smells and impressions with her and left me with a sinking sense of my aloneness.

The weight of that moment and the recent memory of Ciara Franklin's red hair and emerald eyes, identical to Keevah's, threatened to overwhelm me with the grief and despair I had struggled with for years. At other times like this, my means of survival was to answer the gnawing in my heart by getting out and driving myself to search for Keevah and my son—my family.

I couldn't do that now. I couldn't even get out of bed. I felt imprisoned by my own frailties in a prison without bars or locks but from which there was no escape—not for me. This place plagued me with constant reminders of what I had lost. I couldn't sleep. I couldn't toss, I couldn't turn. Because of my injuries, I had no way to fight the loneliness. This night was worse than waiting for my hanging in that New Orleans jail cell.

To get my mind off my situation, I tried recalling everything I could about the dream, the boat, and the people I met on my voyage to America.

The brig *Muireann,* 1816

The two-masted sailing brig, *Muireann,* was not a large vessel. Master McDowell allowed me to roam about her at will. I am certain that he sensed tension between his daughters and me within the confines of the adjoining cabins. I tried not to worsen the situation, so I spent most of my time on deck or went below with other passengers during the day.

Of course, we all took our meals together in the great cabin, which served as both a dining hall and sitting room. It was not great at all. Situated forward of the captain's cabin and officers' wardroom and between the four small passenger cabins, two along each side of the ship, it also served as the landing for the aft companionway. Wide enough for only one long table and ten chairs, it quickly became crowded with more than a few people.

Even to my untrained eye, it was obvious from the many scars and scrapes that someone had moved, repaired, and repainted the forward bulkhead many times. Master McDowell explained that on the trip from Europe to America, the bulkhead served to separate first-class passengers like us from the tens of dozens of immigrants crowding the forward hold with whatever belongings they could carry in one bag.

In America, that scarred bulkhead would be moved aft to enlarge the hold into the space taken by most of the great cabin. The entire hold would then be filled with lumber for transport back to Europe. Thus, the ship was able to make a profit on each trip between continents.

After the evening meal, his daughters would stay with Master McDowell in the passenger cabin he and I shared. I would go on deck and watch the crew, the sunset, or the stars until the girls had retired to their own cabin for the evening. Blaire's subtle hints kept me reminded—I was the one who had everything to lose from any malicious word or act from either her or Mairi.

Despite his daughters' hatred for me, Master McDowell and I grew close. During the first few days of the trip, he would find me and engage me in conversation—never about the past or his strained family relationships. His talks would be about the ship, weather, or something about America. I became certain he made deliberate efforts to find and talk to me.

After three days of such encounters, we agreed to meet in the boat's deckhouse after morning breakfast. A small part of the deckhouse served as a chartroom, limited to the ship's crew, and the larger part as a concession to first-class passengers who wanted to be on deck and yet be out of the wind or weather. Master McDowell could smoke there too. Each morning, we talked until his leisurely puffing consumed the tobacco in his pipe. Then, he would promptly leave. Only on rare occasions did he refill his pipe and continue our conversation.

I did not consider our meetings unpleasant; indeed, I began to look forward to them. I realized these get-togethers were more than social; he had a purpose for them. Master McDowell was preparing me for my future. It didn't sound as though he planned servant duties for me in America, so I began to pay attention when he spoke. We hardly knew each other all those years living in the same house. Now, in the confines of the deckhouse of a rather small sailing brig, I began to learn the character of the man, and he, in turn, began to see me for who I was.

I encountered an old sailor several times during my explorations of the ship. His twisted foot and severe limp would make it impossible for him to work the sails and lines, much less scramble aloft in the rigging, but never had I seen him idle. He clearly paid attention to his close-cropped beard, snow-like against his tanned face and greying hair, and he was always repairing or polishing some equipment item, refilling lamps, or keeping himself busy at tasks often done by cabin boys. Yet I witnessed other sailors querying him about the ship or listening to his seafaring tales.

The old sailor approached me on the evening of our second day at sea as I stood at the deck rail, savoring the symphony of rhythm composed by our boat as she rode the ever-present sea swells.

"So, Laddie, what be ye thinkin' about our boat, the *Muireann*?"

His piercing blue eyes sparkled when I responded with a multitude of questions. He took obvious pleasure in answering each one. Soon, he was teaching me everything I could learn about the ship, as well as several other sailing ships we saw at sea.

Whenever I approached him with my questions, he would put his work down and with obvious passion, tell me all I wanted to know, and more than I could absorb. His Scottish Highland accent was unfamiliar to me, but he was patient and helped me understand.

I learned he had chosen to work sailing ships as a cabin boy for several years before gaining full standing of an ordinary seaman.

After many years on boats of all types, he earned the position of able seaman and then the authority of bos'n. A proud grin creased his leathery face when I answered his nod toward the empty space on the bench beside him with my imitation of a sailor's hearty response.

"Aye, aye, Bos'n."

He waited for me to sit. "A boat can be havin' only one bos'n, me Laddie. And an important job it be. But this boat be havin' one already. I'm not bein' one to cause any *stooshie* or commotion on the boat. So, ye just be callin' me Chad."

"How about if I call you Bo—short for bos'n?"

The old sailor nodded as his grin spread. "I'd be likin' Bo. Yes, Bo, I'll be."

I repeated the name, slowly and reverently, as if God himself had ordained it. The old sailor clearly sensed my pride at the privilege of addressing him by a nickname. I never did ask or discover his given name. He became my friend—he was still Bo when we parted.

From his stories, of which I never tired, I learned he had been sailing since he was about my age. His disfigured foot and limp, which he suffered years past, would have disqualified any other sailor. Yet, the ship's captain, with the owner's approval, kept the old man as a regular member of the crew, supposedly out of respect for his service.

Bo chuckled before voicing his opinion for the real reason he was still aboard. "The skipper be lovin' to hear me tellin' tales. I be havin' some adventures for sure. He be hearin' most of 'em; so, to keep things interestin', I be changin' some of the facts every so often."

My puzzled glance prompted an explanation.

"Course I don't be havin' any trouble with that, mind ye," Bo said. "Me memory be getting' better as I be gettin' older. Why Laddie, I be rememberin' things now I once forgot ever happened."

Deepening wrinkles at the corners of his eyes appeared to be laughing. They gave me courage to challenge him.

"Whether they happened or not?"

Those blue eyes focused on mine with deliberate intensity. "Ye be a sharp one alright, Laddie. Ye remember that now. It'll be servin' ye well." A slow wink and grave nod confirmed a lesson taught and learned.

But I had seen many of the younger sailors talking to him in serious conversation. They were not interested in tales of adventures. It was wisdom and learning they sought. I became certain the ship's captain kept the old sailor onboard—despite Bo's excuse of telling tales—because after years of depending on and trusting each other through hardship and danger, he valued the old man's knowledge. Moreover, the two had become friends. I would discover later such friendships between officers and crews of sailing vessels were rare—unheard of on the vessels on which I would find myself serving.

By our third day out of Greenock, I felt good about the *Muireann*. Bo had taught me a great deal about the boat and the working of the sails and rigging. When I first boarded, all the ropes, poles, and hardware looked so haphazard that I couldn't understand how it all worked. I was certain no one could know the reason for every line, block, or belaying pin. After several days, Bo's explanations helped me see everything had a purpose and was in its proper place. I quickly grasped the names of all the different lines and sails and under what weather conditions the crew used them. I even entertained thoughts of becoming a seaman myself.

For the diversion and edification of interested passengers, several charts of the waters the *Muireann* plied on her voyages between America and Europe decorated the inside walls of the deckhouse. Bo showed me how to read the charts. By his instruction and with the navigation data he obtained from the first mate, I was able to fix our current position each day and thus follow our course. Several of our fellow passengers noticed my course markers and began meeting daily to engage in thoughtful discourse on our progress.

With nods and winks, Bo often reminded me to remain silent during those times. He took pleasure from knowing a thirteen-year-old lad, on his first-ever sea voyage, was placing those position markers that fostered so much pretentious discussion. When alone, we often laughed at our little secret.

Bo also introduced me to a different method of navigation, which was more challenging and, to me, more rewarding. With the participation of the first mate, who gave us raw data on the compass headings and the ship's speed at several times during the preceding twenty-four hours, Bo showed me how to calculate the ship's position. We then compared my work against the accurate position fixes on the chart. My calculated positions were never an exact match but did place us in the general vicinity of the first mate's positions. As my calculations improved over time, I sensed Bo felt pride in both his teaching and my performance. He called the method, "Dead reckonin'" and told me to never forget how to do it.

***

We had cleared the Saint George's Channel a day ago, and according to the charts on the wall, we had open waters all the way to America. Something didn't seem right. From early boyhood, I had known my directions, and the sun told me we were continuing to sail more southerly than westerly. America lay across the Atlantic more to the west—not on our current heading. I went looking for Bo.

He was nowhere below deck. I even stole through the immigrant passenger hold, avoiding conversation traps with the boys I had met. The only place I could not check was the fo'c'sle, where the crew berthed and which was off-limits to all passengers. Besides, I knew he wouldn't be there—he was too busy finding things to do elsewhere. I scrambled up the ship's narrow forward companionway to the main deck and searched my way aft. He was not on either of the small benches mounted on the sides of the deckhouse. Those were his favorite places, so I continued my search.

When I found him, I froze. In a moment, I recovered enough to close my gaping mouth and restore my bug-eyed expression to as near normal as I could. Bo, his unlit pipe clenched firmly between stained and aging teeth, sat, not on his favored windward side but on the short bench attached to the aft wall of the small deckhouse. Close beside him sat a thin, red-haired girl of about my age. Both Bo and the girl were intent on something Bo held in his left hand. With a delicate touch, his right hand worked on the object with a short-bladed knife. She never took her focus off the thing, whatever it was.

Though I could not see what he was working on, I stood frozen in place and watched. When my gaze drifted to the girl, my knees weakened. For a moment, I feared they would fail me. I put a hand on the ship's rail to steady myself. Everything around me faded from view as if a dark tunnel were closing my vision—except for this twig of a girl sitting beside my friend. Even as I watched, several wayward zephyrs sneaked around corners of the deckhouse to play in her hair. Delicate fingers brushed the wind-tossed locks back without the girl ever taking her gaze from Bo's work.

Her hair seemed to intensify in color, becoming almost luminous the more I stared at it. Every tiny stitch and fold of the green dress she wore complimented and magnified the intense emerald of her eyes. Her face glowed with radiance such as I'd never seen. No one had ever affected me like that.

My faculties returned when Bo placed his knife aside, blew any debris off the object that held such fascination for them, wiped it with his work-worn sleeve, and held it up for the girl to see.

Her emerald eyes widened with delight at what they beheld. Never had I seen such eyes. My breath caught in my throat at the sight. I felt helpless, unable to tear my gaze away. Framed with wind-blown red hair and filled with those enormous green eyes, her face ensnared my very soul.

Unable to speak or move one foot in front of the other, I could only stand and watch. I was completely mesmerized at the sight of this girl. After a minute, she looked up at the old mariner's grizzled face. As their eyes met, she smiled and nodded her approval.

His return grin made it clear I was not the only young friend the old sailor had aboard this ship.

A moment or several minutes might have passed; I lost all sense of time before the two noticed me. Without a word, the old man gestured for me to join them. I hesitated, expecting the girl to oppose any such move. Blaire and Mairi, had they been in her place, would have made it clear I was out of place and not wanted.

She surprised me. Instead of deeming my presence an intrusion, she invited me with a smile and slid closer to the old man, leaving room for me on the rather short bench. I was already embarrassed, aware my flustered reactions must be obvious. Her hospitality only confounded my predicament. I could feel my face flushing as I shook my head to decline her offer.

After gathering my composure, I directed my question to Bo. "Why are we headed southerly when America is to the west?"

The old sailor didn't let me down. He pulled his pipe from between clenched teeth and nodded as his grin grew. His grin restored my confidence. It always had before; he knew that.

"That be a good question, me laddie. Ye'll be makin' a seaman yet. Why don't ye be sittin' next to the bonnie lassie here? It'll be takin' some time to explain."

I still felt awestruck by the girl, but to me, any of Bo's suggestions might as well be a command. I attempted to marshal my disordered emotions and stepped toward the narrow end of the bench she left for me. She couldn't have taken up much space, as thin as she was, but even so, there didn't seem to be enough room on the bench for the three of us. I sat on as little as I could, careful to avoid touching her or the skirt of her dress.

Bo watched my painful struggle with an encouraging chuckle.

"Now, Laddie, why don't ye be askin' the bonnie lassie your question? She can explain it as well as me. It's bein' her daddy who owns this boat."

CHAPTER 2

The flush was returning to my face—I could feel the heat of it—but there was no backing out now. I turned to address the girl and repeated my question.

"Oh, but first, you have to see what Bo is making."

"You call him Bo?"

My surprise and a little of my dismay at anyone else calling my friend Bo must have been obvious to her. I thought that name was something special between him and me.

"He told me about you," she said, "and that you started calling him Bo. I like the name you gave him, so I began calling him Bo, too."

She rested a hand on my arm as her emerald eyes queried mine.

"I hope you don't mind."

I struggled to keep from betraying the thrill coursing through my body at her touch.

"It's a perfect name for such a great friend," she said without revealing if she sensed my twinge of fear that she would read my every thought and feeling. I didn't dare speak for fear of further exposing the effect she had on me, so I only nodded my approval.

She lifted her hand from my arm and turned to grasp Bo's hand—the one holding the thing so fascinating to her. With care, she eased the ivory-colored object from Bo's gnarled fingers.

"Here it is. Bo is making this for me. Isn't it beautiful? Look." She held her treasure up for me to see. "It's the *Muireann*. He's carving her on a piece of a sperm whale's tooth. It's called scrimshaw. Lots of sailors do it, but Bo's is the best I've ever seen. I think he has a special gift."

I examined the intricate carving. At first, many of the carved lines seemed random and incoherent. As I studied it with a little imagination, however, the picture the girl was so pleased with began to take shape. The resemblance to our ship was remarkable. It needed more work, but every hull feature and both masts were correct. She was in full sail—with some sails I didn't even know existed. Most of the rigging lines and hull details were yet to be carved, but the girl was right—it was beautiful. I was amazed at the old sailor's skill.

"He's been working on it for weeks, ever since he heard Papa scheduled me to take this boat to America."

I shot Bo a surprised glance, but my gaze was compelled to return to the girl.

"You know each other from before?"

"Oh yes, this is one of Papa's boats and Bo has sailed for us a long time—since I was a baby." She shot a mischievous grin at the old sailor before lifting a hand to shield her mouth from his view. "At least is what he tells me, but you know him and his tales," she whispered loud enough to prompt a corner of the old sailor's mouth to turn upward. With a mischievous grin, she again faced me.

"But you asked about our course to the south instead of heading directly to America. I can explain. May I?"

"Please do." I hesitated for a moment—but it was already obvious. "I don't know much about sailing."

"Oh, but you do. Bo has told me about you. He says you are smart and a fast learner. He says you already know more about the *Muireann* than most passengers learn during an entire voyage. And you already know we're not heading straight for America. So, see, Bo is right. You would make a seaman."

"I guess I was looking forward too much to getting to America to think we would be stopping between Scotland and there."

"We're not stopping anywhere until we get to Boston." Her initial look of triumph changed into smiling concern. "Don't look at me like that." She laughed. It was a friendly laugh. I took no offense.

"We are sailing non-stop to Boston. Trust me; this is the fastest way to get there."

She then explained about currents and trade winds. "We'd be sailing against both if we took a compass heading straight to Boston. By sailing south, all the way to the twentieth Parallel of North

Latitude, we will find both currents and winds to help us make our way to the Americas. We'll then sail westward first and then northwest toward the American coast until we arrive at Boston."

"It seems we're going far out of our way." More words formed in my mind as I thanked Professor Muir for his lessons on latitude and longitude. I was grateful to Bo for making the abstract become real as we plotted the *Muireann*'s position on the chart.

"You're right," Her eyes brightened as her face lit with approval. "It is a lot farther, but it's also a lot faster. When boats sail from America to Europe, they stay north to let the currents and winds help them sail fast in that direction. From Europe to the Americas, it's the opposite. We need to go far to the south to find our favorable winds and currents."

I nodded my understanding. She grinned with pleasure before handing the piece of whale tooth back to Bo.

"Watch how he does this. He's really good."

Bo went back to his creation, carving each mark and line with precision I would never have expected from his aged fingers. The girl and I crowded close to avoid missing a single stroke or cut. In a moment, a small sail emerged atop the foremast, right below a horizontal cut I hadn't recognized as a yardarm. A few strokes later, a similar sail materialized at the top of the mainmast. Bo handed the scrimshaw to the girl.

"Ah . . .," she sighed. "Look, she's flying so many sails. What are they all called, Bo?"

Bo chuckled. "I be addin' a few sails ye haven't seen on this boat. We haven't needed 'em, but our bos'n's be havin' these and more in the sail locker." He pointed to each sail with the tip of his knife as he moved up the mainmast. "This be the mainsail, or as some call it, the course. Next, be the lower topsail, the upper topsail, and the topgallant. The ones on the foremast be havin' the same names, with the word "fore" bein' in front of 'em. These three-cornered ones at the bow be the flyin' jib, the jib, and the forestaysail. This big stern-most sail be the spanker."

"And the little ones at the very tops of the masts are the . . .?" The girl looked into his eyes.

"Those be the royals. See, each mast be havin' one, a fore royal and a main royal."

"It's beautiful. Now I remember the main, the topsails, and the topgallant, but I've never seen a royal before." She turned to me. "Did you know the names of those sails?"

When I didn't respond, she focused on my eyes and nodded her head to reassure me.

"My Papa . . . and Bo taught me about boats and sails. I've sailed before, twice to France and back to Ireland, and once across the Atlantic to America, and then back to Ireland again. This will be my second voyage to America."

She dropped her gaze to the deck before slowly looking up to study the waves and horizon. Still looking at the sea, she spoke.

"I hope . . . I can stay this time. I must be going; my warden will be having a fit if I'm gone too long."

W-warden?

"My cousin, Una. She is supposed to be my traveling companion. She takes her responsibility seriously—far too seriously. She acts more like my warden." She handed the scrimshaw back to Bo and rose to leave.

"Wait," I said. "Will you let me see the scrimshaw after Bo finishes it?"

She turned around to face me. Seated as I was on the bench and as close as she stood, she had to look down at me. Her slight smile accentuated her beauty and resurrected my dizzying emotions. She said nothing about me ever seeing Bo's finished work.

My heart sank as I grasped her intent.

After studying me in silence for a moment, she leaned over to Bo, kissed him on the head, and then turned to leave. In apparent afterthought, she turned back to me.

"You're Scottish, aren't you? You speak well; you've had fine schooling, but I can tell by your accent. You can tell I'm Irish. If Una had her way, I would have a French accent. In fact, I'd speak nothing but French."

Then, she skipped away.

I often wondered if my family felt betrayed seconds before the earth crushed them in that coal mine. Now I knew how betrayal felt. I sat on the bench next to Bo with unseeing eyes directed to the deck. There was nothing to say. I had been devastated before with loss and disappointment, and now, with humiliation.

Bo remained silent as I rose and walked away as if nothing had happened.

A good hiding place on a boat full of people is hard to find, but I did find solitude among the huge coils of rope and extra sail material in the crowded sail locker under the forward companionway steps. Although immigrant passengers were required to use the forward companionway to board and leave the boat, they were restricted to using it only at certain times when at sea—to not interfere with the crew. I would be alone in my mortification, at least until after the next watch change.

As far back as I could remember, everyone I knew proclaimed the Irish were an untrustworthy and immoral people. Worse, they were arrogant and snobbish, deeming themselves better than we Scottish. In fact, they reviled us. In my home country, I never knew any Irish. From what I'd heard, I would have avoided them like poison had I met any.

Then, this girl, daughter of a wealthy ship's owner, who had so captivated me with her beauty and, at first, treated me as a friend, tells me she is Irish and knows I am Scottish by the way I speak. That hurt, but I could deal with it—I'd been shamed before. The real hurt came when she never answered when I asked to see the finished scrimshaw. Bo was my friend—the only real friend I'd had for a long time, and now she flaunted her position by denying me sharing in his finished handiwork.

Immersed in the smells of new rope and canvas in my dark refuge, I almost convinced myself I didn't care if she was Irish or what she thought about me. She made no difference to me, but this I came to know—I hated this boat, I hated America, I wished I were back in Scotland.

I would be alone there, but I knew how to be alone. I'd been learning every day since McDowell Pit Number 2 collapsed.

***

The creaking of heavy bronze hinges awakened me—an invader entering my sanctuary. I remembered shedding angry tears but hadn't meant to fall asleep. I hurried to wipe away any evidence lest I be further embarrassed.

Bo, with the light of a small whale oil lantern, slowly entered the storage locker and selected the coil of rope next to me to sit on. To my gratitude, he extinguished the lantern, leaving the two of us in the dark. He may have seen tear trails on my face, or he may have known. I think he knew long before he ever saw me.

"Laddie, I be thinking ye be on the wrong tack, so I'll be stickin' me nose in yer business here."

"What do you mean, wrong tack?

"Ye be like a boat on the wrong tack—sailin' in the wrong direction. Ye be thinkin' wrong about what she said."

"She said I'm Scottish because of the way I talk. She's Irish, and her rich father owns the boat. She doesn't even want me to see your finished scrimshaw. And her talking about speaking French, like she's so sophisticated. She thinks she's better than me." I kicked a pile of canvas near my feet. It didn't help. "Why did you even tell her about me, Bo? You knew she was Irish—they hate us Scottish."

"The lassie didn't mean to harm ye by sayin' ye're Scottish. She don't be holdin' to such notions. After all, me and her be friends and I be about as Scottish as they come."

He paused. In the long silence, he sucked on his unlit pipe. After a sigh, He spoke. "Laddie, I told ye I be about yer age when I started sailin', and that be the truth. But I didn't be tellin' ye everything."

Another long pause before he continued. "Me family and me, we be livin' near a wee fishing village called Lochinver. A cousin and me be returnin' from deliverin' a skiff he made to a shop in Ullapool. We be comin' home to grim news, Laddie. Both our families be dead. People said it be the food poisonin.'

"There bein' no one to take is in, we be goin' back to Ullapool. He be gettin' on a brig as an ordinary seaman. Even though I be workin' the boats around Lochinver for couple of years, I be small for my age—no one be wantin' me for a seaman. I soon be beggin' and stealin' to eat and be gettin' caught.

"I be spendin' some days in jail before the magistrate be givin' me a choice. He be sayin' the town don't be wantin' no thief from Lochinver hangin' around. And they don't be wantin' to feed one in jail either, so I be havin' to leave—on board a ship as a bonded cabin boy or be goin' to prison. If it be prison, the only hope I be havin' is for someone to pay my fine in exchange for me bein' indentured to him. I be havin' to pay my debt back to him to be free again. Indentured servants don't be getting' paid enough to ever pay off a debt. I be agreein' to serve on a ship.

"It wasn't a real ship—just an old fishin' lugger the captain be usin' to take passengers and goods between Scotland and Ireland. That captain be takin' me on as a cabin boy before he be learnin' what I knew about sailin' and what I could do. Then, he be givin' me the work of a full seaman—just him and me crewin' the boat.

"He be tellin' me not to be askin' or talkin' about what we be carryin', and I didn't. All I know was we be carryin' a lot of sail on that little boat, and she be fast. We be out-sailin' a fleet-worth of English ships. Seems like they always be tryin' to catch us. Those English be wantin' some of our Irish passengers bad, but we be getting' em wherever they be wantin' to go, and then we be forgettin' we ever seen 'em.

"After my bond debt be paid, I be stayin' on with that captain for a couple years until I be a near-growed man. When we be gettin' word the English be settin' a trap for us, he be sellin' the boat and be goin' his way. I be gettin' myself on a real sailin' ship. I be sailin' ever since.

"My point be that I know how ye be feelin' about yerself—bein' a bonded servant. I once be the same as you. That don't be makin' ye less of a man. That only be the circumstances forced on ye. What be makin' ye a man is how ye be risin' above those circumstances to be the man the Almighty meant ye to be. I be thinkin' ye're already makin' to be that man."

In the silence following, I heard him suck his pipe a couple of times, giving me time to think about his words.

"Laddie, I didn't come to be stayin', but I will be leavin' ye with somethin' to think about. Don't be getting' yerself in a *stooshie* over a little misunderstandin'. Talk to her—be settin' things straight between the two of ye's."

Bo lit his lantern and stood. He opened the door but stopped and turned back. "Might be, me Laddie, she be more in need of a friend than ye be."

Alone in the dark again, I tried to make sense of it all. Bo's few words made me doubt my previous convictions. Now, I was truly bewildered. Unable to reconcile my conflicting thoughts, I decided to slink from my sail-locker sanctuary to my favorite niche on the bow. I had spent many hours staring at the seas from there. The foredeck crews knew me. They would leave me alone. Much as I wanted to believe Bo, I found it difficult. I wanted to see her again, but I had resolved. I would not accept scorn from any Irish—not even her.

***

Two days went by without seeing the girl. That was not unusual, as I'd only seen her once during the entire voyage. Bo and I continued our routines of plotting the ship's course, telling tales, and him teaching me about sailing the *Muireann*. He even got me started going aloft in the rigging.

Within an hour, I was scrambling up and down the rigging from deck to crow's-nest. Most of the crew cheered me on, and before long, I could do as well as many of them—better than some. Bo laughed at my antics. His encouragement spurred me to listen to and learn from my audience of sailors.

"Ye be a natural," he said. "Before long, ye'll be workin' the yards like a regular topman."

He never mentioned the girl. For my part, I tried to act as though she were a forgotten memory. Inside, however, my thoughts and feelings were in constant turmoil. She had hurt me—Bo said she didn't mean to—but she had. She said I was Scottish as if I was lower than her. But Bo said she didn't believe that way about people. She had captivated my heart and mind with her beauty and manner; I desperately wanted to see her again—to be friends. But that would be impossible.

The differences between us were too great. She was a rich man's daughter, and I was an orphaned bondservant. Despite what Bo said, I had learned social status was all-important to those who possessed it. I watched Mrs. McDowell forsake her daughters for it. Those daughters drilled it into me during the five years I lived in their household. I had no hope of ever rising above what I was born to—a peasant laborer and an orphaned one at that.

The girl would never befriend the likes of me. I, on the other hand, could not erase from my mind the image of her mesmerizing green eyes and enchanting smile.

Following the evening meal of the second day after I had met the girl, I went on deck, as was my usual habit. Bo was waiting for me. Without a word between us, I sat next to him on the windward deckhouse bench while he prepared his pipe. The only place I remembered seeing him smoke was when he was below or in the deckhouse—never on the open deck. He had no intention of smoking. Flying embers from cigars or pipes were the last thing anyone on a wooden ship with yards of combustible canvas hanging above the deck wanted.

The tobacco was a distraction to keep his hands busy while he waited for me to speak. He gave me the time I needed. After several aborted attempts, I mustered courage and laid my soul bare.

"Who is she? I've never seen her before—just one time. Why doesn't she ever come on deck? Why did you even tell her about me?"

Bo said nothing. He silently tapped the tobacco in his already-filled pipe.

Why had he told the girl about me? He knew she was Irish and how they blamed the Scottish for all the ills of Ireland. Their hatred ran deep—almost as deep as it did for the English. He must have known what she would think of me.

"Laddie," he looked up to meet my gaze. "I'll be answerin' yer questions one at a time, but ye need to be listenin' with yer head, not jest yer ears. Know what I be meanin?"

I wasn't sure, but I nodded.

"Her name be Keevah Ferguson. I already told ye she be the daughter of the man who owns this boat, and three others like her. This one be the best of the fleet, and it surely be havin' the best Captain of the lot. That be the reason she be on this boat."

He paused to examine his unlit pipe. My questions were not all answered, but I thought it best to be patient.

In time, he continued. "Her daddy be goin' to America ten, twelve years ago with the English bein' hot after him. Seems he bein' some sort o' leader of the revolts and such to unite the Irish against England. With them bein' close on his tail, he be havin' to flee. He be takin' Keevah's three older brothers with him and leavin' baby Keevah and her mother in Ireland—them bein' in no danger like him.

"After a time, he be gettin one ship, like this one, and be bringin' Keevah and her mother to America. With it bein' too hard to make a living for all the family, he be sendin' Keevah and her mother back to Ireland. He and his sons be workin' hard and buildin' up his shippin' business. When her mother be comin' ill of the consumption, she be sendin' Keevah to stay with a cousin in France. Her mother be dyin' while Keevah be away. The poor young'un never be there to attend her mother's wake or mourn at her grave."

He paused again until I met his gaze with my own. "Ye and the wee lass be havin' somethin' in common there, me Laddie."

I tried to stifle emotions welling within.

"Don't be sittin' there like a *stookie*, ye needn't be tryin' to hide anything from me. I know about yer family and the tragedy it be. But ye need to know this—Mister McDowell be speakin' to the captain about ye, and the captain be speakin' to me. Ye be havin' us on yer side, me laddie. Don't be forgettin' that now."

My voice deserted me. After many minutes, I nodded my grasp of a thought so foreign to me as to be inconceivable.

"That lassie might as well be a prisoner of her older companion. I know her to be as full of life as anybody. Why, she'd be all over this boat seein' and learnin' everything she could, same as ye be doin' if she had her say about it. Ye don't be seein' her much 'cause she's bein' stepped on by that cousin she calls a warden. Why, to my mind, her cousin be worse'n any warden. So, it's not bein' the lassie's fault if she's not bein' sociable and friendly. Before long, she'll be gettin' out, like the time you saw her with me. Ye be watchin' and don't be hesitatin' to talk to her. I be thinkin' ye'll be the first one she be lookin' fer."

⁂

Bo was right. Mid-morning, two days later, I found the girl standing at the windward rail, watching the angry sea roil from yesterday's squalls. As often occurs, every third of the storm-whipped swells was larger than the previous two. The ship's bow would pitch into those higher swells and fling wild spray into the air. The foredeck crew wore tarred clothing to protect themselves from the spray and mist, drenching the foredeck until seawater poured out the scuppers.

Most of the spray fell before reaching the rail where the girl stood. Even so, I was surprised she'd be on deck. Where she stood, she would still taste salty mist from the bow-spray and the wind-blown seas. She acted unconcerned about the pitching and rolling of the boat or anything around her.

I approached her side cautiously. Unlike the vivacious girl I had seen with Bo, she appeared pensive and frail—a wind-blown willow against the heavy deck rail and massive waves. I longed to see her as I had before.

"Keevah?"

Not knowing if she heard me, or how she'd react, I stepped close beside her and tapped her shoulder with a finger.

"Keevah?"

"Oh . . ." She turned with a start. "I'm sorry, I didn't hear you coming. Forgive me, Lansdale. I'm afraid I was preoccupied."

"You know my name?"

"Bo told me . . . he has told me quite a bit about you."

"He would. I see you got away from your warden. How did you manage that?

"It was quite easy this time—with her being so seasick for the past two days. Your older sister, who is caring for her, thinks I'm in the way." She turned to face me and thrilled me with a smile.

"Lansdale, a nice name, but a bit formal. May I call you Lanny?"

She may as well have jabbed me in the gut with a belaying pin. I tried to hide it.

"Oh!" Her hands flew to her mouth as emerald eyes apologized. "I didn't mean to say anything wrong. Lansdale is perfectly fine with me."

"No, it's okay. Lanny is good. No one except my sister ever called me that. I—It caught me by surprise. You can call me Lanny. I like it."

"Great! To me, you will be Lanny. I like that name." She paused, turning her head to examine the seas for a moment, before looking me in the eye. "Lanny, your sister Blaire, the one taking care of my cousin, doesn't call you Lanny. In fact, she says you are an orphan, not even part of her family. And she claims you are a servant. Is that true?"

My gaze dropped to the deck as my heart sank. "Yes," I confessed. Blaire would be gloating in her victory. "It is true, but she's not my sister. My only sister was named Bridget; she died in a coal mine collapse, along with my parents." I turned, mumbling as I stepped to leave. "I won't bother you anymore,"

"No! Lanny, stop!" She grabbed the front of my shirt with both hands. "Lanny, stay . . . please. I don't care what she says. I don't care about her family, not about any of them."

"Keevah, I am a bonded servant. I might as well be a slave, and there is nothing I can do about that. I'm not fit to be your friend."

"Lanny, that's not true." She riveted her focus on my eyes and clasped a hand to each side of my face. Her strength surprised me. "I know you, and Bo knows you. He has told me a great deal about you—the kind of person you are." Her words became less forceful—almost pleading as she lowered her grasp to my shirtfront.

"And Bo is right. It is, as he says, being a servant is what you do; it is not who you are. He knows who you are, and I know who you are. I saw who you are when we were with Bo. And I like who you are. I want to be your friend. I want you to be my friend too."

"I would like to, Keevah. But Blaire will tell others about me. Everyone on this boat will know about me. They won't allow us to be friends, no one will like it. They will say it's not my place."

"Not everyone." Her words came with conviction. "Yes, my cousin Una will have a fit if she ever gets well enough to take her mind off herself. And Blaire will explode with rage; she hates you for some reason. I saw through her in an instant. But Bo, as will Captain, will be on our side, and I'm almost certain Mr. McDowell will approve. Captain asked him if his daughter would help care for Una while she is sick. I met him when he accompanied Blaire on her first visit. He seems a decent man.

"Look at me." She put a finger under my chin and lifted. "Lanny, I am not like them. I've had a taste of how you feel. When I was sent to France, I was the pathetic little waif from Ireland—the wastelands of the world, at least in their minds. All my cousins looked down their noses at me as if I were a homeless barbarian. Their condescension made me furious. Cousin Una saw an opportunity to get one up on her sisters by becoming a righteous martyr, so she appointed herself as my tutor and guardian.

"She taught me French and all the social propriety she could, but it didn't work out as she'd planned—she had no intention of sailing to America with me. My father wrote to Una's mother he wanted someone to escort me. It was logical she selected Una. I think the reason she's so controlling is her way of making me pay for what she sees as her misfortune. It certainly didn't result in the acclaim she expected . . . and it's making me miserable."

It shocked me that someone of her status could ever feel miserable. Then, I remembered Bo's words from two days ago and earlier in the sail locker.

"Bo told me about your mother, Keevah. I'm sorry."

"Thank you." Her emerald eyes started to tear as she stared into mine. "I know about your family too, and I'm so sorry."

Neither of us knew what to say for a long while. We turned to the rail to stare at the rolling waves. Standing shoulder to shoulder, each wrestled with our silent sentiments. I felt sympathy for her. When she reached out to place a hand on my arm, I was certain she felt the same for me.

"Lanny, I want to see you and Bo every day. He's still working on my scrimshaw, and I want us both to see it all the way to its finish."

"I would like that, but can you get away from Una every day?"

"Yes. I will tell her the way it's going to be from now on—whether she likes it or not."

"That means defying her authority. Are you prepared?"

"Lanny, I can't take any more of being cooped up in a tiny cabin with her. I will use my father's name and position if I need to. I don't think it's right for me to do it, but neither is it right for her to treat me like a prisoner. I expect Captain will see it my way, and he's the one who is really responsible for me."

"Bo will be happy to spend time with us both," I said. "He likes you very much."

"I know, and I like him. We go back a long way. Every time I sail, my daddy makes sure it's with Bo and Captain Johansson. But I want to be with you sometimes too—without Bo. I want a place where the two of us can meet and talk. It seems forever since I've had a real friend, especially one my own age."

"I know a place in the bow. It's forward of the port foresail locker. The foredeck crews know me, and we'll be out of their way; they'll let us talk there. It's a great place to watch the seas too."

"That's it then. I'll see you there tomorrow. What time?"

"Four bells, forenoon watch."

"Bells and watches? My, you are becoming a seaman." Keevah's delighted laugh drew a smile from me. "I'm proud of you already. I will be there, my friend. And no more eating in my cabin with Una; I'll join you and the others for dinner in the great cabin this very evening. Right now, I'm going to inform Captain of the new arrangements."

She flung her arms skyward as if flinging off hated shackles. "Oh, Lanny, I so love freedom."

She skipped her way to the companionway. I never doubted she would persuade the captain to see things her way and I would see her again. My spirits soared higher than the main royal of the *Muireann*.

Bo had been right. I loved that old man.

CHAPTER 3

Henrysville, Indian Territory of the United States, 1850

I awoke to the glow of an evening sun stealing its way through the odd-shaped window in the wall of my room. As I studied the window, it became obvious that it was too large for a jail cell. A determined and resourceful man could climb out—if he didn't have a broken leg. Though it allowed more light to enter than I expected, the white ceiling was to be the only place in the entire room adequately lit. Walls and furniture became darker as my gaze drifted to the floor. I found it depressing.

Muffled women's voices and brisk footsteps approached and then stopped. A soft knock preceded a slow opening of the door. Ciara Franklin eased into the room. Hesed, the Indian woman, followed immediately with a basket that smelled of food. I was beginning to feel hunger, so the smells were welcome. It was also becoming obvious I would have little privacy with these two around.

"I see our patient is awake," Ciara said. "You had quite a nap. That's good. Hesed brought food; we hope you're hungry, but you don't have to eat it all. Generosity is one of her virtues . . . sometimes to a fault."

While Ciara lit one of the oil lamps, the Indian woman stuffed pillows behind my back to help me sit up. I noticed my chest had been snuggly wrapped with bandage material. If I moved carefully, the pain in my ribs was tolerable—much better than before.

Ciara moved the lighted lamp closer to the bed. "Jack says wrapping your chest will lessen the movement of your ribs so they won't hurt so bad, and you may heal faster."

"You did this while I was sleeping?"

"It was better for you that we did it then. Hesed did the real work; I helped when I could. Perhaps I should tell you now that she also helped Jack sew up your scalp wound. I stayed away to avoid seeing it, but if I know the two of them, she did most of it herself."

I looked at the Indian woman. Her raven hair lay smoothed and parted, a braid falling forward over each shoulder, as was common among Indians. A broad forehead, prominent cheekbones, slightly hooked nose, and a strong jaw that tapered into a sharp chin sculpted a face conforming to the Indian princess of eastern newspaper fable. Her steady gaze, however, with dark, almond-shaped eyes under level brows, gave her a no-nonsense appearance. I judged her more handsome than pretty.

"Hesed, you must be a woman of many talents," I said. "You work for a newspaper, cook such good-smelling food, and practice medicine as well. My chest and head thank you—they both feel better."

Her copper complexion made it impossible to tell if she blushed or not. She directed her eyes to the floor and murmured a soft, "Thank you, sir."

I was not surprised at her awkward modesty. From what I had seen, Indian women acquired scant experience in responding to compliments.

She left the room for a few seconds before returning with a short-legged bed table, which she set close to my waist. Without saying a word, she put an extra pillow behind my back and placed a bowl of beef stew, two thick slices of freshly baked bread, and a glass of water on the table. When I winced at my awkward attempt to feed myself with my right hand, I switched the spoon to my left. She took it from me.

"Allow me. Lay back on the pillows."

Ciara relinquished the single bedside chair to Hesed, then stood at the foot of the bed and watched Hesed feed me until I was satisfied. I could have eaten all that she brought were it not for my injuries lessening my normal appetite. After Hesed cleared away the meal dishes, she removed my extra pillows and the table. Ciara took possession of the single chair after Hesed left the room.

"Mr. Grayhawk, I promise, if you wish, I will not write anything about this conversation I want with you right now, but I am curious."

My gut sent warning signals, as it had so many times in battles at sea and land and in dangerous situations from which I might not survive. Seldom had such warnings been without cause. I learned to heed and prepare.

This time was different; it was confusing—no one was trying to kill me. There was no declared or obvious enemy, no flag, no persons, no honor to defend. In fact, the woman before me had demonstrated her intent to help me heal. But she was curious, and that meant she wanted information. She could destroy me. The destruction she offered might not be physical. It would be worse. I feared she presented the greatest challenge I had faced yet. She could weaken me, dull my defenses, and bare those destructive follies I had worked so hard to forget. I wondered if she realized she held the power to do this—that she resurrected remembrances and sentiments of Keevah.

She moved the chair toward the head of the bed to reduce the distance between us. Knowing her intent, I would have preferred she maintained a greater separation. Then, to intensify my angst, she perched herself on the edge of the chair in anticipation. Her intent on getting answers caused me to double my vigilance.

"Before you say anything," I said, "I have some questions of my own. Who is this sergeant you mentioned, why is he here, and what are you and this entire town doing in the Indian Territories? I thought the Territories were limited to Indians—open to whites passing through."

Annoyance flickered in her eyes. It disappeared in an instant. Her poise both calmed and warned me. "Fair enough, but remember, you are here too."

"I am passing through, not homesteading."

"Passing through? To where, Mr. Grayhawk?"

I took several seconds of uneasy reflection. How much did she already know about me?

"I'm not sure . . . I'm searching . . ."

She studied me in silence for a moment before speaking. "Well then, I will answer some of your questions. About what I am doing here will have to wait. I do want to discuss it at length with you but now is not the time. When you are stronger, we will talk. By the way, I don't know your first name. May I address you by a first name?"

"I go by Grayhawk."

"Mister . . . or just Grayhawk?"

"Makes no difference, that's my name."

Her deadpan expression convinced me she would be a skillful opponent at cards.

"Hesed washed your clothes; they had dirt from the street and quite a bit of blood on them. That's not what I wanted to talk to you about. When Jack and Sergeant Kirby removed your clothing, they found this strapped to your body. They gave it to Hesed, along with your clothes."

She reached into a bag and pulled out a stained boot-leather pouch. I had carried it for years, strapped to my chest under my arm, as other men carry a shoulder holster for a weapon.

"She didn't mean to, but as she was preparing your clothes, the flap of this pouch came open. She couldn't help but see this Bible."

"Give that to me!" Despite the sudden pain in my chest, I reached for it. "You have no right to go through my personal effects."

"It was not intentional, sir, and I do apologize for any intrusion."

She offered the Bible; I took it.

"From its worn and tattered condition, I would say you've been carrying it for a long time."

"It was a gift."

"To you, or did you mean it for someone else?"

My answer was a fierce scowl.

"I only ask because I didn't find a name in it, and the fragment that's left of the fly page has some French written on it. Yes, Mr. Grayhawk," she said in response to my suspicious glare. "I do speak and read a little French. My mother taught me. Do you speak French?"

"It was a gift to me, Mrs. Franklin; that is all you need to know."

"Very well, I'll respect that. But it does raise my bigger question. In my occupation, I meet and talk to people from all walks of life and of all educational backgrounds. You came into our town as a wanderer—you yourself claim to be searching for something. Your speech, however, tells me that you are an educated man. And this Bible, this well-marked and notation-filled Bible that you hold so dear, it too tells me you are more than a drifting frontiersman.

"You complimented my friend, treating her as a genuine human being, not merely as an Indian. She is as human as you or me, but most men on the frontier would not consider her so. All these things indicate to me that you are much more than your appearance and, quite frankly, your name would suggest."

She paused, scrutinizing me with emerald eyes like those I had known long ago. "I would like to know more about you—to know the real you. I see I have upset you, but rest assured. I will respect your wishes.

"Tell me about yourself." Her voice softened to a whisper. "Can't we be friends?"

Her simple words destroyed any rational functioning of my brain. My mind was flooded with the memory of another green-eyed, red-haired girl who asked me to be friends.

"I can't . . . not now." Pushing my head back into the pillow, I closed my eyes and slowly shook my head to fight away the resurrected grief threatening to overwhelm me.

I vaguely recall her touching my shoulder and murmuring something too softly for me to grasp.

When I opened my eyes, she was gone.

I laid the Bible on the bed next to me. I could not reach the desk.

Hesed's meal agreed with me. Despite Ciara's upsetting visit and the multitude of memories tumbling about in my head, I began to feel drowsy. Sleep would be a welcome reprieve. I closed my eyes. From within the cobwebs of my mind came the realization that she asked her questions and answered none of mine. She did manage to torment me yet again, for she resurrected vivid memories of that other red-haired girl. The one who, long ago, did become my friend—the best I have ever had.

The brig, *Muireann*, 1816

Keevah was as good as her word. She convinced the captain to exert his influence on Una to slacken up her control, which she reluctantly did. She had nothing more to gain from her escort duties and was no doubt tired of overseeing the high-spirited girl every minute of her day. Keevah joined the rest of the passengers for meals in the great cabin and had the run of the boat for several hours each morning and afternoon. The rest of the time, she was confined with Una in their tiny cabin. She never said, but I suspected Captain Johansson determined her hours of liberty as a compromise.

Within a day after gaining her newfound freedom, Keevah knew every crew member on watch during her hours of freedom. Knowing each of their names and home countries was important to her. Both foredeck and main deck crews accepted the girl and me as more than regular passengers. Neither crew voiced objection to our meetings at my spot forward of the foresail locker. No doubt, my association with her was why I was included. That made me admire her even more.

Sailing with steady and fair winds meant no tacking, and there was little need for sail changes. When the occasional change in wind direction occurred and when winds were light, the men allowed Keevah and me to help work the sheets for the jib and flying jib. These lines controlled the position and shape of two of the triangular sails at the bow to help the ship gain whatever power it could from the winds. At those times, we were always under the watchful eye of the man in charge of the foredeck crew. Keevah told me he was a jack-tar, a sailor of long experience and depth of knowledge. Even so, I noticed that Bo also happened to be close by every time we touched any lines, idly observing the crew as he kept a watchful eye on us.

Each afternoon, Bo continued his work on the scrimshaw, always in our presence. I was certain he would have finished it quickly were it not for Keevah's demands to let her see every cut and scratch of the carving. He derived a great sense of joy from seeing her happy. I had never witnessed a friendship like theirs. No doubt he would have done about anything to please her.

On the day he promised to finish the work, an excited Keevah and I crowded close on either side of him to witness every single cut. A woman's scream suddenly erupted from the forward companionway.

"Fire! Fire! Oh God, help us!"

Bo sprang to his feet, stuffed the scrimshaw into his pocket, his knife into its sheath, and told us to remain seated on the bench. Along with other crew and the ship's officers, he rushed to the forward companionway as fast as his crippled foot would allow.

Two seamen descended the steep steps. In an instant, one end of a canvas hose flew up to the deck, where other seamen grabbed it and attached it to the deck-mounted seawater pump. The pump crew dropped the free end of another hose already attached to the pump into the sea for a source of water. Long handles appeared from somewhere and went into the two pump sockets. Another man poured a bucket of water into the opened priming port. He then closed the port as two seamen on each handle started pumping. When seawater began squirting from a small spout on the pump, they closed the spout and waited for a call from the men below. When the call came, the four sailors started pumping with all their strength. Other seamen moved into position to take their turns.

I was in awe at the quick action. Not a motion or moment was wasted. My stomach dropped a bit when it occurred to me that we were in a boat made of wood with yards of combustible cloth hanging from the rigging. I was thankful for this crew of men and officers.

Keevah and I left the bench and moved to the side rail to see the action. A plume of dark gray smoke rose from the companionway before dispersing into the wind. Most frightening was the frantic immigrants trying to scramble up the narrow companionway. The boat's crew could reach down and help a few up to the deck. It soon became obvious from the cursing and screaming that the companionway was so crowded and blocked that no one could escape. We saw the captain speak to his first mate and gesture toward the aft companionway.

The mate selected a couple of seamen to join him. The three men ran aft and scrambled down the steep stairs. In a few moments, immigrants started pouring up the aft companionway and onto the deck. Sharp commands from below, though indistinguishable, told us the first mate and his crew were effecting an orderly evacuation.

Bo moved near the aft companionway and worked among the coughing and panicked immigrants, reassuring some and instructing others, trying to maintain order within the jostling swarm of frightened people. His appearance and demeanor had a calming effect on the group. I was proud of my friend. When a frightened mother emerged from the companionway with a baby and blanket in one arm and a screaming child in tow, Keevah tugged at my shirt sleeve.

"Come, Lanny, we can help too."

I followed her to the woman's side. Keevah picked up the little girl and started cooing into her ear. Freed from the clinging child, the mother quickly wrapped both arms around the baby.

"Thank you," she stammered.

"Come this way," Keevah said. "You'll be safe."

Between the two of us, we cleared a path through the crowd and sat the frightened mother on the deckhouse bench. Her older child clasped onto her mother's leg as soon as Keevah set the terrified little girl down.

"I'm going back," I said. "There are others who need help." I left Keevah to her task of assuring the mother that her children were safe. She caught up with me before I reached Bo's side.

"We're here to help," I yelled. Before Bo could answer, we saw people who needed us. Confusion and separation from family caused near panic among many young and elderly. Keevah and I talked with the frightened, held hands with those who needed a touch from another person and tried to reunite panicked family members as best we could.

Soon, the last immigrant made his way on deck. The first mate emerged from the companionway and declared the hold clear and the fire out. Calm began to settle throughout the crowd. Two coughing and soot-covered seamen who extinguished the fire were the last to emerge.

Keevah and I returned to the side of the deckhouse. The mother, clasping her baby with one arm and pressing the older child's head against her leg, rose from the bench. Through tears, she tried to thank us. Keevah simply stepped toward her with outstretched arms and embraced both mother and baby. I stood by in awe.

This was not the way I thought things were done—that the daughter of a wealthy ship owner would consider hugging a lowly immigrant. But she had also befriended me, a bondservant. I was convinced this thin, red-haired girl was different from most people.

The woman moved back into the crowd of immigrants as the first mate started counting heads.

"That was kind of you," I said, "to hug one of these poor people; she needed that."

"They are not poor people, Lanny. They are good people . . . and brave people; they just don't have money."

I searched my friend's eyes, attempting to peer into this girl's mind and heart. No doubt, she was right. I had so much to learn.

As Captain Johansson and his first mate questioned immigrants to determine the cause of the fire, the bos'n organized volunteers from among the crowd to clean the hold of burned bedding, clothes, and smoke residue. Keevah and I stood by the rail, transfixed on the events and the now well-behaved immigrants.

Bo returned and gestured toward the bench to finish the scrimshaw. He reached into his pocket for the piece of whale tooth. I glanced at his face, expecting to see his usual grin. Instead, my friend's face distorted in anguish. He pulled Keevah's treasure out and stared at the broken halves.

I glanced at Keevah, sensed the depth of her disappointment, then returned my focus to Bo. My heart sickened at the sight. My old friend had poured himself into this scrimshaw to gift Keevah with a finished work of his art. He knew how she prized it. The old sailor loved this little red-haired girl as if she were his own family. Then it struck me—she was family—the closest to any family he knew and would likely ever know. The scrimshaw, and all it represented, was a symbol of the love he had for her and she for him. He would have done anything for her. Instead, all he had to offer were two pieces of a broken whale's tooth that lay in the calloused and soot-stained palms of his hands.

Keevah didn't hesitate. She took the crestfallen old sailor's hands and pressed them and the scrimshaw pieces together between her own. Continuing to clasp his hands, she looked into his eyes, with tears in her own.

"I will always treasure your gift, Bo. It makes no difference how many pieces there are because you made it, and you made it for me. That is what matters."

I realized that her tears were not for the broken scrimshaw but for her devastated friend. The scrimshaw couldn't be mended; Bo could be. With awe, I watched this young girl put aside her own loss and reach out to heal an old man's broken heart.

"Perhaps it's better this way, Bo," she said, "because now I can share your gift with Lanny. He loves you too, and now we can each have a part of you to remember forever. Our memory of this friendship won't die when this voyage is over. It will be with each of us for as long as we live."

Bo continued to gaze at her, his own tears wetting his soot-stained beard, but the pain in his face was gone—replaced by adoration. He tried to speak. All he could manage was a faltering "Thank ye, child, thank ye."

***

Lively opinions of immigrants and fires dominated the evening meal in the *Muireann*'s great cabin. After Keevah and Una went to their room, I headed for my spot in the bow. Within a few minutes, Keevah surprised me.

"How'd you get out? I thought you were in chains at this hour."

"I talked Una into granting an exception. I must be back at the quarter hour. Rolling her eyes, she said, "How am I supposed to tell the quarter hour? Ships bells are only rung on the half hour."

She locked her gaze on me and grinned.

"Keevah, that was kind—what you did for Bo. He felt terrible about the scrimshaw breaking. You turned disaster into victory—for both him and you."

"And, for you too, my friend."

"What do you mean, for me?"

"Lanny, I meant what I said about sharing the scrimshaw with you. I had already decided that I would give the whole thing to you anyway."

"What? Why, Keevah? He made that for you."

"He is your friend too, I know that. But that is not the only reason. I wanted you to have it so you would remember me. Now, don't you see? This is even better. If we each have a piece, we each have something of Bo and of each other too. I want that, Lanny because you are the best friend I've ever had. I want to share something important with you."

"Keevah . . . I . . ." No words came. No one had ever done anything like that for me.

"Here, Lanny, take this."

She held out one piece. I took it from her hand as if it were the greatest treasure on earth. She took my hand and held my piece up to match hers.

"See, we each have half a ship, but when we put them together, we have a whole ship. This will be our ship, Lanny. And it will be a whole ship only when we put our two pieces together."

We admired our ship for a long time before putting the two fragments away into safe pockets. With our backs pressed into the corner formed by the top of the foresail locker and the foredeck railing, we talked and laughed till dusk. A seaman lit the oil lantern fastened to the rail forward of us. Light from its red lens bathed a portion of the ship's rail. He then lit its green-lensed companion on the starboard side for the ship's running lights.

Under the protective eye of the on-duty crew, we watched as golden echoes of a setting sun set fire to the foaming tops of windblown waves. Too soon, the flames waned and gave way to lacy fragments of silver dancing across the sea. Scattered whitecaps glowed their ephemeral lifetimes away with captured moonlight before vanishing back into the darkening waters.

Leaning against each other for warmth as the evening cooled, we talked well past Keevah's curfew time. Our conversation seldom paused, but when it did, we simply enjoyed the motion of the ship as she rose and plunged in cadence with timeless ocean swells. We were comfortable with each other. Those moments imprinted themselves forever in my memory. Only at six bells into the first watch, when we could scarcely keep our eyes open, did we retire to our respective cabins.

I never knew how it came about—Keevah never told me—but every evening after that night, within minutes of the sounding of six bells of the last dog watch, we joined each other near the bow to take in the evening activities of the crews. Often, we watched enthralled as the men scampered aloft in the rigging to shorten sail for the coming hours of darkness.

A half-hour before sunset always found us huddled in our spot, out of the way of the working sailors, our backs pressed against the sheltering bulkhead of the foresail locker. With eager anticipation, we waited to witness the incomparable world of sunset on the open seas. Often, the sun cloaked itself behind a distant cloudbank before sliding under the watery horizon. Other times, explosions of pink, orange, and scarlet lit every cloud in the sky before they surrendered their brilliance for darker shades of ruby and purple and, finally, dusky gray. On cloudless evenings, our boat sailed into waves reflecting the uniform blushes of a crimson western horizon. Muted fascination took over until the darkness of twilight settled in and again permitted whispered conversation.

We were never disappointed. Nothing could mask the predictable pitching and rolling of our boat as she made her way through ever-present seas. Tucked safely into our spot in the bow, often with tarred weather gear offered by the crew to keep us dry from any spray, we relished the sights and sensations. Thoughts of petty conflicts and quarrels of the people around us faded as we shared in witnessing the power and majesty of God's eventide creations. Moreover, we always had the company and security of our best friend close to our side.

Keevah was right about many accepting our friendship, but I was also right about others resenting it. Blaire launched a vicious campaign to destroy me. It mattered not to her if she also destroyed Keevah in the process. After some of the crew heard some belittling remarks between the girls about our friendship, Captain Johansson intervened on Keevah's behalf and spoke to Master McDowell, who in turn reined in his daughter.

Keevah benefited. Blaire, however, simply began using more veiled tactics against me. Master McDowell was either unaware of or ignored her efforts. I felt it would serve no purpose and would only hurt others, so I resolved to let the onslaughts roll off my back as sea spray off a sailor's tarred and oiled foul-weather slicker.

As Blaire saw her efforts become less effective, her frustration became greater. She and Una became allies against me. Their combined efforts to keep us separated were ingenious, but spunky little red-haired Keevah would have no part of their schemes. With Bo and Captain Johansson in her corner, she would continue to defy her older escort and insist on her freedom.

Every time we met, even for meals or our evening ritual at the bow, we united the two parts of the scrimshaw. Blaire's and Una's irritation visibly intensified each time they saw our ship come together. The two girls resembled the occasional thunderheads we saw, growing more threatening until they could no longer hold themselves together. When they did burst, they dumped their ire on everyone, innocent and guilty alike.

Like the crew of the *Muireann*, the wise thing for Keevah and me at such times was to reduce sail and weather the storm until it passed. Through it all, Keevah's enthusiasm for our friendship never dampened.

Up to this day, I would equate the motions of ships on the seas with those evenings I spent in the bow of the *Muireann* with that red-haired, green-eyed girl who befriended me on my journey to America. Little did I know it would be a friendship replete with joy and pain.

Chapter 4

Henrysville, Indian Territory of the United States, 1850

Hesed rapped softly on the door, but not until she had eased it open, stuck her head in, and determined that I was awake. I wondered why she bothered to knock at all; she was coming in anyway. I felt no ill will against her; increasing pain left me no energy for that, only a mild spark of curiosity.

"I brought breakfast, Grayhawk. How are you feeling today?

"Better."

She put the tray of food on the chair. "Excuse me for a moment. I need to get the bedtable." Her moccasin-shod feet padded quietly from the room, accompanied by soft rustlings of her aproned frontier-style dress. Though she dressed in white-woman's clothing, she still wore Indian footwear. I wondered if her moccasins and braids were more to honor her forebears than the choice of current comfort or fashion. I felt for her—having her traditional family and tribal customs, not to mention her parents and childhood homeland ripped from her, while she straddled a future between two cultures—never, I feared, to be truly at home in either one.

Hesed's food focused me back onto my own situation.

This was my third day in bed, and still no doctor. How could I convince these women that I needed out? Even if I could make my case, how was I going to get out? My leg was not getting better; in fact, the ache and throbbing were worsening. I could not move it at all without severe pain. My occasional use of the chamber pot was an encounter with torture.

I was glad Ciara Franklin had not come. I could talk about my injuries with Hesed. I refused to admit anything to Ciara. She meant me no ill. I was certain of that, indeed, quite the opposite. Even so, I could not dispel my feelings of resentment toward her. I knew it foolish of me, yet her very resemblance to Keevah was like a razor slicing into my heart. Every time I saw her, I expected Keevah's musical Irish lilt to fill my heart with hope.

When Ciara spoke her direct American words, I felt betrayed. Any hint of Irish, however, would make her resemble Keevah more, and make me feel worse. She had done nothing to deserve hostility, and I could not explain it, yet neither could I help but feel it. My conflicted emotions would never let my enmity die.

Hesed returned and set up the bedtable and food. Then, she sat and watched me spoon the thick soup into my mouth. She didn't say a word until after I'd eaten my fill.

"You're doing better," she said as she removed the dish and table, "at least at eating."

The hair on the back of my neck sent warnings when she slid the chair closer beside me. Was that a tactic picked up from Ciara—to set off alarms in my gut, to unsettle me, before grilling me? She worked for Ciara, and Ciara wanted information. I was not about to be outwitted again in another question-and-answer session to satisfy the curiosity of a newspaper reporter.

She fixed her gaze on the blank wall above my head for a second before looking me straight in the eye. I resolved not to let my guard down.

"Grayhawk, we have no word from Dr. Kendrick. It might be days or even weeks before he can return to us. Your leg needs medical attention now. I'm guessing it hurts you more now than before; am I correct?"

Her question and direct manner caught me off guard. Those unwavering dark eyes under no-nonsense level brows forbade lying. She expected an answer—a truthful answer.

"Yes, it does hurt. Even the slightest movement—"

"I suspected as much."

"Can the barber do anything with it?"

I am sorry. He says he knows nothing about mending broken bones. However, I have talked to one of my people. He is not a doctor, but he has studied and worked with several doctors in Georgia before he came to the territories."

I looked askance at her. Her shoulders squared, and her back stiffened, though her face showed no emotion.

"No, he is not an Indian medicine man, if that is what you are thinking, though he is Cherokee. He was accepted by the whites because of his skill and knowledge. He would have been allowed to stay in the mountains of northern Georgia but decided to come here on his own accord. We are his people; he heard of our needs and came to serve."

She grinned, knowing she had discerned my thoughts even before I spoke. No western Indian I was acquainted with would openly reveal their feelings or thoughts as she had. Such a display would be considered a betrayal of oneself. In some arrogant way, it pleased me I had read her like a book—no stoic Indian she.

It then occurred to me she had perceived my opinion of her Cherokee healer before I said a word or moved a muscle. Perhaps I was not as clever as she after all. What else did she know about me?

"His name is Jeremiah Bearstriker. He will come to town to see you but will not enter the doctor's house unless the doctor invites him. So, what do you want to do? Stay here and wait for Doctor Kendrick, or move to another location and have Bearstriker look at your leg?"

"Move? To where—that place they call a hotel? Why it's a—"

"I know!" Her lifted finger and raised eyebrows silenced me. "I may have an answer. I live in a small house right beside Ciara's place. It has one bedroom, which you can have. I will move into Ciara's house. She has three bedrooms. My place has a kitchen. Ciara and I share a well, so we won't have to carry food and water so far, and you will be closer."

"Closer? Why closer, so you two can grill me with more questions any time you take a notion—day or night?"

Hesed leaned back in her chair with an impish grin.

"Why yes—if that's what we want." Her smile, now wide and laughing, displayed some of the whitest teeth I'd ever seen and convinced me this Indian woman had no intention of hiding her thoughts as many of her cousins deliberately did.

"I hadn't thought of that. I'll have to suggest it to Ciara. If I know her, she'll love your idea."

My response was a half-hearted chuckle. I said no more as I explored the face of the woman sitting next to me for more clues about her character. Her humor had surfaced easily, a pleasant facet of her personality, though I could not ignore the kernel of truth in her jest. Her broad smile diminished into a grin, wider on one side where her lips remained slightly parted as if poised to reveal one of her secrets. I wondered if her intent to repress her grin worked better on one side of her face. Pleasant enough, but it gave me the feeling she was not telling everything she knew. Her grin disappeared when she spoke again.

"Of course, I'll have to get Ciara's approval. I haven't spoken to her about any of this."

"You seem sure of yourself to tell me your plans before even speaking to Ciara."

"She will approve. We know each other well enough to almost tell what the other is thinking."

"The two of you are quite the pair." I shook my head. "She is merciless at interrogation, and you are shrewd at planning and doing . . . a formidable duo."

It was her turn to study me, furrows growing in her forehead as her brows raised a bit, but with thoughts veiled behind impenetrable eyes. She could become Indian when she wanted to. I couldn't help but like her.

"Hesed." I uttered the word slowly, to savor the sound of it. "Hesed. Is that your true name?"

She nodded.

"I've never heard that word as a name before. It means something quite unusual in a different language, an ancient language. Did you know that?"

"I know." Her expression never changed.

I continued my scrutiny of this woman. She couldn't know that I knew something about Cherokee naming traditions—that an initial name given to a baby often was changed later to reflect a significant trait about the person.

"I've been told," she said softly, "that my grandmother gave me that name when I was about five or six. I supposedly tried to protect and heal every hurt thing I could find, from baby rabbits to birds, even a rat that our cat tried to kill—so the story went." She offered no more.

I continued. "Do you have a last name?"

"Of course I do. Bluefeather."

"Hesed Bluefeather. That certainly makes sense. You're Cherokee, aren't you?"

"That should be no mystery. This is a Cherokee region of the Indian Territories. Most of us here are Cherokees."

"But not all."

"Then what makes you so certain that I am Cherokee?"

"Your name. And I would venture," I spoke my inquiry gently, "that you are of the *Ah-ni-sa-ho-ni* clan—the healers?"

She made no effort to hide her astonishment. Civilization had tempered many of her native reflexes.

"Hesed," I said gently, "I don't mean to speak when I shouldn't, but I think you bring honor to your clan and to your family."

"How do you know about the Blue Holly clan?"

I sensed a wall rise with her challenge.

"And what makes you think I bring honor to them?" She challenged again before I could mouth my first word. "How do you know anything about us?"

I spoke in the Cherokee language to say I held the Cherokee people in high regard and meant them or her no offense. I even addressed her as *"usti vgido,"* my little sister. She relaxed a bit and continued to stare at me in silence, her defiance melting into a mingling of amazement and curiosity. The wall, so abruptly erected, began to crumble.

I remained silent, so she spoke. "Grayhawk, or whatever your name is, you obviously know quite a bit about my people. Ciara and I, on the other hand, know little about you. You are an enigma to everyone in this town. You came here with nothing but a horse, saddle and tack, some trail supplies, one change of clothes, and of course, your Bible, which Ciara says you refuse to talk about. Yes, in case you are wondering, we checked the livery and the hotel. Oh, before I forget, the liveryman says he'll board and care for your horse for as long as you need him to . . . in gratitude for what you did. He is Cherokee also."

"Thank you, Hesed, you too are an enigma to me anyway. You are Indian, living in the Indian Territories, yet you speak English better than most people I know, and you are well educated and are capable of everything you do. How did that come about? I would like to know."

"And you, sir, are Scottish; at least Ciara tells me your accent, though faint, is Scottish. And you too are in the Indian Territories, and you too speak English quite well—for a Scot that is." Her disarming grin precluded my taking offense. "You too are, obviously, well educated. And I, likewise, am curious about you."

She leaned back in her chair and raised her eyebrows.

"So," she said, "it appears we each want information about the other." She paused as if to allow me time to digest her meaning. "I am willing to share my story if you will share yours. *Dadanetselá?*"

"Yes, *Dadanetselá*," I said, pleased that she asked in her native tongue. "We have a deal."

Without speaking further, she lowered her gaze to the floor before glancing upward. I wondered if she were asking permission from her ancestors to speak of them or steeling herself against memories her words might resurrect. In a moment, she started.

"I was born and raised in a small community in western North Carolina." She spoke easily but deliberately, pausing for short moments to select her words. "My parents lived on a small farm, a few acres for a garden and some pasture. Their real vocations were in education. My mother was a primary teacher. My father taught older students, but he spent most of his time as superintendent of the community school system. He was one of a group of educators whose dream was to have schools based on the European pattern throughout the Cherokee nation.

"My parents taught me from early childhood and later in school to speak, read, and write both Cherokee and English. Did you know we Cherokees' have our own alphabet and written language? My father was also the pastor of our church. We have been Christians since the time of my grandparents.

"Grayhawk, are you alright? You look upset."

"I'm fine." I resolved she would not learn the cause of my angst. "I understand how you were educated . . . but."

I scrutinized her face for some hint of the pain she must feel when sharing her past with me—a stranger and a white man—the race responsible for her loss and current circumstances. Those dark eyes concealed every emotion I expected to see except the kindness of her spirit. That, she could not hide. She waited patiently for me to continue.

"Hesed, when did you come out here . . . to the Indian Territories?"

I regretted asking when her gaze drifted to something far beyond the walls of my room. Long seconds went by.

"Twelve years . . . I was thirteen years old."

"Your parents . . . ?"

I was certain she wasn't going to tell me more, but after a short pause, she again looked me in the eye.

"My father was murdered in North Carolina in 'thirty-eight, when they took us away. He had been active on a commission for several years, working to present the Cherokee claims to our lands to the United States Congress. I believe his efforts made too many enemies among those who wanted our lands. They killed him and then burned our house and barn, and even the church, to the ground."

"I am sorry,"

"Even while our home was burning, soldiers with guns rounded us up and marched us to a place near the outskirts of town. It was like a prison camp. Neighbors and many other Indians I didn't know were all there. Some had wagons and belongings, like they expected this to happen. My mother and I had nothing but the clothes we were wearing." She dropped her gaze to the floor and sat silent for a long time. I didn't know what to say.

When she looked up, there were tears in her eyes.

"I was terrified . . . that was the beginning."

"Hesed." I tried to reach her hand. The movement of my body sent bolts of pain up my leg. "I know enough. You needn't say more."

Glistening tears veiled any clues as I tried to read her emotions. Those Indian eyes appeared almost black as they bored into mine, trying to ferret out the meaning of my words. How could I possibly know enough of her story? I hoped she wouldn't ask.

"My mother died on the trail . . ." Her voice, soft and low, faded as she again dropped her gaze to the floor. Finally, she rose and stepped toward the door. I could barely discern her distraught mumble, "Excuse me. I am sorry." Keeping her face hidden from me, she slipped out of my room.

I understood. Cherokees refer to those brutal marches from their homelands to the government-established Indian Territories as *Nunna dual Tsuny*, the trail where they cried. Hesed's tears still fell from her tragedy on that trail. Over the years, I had hardened myself to contain mine. Even so, I could no more forget the grief of that trail than she could.

In a moment, I heard the deliberate latching of the outside door. I was alone again, so I forced myself into remembering more pleasant things—like the *Muireann* and Keevah.

The brig, *Muireann,* 1816

By my reckoning from our daily position fixes on the chart, the *Muireann* was three days out of Boston. Master McDowell arrived early at the deckhouse for our customary discussion. When I arrived, the pipe in his mouth was unlit. He arose, slipped his pipe into a pocket, and stepped to the door.

"Follow me, Lansdale."

It was an unusual request. I complied without question. My stomach fell when he descended the aft companionway and stopped in front of the captain's cabin. His knock on the door resurrected all the anguish and loneliness of that day when the men told me that my sister, Bridget, and my parents had died in the coalmine. It was the same thing all over again. This time, they would say the words I had secretly feared for weeks. "Never see Keevah again."

Captain Johansson's call to enter was the signing of my death warrant. Numb with fear and despair, I followed Master into the cabin.

"Are you well, son?" The words, sounding far-off and irrelevant, came from the direction of the captain. I looked up and tried to focus.

"Lansdale, answer . . . lad, are you ill?" Master placed a hand on my shoulder as he bent over to examine my face.

All I remember was staring at the captain and stammering, "I am well, sir."

Why were they concerned about how I felt? Weren't they about to jerk the most important person in my life from me—just as the coal mine had done before?"

Another knock on the door prompted the captain to call out his invitation. My knees almost gave way when Bo entered. The three men on this boat whom I most revered now stood before me—Master McDowell, whom I had come to admire and respect; Captain Johansson, whom I considered a hero for standing up for Keevah; and my old sailor friend, Bo, whom I truly loved. Had they convened to deliver what would be, to my mind, a death sentence? Had Blaire and Mairi won after all? Had they been right all along? Was it true that I would be forever a lowly orphaned laborer and servant—never to rise above my birth status?

Bo stepped to my side. Captain Johansson remained seated at his desk. Master McDowell took position in front of the chart table, straightened his vest, and tugged at his jacket lapels. I tried to steel myself—to hear his judgment.

"Lansdale," Master McDowell stated as if speaking before Parliament. "I have asked these two men to witness what I have to say to you."

He had witnesses. I would never be able to deny his decree.

"When we boarded this ship, the ship's manifest listed me and my family as Baltar McDowell, two daughters, Blaire and Mairi, and one bondservant, Lansdale Grahame. When we step onto American soil in Boston, I want the manifest to list me with two daughters and one son, Lansdale Grahame McDowell. It will read that way forever in my, and in your, family records, Lansdale, if you approve."

Too stunned to answer, I focused on his eyes. After a moment, I became aware of my slack jaw.

Master McDowell, seeing I could not speak, continued. "This will mean you will no longer be under bondage to me. You will no longer be a servant to my family or to anyone. You will be my son, with all the rights and privileges that such a relationship entails. You will be free."

"W—why . . .?" I stammered.

Master softened his voice and stepped close to me.

"Lansdale, this was my intention from the moment I decided to bring you and my girls to America. I felt it would give you a better chance to succeed in your new country. Now, after getting to know you, to see your mind and character, not to mention your conduct and depth of courage exhibited on this voyage, I would be proud to call you my son.

"Captain Johansson has insisted that it be your decision; he will not conduct any such proceedings or approve any manifest change unless you agree. Lansdale, I would be proud to have you in my family. Will you agree?"

All I could think of were Keevah's words as we parted that day at the deck rail, "Oh, Lanny, I so love freedom . . . I so love freedom." What Blaire or Mairi might think, or how they might react never entered my mind. The thought of freedom and Keevah's words consumed my entire thought.

"Yes, Master, I agree."

"Excellent," he said as he patted my shoulder.

"It may take some time to get used to, but you need to call me Master no longer. From this moment on, you may call me Father."

After briefly conferring with Captain Johansson, my new father turned to me.

"You may go now." A wide grin stretched across his face. "I suspect you have a friend you will want to share this with."

I bolted for the cabin door.

Keevah's and my friendship grew with each passing day. When the *Muireann* eased up to the docks at Boston, we were, in Bo's words, "Thicker 'n thieves." Before we disembarked, much to the chagrin and distaste of Una, Keevah towed me into the hold to find the immigrant mother we had helped during the fire. By this time, all the immigrants knew us. They eagerly helped locate the young woman. A long and tearful embrace between the mother and Keevah ensued. The grateful young woman wasn't through yet. With tears flowing, she grabbed me for a long hug as well.

Again, I found myself awed by my red-haired friend and the lessons of compassion and character she continued to teach.

Many well wishes from the immigrants followed as we scampered up the companionway steps. Captain Johansson noticed us as we stepped on deck. He caught my eye with a slight smile and a nod of his head before returning to his ship's business. Though Keevah's actions might surprise me, he expected no less from this spunky young girl whom he had come to know so well during their voyages across the seas.

Bo approached Keevah and me with a grin, but his eyes were too moist. We each hugged him—Keevah's embrace long and tender. I heard her thank him for our scrimshaw and saw his silent nod of acknowledgment. These two treasured friends avoided using the word to convey their final goodbyes to each other.

Keevah's father and three brothers awaited her at the dockside. Before joining her eager family, she turned to me, hugged me, and kissed me on the cheek. "Goodbye, Lanny, we'll write."

She skipped to Una, who took one of her hands to lead her down the gangway.

"No, wait." Keevah twisted away from a displeased Una and ran back. "Lanny, the scrimshaw!" She already had her piece out of her pocket and held it up. "Hurry, we must make our ship one more time!"

I produced my piece. She grabbed my hand, thrust the pieces together, and leaned against me, mesmerized by the intact carving of our ship. I glanced at her face and the tears gathering in her emerald eyes.

"Lanny, you are my best friend ever. Oh, I almost forgot—my father lives in Portland, Maine. That's where his boats and shipping business are. His address is on this paper." Still holding our ship together with one hand, she handed me a scrap of paper with the other. "Don't lose it, and write, so I'll know where to write you back." She separated our ship and turned imploring eyes to search mine.

"Please write, Lanny," she whispered.

"I will, Keevah. I promise."

With her piece of the scrimshaw still in her hand, she threw her arms around my neck. I answered with a long hug. We parted without a further word. She joined an embarrassed and exasperated Una. Together, they walked down the gangway, and Keevah jumped into her family's open arms.

Subdued at our separation, I tagged behind my new father and sisters as we strode down the gangway. We followed our porter to the line of carriages waiting for paying passengers. I looked back, hoping to catch a glimpse of Keevah. She was lost among the mass of people, but I did see Una holding one dour-looking fellow by his jacket lapel and pointing in my direction. Her mouth was going like a runaway coal wagon. I was thankful I couldn't hear her tale, though I was certain I knew every condemning word.

Seated beside my new father on the carriage seat, I pondered about all that had happened since we left Scotland. I was in a new land with a new family. Never mind that my new sisters despised me. I was facing a new future. Never had I felt, or fully understood, what it meant to be free—nor had I treasured any possession like my piece of Keevah's broken scrimshaw. That piece of whale tooth was the world to me.

I could not know the course it would set for my life.

Henrysville, Indian Territory of the United States, 1850

My questions to Hesed had reopened painful wounds; I should have known better. I had promised to tell her about my own education and background, which I would after I organized my thoughts and developed my story. I knew that could lead me to tell her more about myself, more than I wanted to share. Yet, she deserved to know something. It was my clumsy questioning that led to her tearful retreat.

I wanted to pray for her, but it seemed God hadn't listened to me for years, not after all I had done and failed to do. I glanced at my Bible lying on the desk. Hesed hadn't mentioned it when she moved it from where I laid it on my bed. I noticed her gaze lingering on it as she placed it on the desk out of the way. I had carried it for most of my adult life because it was a gift from Keevah. I couldn't remember the last time I'd opened it. I doubted I would have the courage to do so now. I wouldn't know; my current disabilities kept it out of my reach. Gratitude for that small mercy resurrected forebodings of my spiritual plight.

The odd window at the top of my room offered no answers. I continued staring at it, demanding an accounting from myself for the *Dadanetselá,* the bargain I'd agreed to with Hesed. I would have to keep my promise to tell her my story, but I would not tell her about Keevah. I had never revealed Keevah to anyone but one friend, and that was many years ago. I didn't have her any longer, only memories. I feared, for reasons I could not understand, that if I shared them, they would no longer be mine. Memories were my only thread to those whom I considered family; every one of them now lost to me. I could not bear to lose those last tenuous threads to those I had loved.

Boston, U.S.A. 1818

Neither had I shared with anyone about my crushing disappointment at never receiving a return letter from Keevah. I never doubted her sincerity when she asked me to write before we disembarked the *Muireann*. I eagerly wrote her as soon as Father McDowell established a home and address in Boston. At least a half-dozen letters followed that first one, each resurrecting fervent anticipation, which lasted several weeks—until disappointment ushered in the bitter taste of reality.

Determined not to give my new sisters more ammunition against me, I took pains at concealing my misery from them. I am certain Father McDowell sensed my unhappiness despite my attempts at secrecy. I am equally certain he knew the reason for it. He earned my gratitude by keeping me tasked and letting me deal with my distress in my own time and way.

I attended school by myself because girls were neither required nor permitted in public schools. Father McDowell again hired a private tutor for the girls. There were private schools for young ladies in the Boston area, but he could find none that met the standards he demanded for his daughters.

My resolve not to give up Keevah resurrected my hopes such that after each period of despair, I would write another letter. Throughout the winter, my letters to Keevah dwindled to one every other month. By spring, I stopped writing altogether. The sting of being forgotten so quickly by the one whose friendship I treasured so deeply never diminished. Whenever I thought of her, the image of Una's pointing finger and accusing mouth interceded—to crush any dream of ever seeing Keevah again.

I hoped it was Una's doing that she did not write. I could not bear to entertain thoughts as to what other causes might keep her from responding. Every other possibility seemed dreadful. I prayed for her often—that she was safe and well and had not succumbed to the clutches of her vengeful French cousin.

The McAllister estate on the outskirts of Boston became an obsession with Father McDowell. Formerly owned by an enterprising and well-to-do sea captain, its once elegant buildings and grounds had fallen into disrepair after the captain, his ship, and crew disappeared at sea. After the eventual declaration of his death, the captain's heirs sought to divest themselves of the financial burden of maintaining a non-profitable property.

Although we didn't understand the why of it, we celebrated Father's negotiating skills when he claimed to have purchased the place at a real bargain. Three months later, even before craftsmen were finished restoring the property to near its former grandeur, we moved into the estate mansion. That very evening, on the first anniversary of our landing in America, Father shared his dreams with us.

He had become quite disillusioned at the American system of education for failing to include girls in public schools. For years, Scotland had required at least elementary education for both boys and girls and provided public schools for all, even the peasantry. He thought it should be so in America as well.

He had always provided tutors for Blaire and Mairi, and he would continue to do so. Only now, they would be in the company of approximately twenty other girls. His new estate and spacious mansion would become a private school for young ladies. He could not afford to school the masses, but he could provide private education for select girls at the same level as he insisted for his own daughters, at least for families who could afford his sizeable tuition fees.

I thought it an ironic twist when he told me that I, who had started in a public school in Scotland with dozens of other peasant children, would now have a private tutor, unshackled from my sisters. Blaire and Mairi would lose their private tutor and would join other children in a classroom. I thought it wise not to gloat over my good fortune. It never occurred to me at the time that my sisters would gain an army of allies with so many girls living together in the same house.

Another flurry of letters to Keevah pursued those written from the Boston house. I could not bear the thought of her not knowing where to write me, should she ever want to. Over the following months, it became apparent she did not. Again, I stopped writing.

One year with a fourteen-year-old male confined to the same house with twenty-two female students, ages thirteen to seventeen, not to mention a half dozen female instructors, was all Father McDowell could take. At vigorous prompting from his teaching staff, and I suspect some threats of resignation, he agreed I should attend a private boarding school for boys for the remainder of my education.

I met his proposal with unreserved enthusiasm. At fifteen years of age, I enrolled with twelve other boys for year one at the Aberdeen School of Grammar for Young Men. The school, which boasted a total enrollment of thirty-two, had achieved great success in preparing students for religious studies at Harvard. It offered a perfect opportunity for me, as I had developed a keen interest in those matters. My personal mission was to graduate from Harvard with honors. The Aberdeen school would be my first step.

As I had with the aged Professor Muir in Scotland, I thrived under the intense curriculum and discipline. Latin offered no challenge; Hebrew, I managed with difficulty. French, though not required, became my favorite. I became fluent in my three years there.

French studies reminded me of Keevah. With apprehension because of the years gone past, I sent her three more letters—one at the beginning of each school year. No answers came. I was disappointed but not surprised. I did not write again.

Before my final year at Aberdeen, my goal of attending Harvard went by the wayside. Passionate and occasional acrimonious debates among college leaders over doctrinal issues with which I did not agree turned my attention from Harvard to a small seminary led by the head pastor of one of Boston's larger churches. Tuition was minimal, and I would be earning my keep by working for the McIntyre Church and Seminary.

After depending on Father McDowell for so many years, I was making my own way; at least I thought so. My sisters were overjoyed to see me leave, though our goodbyes became the sincerest moments between us in all the years I spent with them.

Father McDowell and I had a more difficult time. Our relationship had never been as a bond between father and son, more like a revered mentor and prized apprentice. Nevertheless, we were close. I was grateful to him for all he had done for me. He, in turn, I am sure, felt liberated from the burden of guilt at being the owner of the mine where my family died. I sensed a veiled sadness as well as pride when he wished me well. His lingering handshake said more than his words. We parted treasured friends.

✲✲✲

Henrysville, Indian Territory of the United States, 1850

Light from the window was fading when Ciara knocked. This time, she waited for my invitation before entering. Aromas from the basket she carried indicated food—no doubt prepared by Hesed. I would have preferred eating in the company of the Indian woman—the very sight of Ciara never failed to upset me. But, after having driven Hesed to tears, I didn't blame her for staying away. I resigned myself to putting up with Ciara's visit.

"How are you feeling?" she said. "I brought your supper. Hesed didn't feel like coming this evening."

"I don't blame her. Will you tell her I'm sorry?"

"Don't blame yourself." She set the food before me and then sat in the bedside chair. "She told me of your conversation."

"It was stupid of me. I knew the answers to my questions the minute I realized she was Cherokee. I didn't need her to retell all the dreadful details."

"She will be all right; she's strong."

"That is obvious, but what I can't understand is how she can be so kind to me, a white man, after what whites have done to her. Even in her conversation, she seems to hold no animosity toward anyone. I am not certain I could be so forgiving."

Ciara's brow furrowed as she glanced at my Bible lying on the desk by my bed. I could almost see questions forming in her mind. She spoke none of them.

"You've glimpsed a facet of the person she is—extraordinary. I am blessed to have her as a friend."

Her pause, as if preparing to change the subject, rekindled the tension I had felt when she questioned me. Yet, I sensed no challenge or threat from her this time—she did not have her notebook. I resolved not to be defensive.

"Hesed said she made an agreement with you to share your life histories, or at least some of it, with each other. She . . . we both want to know more about you, right now she—"

"I did agree, and I understand."

"She thought you might share with me. Will you?"

My affable snort brought a smile and nod from her.

"Why not? It makes no difference which one of you I tell. The other will know every detail the minute the two of you get together." I paused a tense moment to gauge her reaction. Her answering chuckle put me at ease. "Yes," I said. "I will keep our agreement. I will tell my story."

"You are right about one thing," she said. "We are close. We share about everything with each other. Some people accuse us of being like sisters—little girls with secrets between us."

The smile faded. A level gaze of her green eyes secured my focus.

"Mr. Grayhawk, I know her to be worthy of my trust . . . and yours."

I nodded. She allowed me time to shape my story. I began with my boyhood in Scotland, the coal mine tragedy, my servanthood bondage, and the voyage to America. A summary of my education and eventual enrollment in the seminary in Boston followed.

When I paused, she urged me to continue, so I did. I told her of the letter I had received from Father McDowell's lawyer telling me of his unexpected death and that he had willed his entire estate to his daughters.

I did honor Hesed's and my *Dadanetselá*, but I said not one word about any girl, especially the red-haired girl that I met on the boat. Those memories I would share with no one—especially not with her. After hesitating, I concluded by sharing my failed intentions of becoming a man of the cloth. I didn't tell her why.

At first, I took Ciara's intent gaze and long silence as disbelief. She crumpled her brow as if trying to comprehend a puzzle that had too many missing pieces. In a few moments, she spoke,

"I was certain you were more than a frontiersman, but I had no idea. I am dying to know more. And, about your name, it seems more Indian than Scottish."

"Another story altogether," I said.

"I accept." Her voice softened to a gentle whisper. "Why did you not become a minister? That is something you dreamed of . . . and worked so hard for."

With a lump growing in my throat, I diverted my gaze to my feet and remained silent.

"I'm sorry," she said. "That is none of my business; I don't mean to pry."

In an impulse of compassion, she reached out to touch my shoulder. At the same time, I raised my hand to wave off any need for an apology.

The moment our hands touched, quite by accident, I sensed a foreboding link toward this young woman whose very appearance caused me pain every time I saw her. My bones chilled. Her persistence in uncovering my past felt like a snare closing on me—a vulnerability which I could not identify—or from which I could not flee. The worst of it was that I had no idea of the reason for my trepidation—only that she was at the core of it.

After a minute, she broke the silence.

"I didn't mean to upset you," she said. "Your supper is getting cold, and you need rest. One of us will pick up the dishes in the morning. By the way, Hesed did talk to me about you moving into her place. I agree . . . if that is what you want. I would recommend it. Under the circumstances, I also recommend Jeremiah Bearstriker. I've heard of his work."

Using both hands, she lifted her swollen belly as she rose. "Thank you for sharing your story. Rest assured, I will share every detail with Hesed. Goodnight." She turned and gave me a warm grin as she stepped out the doorway.

I acknowledged with a nod as she left. Ciara's question evoked memories of my last year at the seminary—mingled with wondering if I would ever see the Indian woman again.

CHAPTER 5

McIntyre Seminary, Boston, U.S.A. 1823

Mrs. Macintosh, the seminary secretary, approached me in the church sanctuary as I focused on one of our students' weekly chores—polishing the massive chair in which the Head Pastor ensconced himself every Sunday.

"You have a lady asking to see you," she said, maintaining an appropriate chilliness and distance from me, a mere student. Turning on a heel, she strode toward the sanctuary doors, never waiting for my response. Her distain was obvious. Students should have no time for or interest in women while engaged in pastoral studies.

"Meet her in the outer office," she said over her shoulder. "Immediately. She is waiting."

Her voice trailed away as her stiffened back disappeared through the doorway.

What misdeed caused this woman to inquire for me? Members of the congregation rarely spoke with seminary students since the church had adequate pastors and staff to handle any situation. However, she asked for me. I had no choice but to go.

Whatever her grievance, I must represent the church and staff in good light. Dismissal from the seminary was a distinct possibility for any transgression—real or perceived. Our student numbers had already been reduced this year for what we thought was a simple matter of poor judgment more than a breach of seminary policy. Would this now be my fate after all my hard work? I dreaded this compulsory encounter, which I knew a church staff would monitor.

Upon entering the outer office, I struggled to maintain any semblance of dignity. Sitting before me, in one of the half dozen straight-backed chairs lined up along the wall, was the most beautiful woman I had ever seen.

Her emerald eyes fairly danced as Keevah rose to greet me. No longer the skinny, red-haired girl who had befriended me on the brig *Muireann*, she stepped toward me with self-assured poise and grace.

I stood stunned, my head felt like it was spinning, with my mouth open as well.

Keevah appeared in total control. She curtsied in a most proper manner, as a young woman would if approaching a respected church pastor. A mere seminary student and intern should never expect such a reverent greeting.

She extended an envelope to me.

"Father sent me to respectfully request you join us at dinner next Monday evening."

My hand took the envelope while my gaze fixed on her face. She flashed a tiny smile for only a second. Even after all these years, I couldn't miss that impish grin that I had come to love so much on the *Muireann* as we plotted our strategies to counter Una's and Blaire's malicious plans. It came and went too quickly to alert anyone. Nevertheless, I recognized her warning to follow her lead and not to voice my surprise about her father ever requesting anything of me. I could ask my whys later.

"I am grateful for his invitation and would love to attend. Monday is my one free evening of the week."

We both stood, simply enthralled with seeing each other after so long.

A polite clearing of the monitor's throat shattered the moment.

Following Keevah's strategy, I fabricated. "It will be good to see and talk with your father again . . . after such a long time."

"He said to tell you he looks forward to getting together; he has missed those long and deep conversations with you. There is also something he wants to discuss with you—something important to him as well as you. At least, that is what he told me to tell you."

"Tell him I look forward to it."

"Oh, and he says to dress informally."

With that, she curtsied in respect before turning toward the door.

"Thank you, Miss Ferguson."

She turned back and smiled, "You are quite welcome, sir," and was gone.

I turned and glanced at the monitor. Her stern expression never wavered, but she did nod her consent—not necessarily of the meeting itself but at least at the propriety of its participants. If only she knew.

This was Friday. I had three more working days and sleepless nights to wait and wonder what my best friend had planned this time. Eternity passed and my Monday evening free time finally came after I completed my studies and chores.

Keevah was waiting for me in the lobby of the fine hotel named in the invitation. I hesitated, as I had not dressed for such an establishment.

"Come with me," she said. "I have a carriage waiting. We can't talk here."

During the ride, after inquiring about my health and happiness, she explained her reason for the deception.

"I felt I had to say Father invited you to dinner in case the invitation was appropriated and read by the seminary staff. One of my friends has a cousin in another seminary in Provincetown. He reports they are quite strict about such things, and that includes young women contacting or socializing with students. I assumed your seminary would do likewise."

"You assumed correctly."

The carriage pulled up to the front of a modest yet respectable two-story dwelling, the type common in working-class neighborhoods of Boston.

"Here we are. Do you remember the immigrant mother we helped during the fire aboard the *Muireann*? She married a German carpenter, Wassermann. He works in the shipyards here in Boston, often on my father's boats. The man saved all the money he could for over two years to pay for her passage from Scotland, hoping she would consent to marriage, which she did. I met her again when she and her husband attended a boat launching after Father had it refurbished. Wassermann did a great deal of the carpentry work, and father likes his craftsmanship."

My step slowed. I felt furrows forming on my brow.

"Lanny." She stopped me in my tracks with a hand to my chest. "She will be thrilled to see you. Don't worry; they are loyal to me. Neither of them will say a word about our meeting."

Keevah was right. The woman hugged me with a joy that brought tears to her eyes. No longer a destitute immigrant with two poorly clothed children, she appeared a confident American mother of four with a husband proud to have her at his side. I recalled the woman Keevah had hugged aboard the *Muireann* and marveled at the transformation. Keevah had seen through the inevitable stigma of poverty to discern the heart and soul of the person within. Afterward, I would often remember and question if I would ever have learned to view people that way—like a man of God should—had I become a pastor.

"I was devastated," Keevah said after the Wassermanns left us alone in their tiny parlor, "when month after month, I received no letter from you."

"But I sent letters."

"I know that now, and I understand how you must have felt, so let me explain. Una stayed with us for years and taught French at a nearby girl's school before deciding to return to France. She left three months ago to sail back to her family. I was sorting through things she left in an old trunk. I found your letters. She intercepted every one of them—I never saw a one. It has taken me all this time to track you down. The kind people at Aberdeen School told me how to find you at McIntyre." She stopped as tears moistened her eyes. "You wrote me for years, didn't you?"

"I did."

"I am so sorry."

"It is unbelievable that she saved those letters."

"She missed France and her family. I was the person she was with most of the time. We naturally became closer as time passed."

"You were kind to her . . ."

Keevah nodded. "She grew homesick. I could help. Although it took years, we became like sisters to each other. I am certain that's why she left the letters where only I would find them."

I could only stare in amazement at my friend.

Her grip on my arm tightened as she spoke. "I felt terrible thinking you hadn't written. I can't imagine how you must have felt to never have received an answer. I am so sorry."

"Can you imagine how I feel now, seeing that you are alive, in good health, and actually here?"

Her emerald eyes started to tear up again as they searched mine.

"Lanny, d—do you still have your half of our scrimshaw?"

I reached into my pocket to retrieve the soft leather pouch I always carried it in. "I keep it hidden in this because I'm afraid the seminary staff will think it is a source of pride. We are not allowed jewelry or any personal treasures because they think such items are vanity and will interfere with our commitment to the Lord." I slid my half of the scrimshaw out of the pouch and handed it to my friend.

She held the two pieces together and stared silently at our ship for several long moments. Several times, I saw rapid blinking as her eyes moistened.

"Six years, Lanny. Six years . . . we can never let this happen again. Lanny, Una has turned my entire family against you, especially my two oldest brothers. Even after we became close, she couldn't undo the damage she caused. I want to see you again, but it will have to be here. I am of age and unmarried, only because I've resisted their plans for me to marry an older man more than twice my age—someone who could be of great benefit to their shipping business. My two oldest brothers are angry about that, but I'm simply not going to do it. It's not who I am."

"What are you going to do?"

"Ha! I've already done it. I've accepted a teaching position at a girls' school right here in Boston. I can stay with the Wassermanns until I get a place of my own. They can't stop me, Lanny. I'm on my own now. And I can visit with my best friend ever, that is, whenever you have time for me."

***

Keevah and I did visit each other often. She was able to rent lodging in an attic room of an elderly German couple who, if they could, would have adopted her as their own. The husband's prosperous boot and shoe-repair business had allowed them to purchase the Greek-revival home in the neighborhood near the girls' school. Keevah fit in well and grew to relish her role as a teacher and mentor of young ladies.

By the end of her first teaching year, I had entered my final year at McIntyre Seminary. In less than a year, our friendship had grown such that we came to depend on each other in many ways. I could voice the concerns, trials, and triumphs of my studies and demands made upon me in complete confidence that Keevah would care and help me keep it all in perspective.

She helped me deal with the news in the letter I had received from Father McDowell's lawyer telling me of his unexpected death and that he had willed his entire estate to his daughters. Neither of us received an answer to our letters of condolence to Blaire and Mairi. Though he was not my blood father, I felt the loss of another member of my family. Through it all, Keevah's friendship became more precious to me.

She, in turn, was at ease in sharing anything from confrontations with parents and school administrators for her spirited ways to the most coarse or sensitive moments with her students, many of whom adored her. We supported and inspired each other. Even with the limited hours we had, we made each other's lives full.

Somehow, without becoming aware of doing so, we got past the ritual of putting our scrimshaw pieces together each time we met. That was merely a childish game that we outgrew in dealing with the issues and trials of adult life. Nevertheless, we each kept and treasured our broken pieces of whale tooth—mementos of a carefree and less worrisome childhood friendship.

Neither of us could tell when it happened. It might have been on the boat *Muireann,* for all we knew. But one winter evening, after receiving a particularly hard-sought recognition, I returned to my room with the coveted letter. In my solitude, I realized I could not enjoy any of life's rewards without sharing with Keevah. In fact, nothing would matter without her. When we met at our appointed time the next Monday evening, I told her I loved her.

She cried.

"I know," she said softly while wiping tears. "And I love you too, Lanny. I think I always have," she said. "That's why it hurt when I thought you hadn't written."

Our courtship, though limited to a few hours on Monday evenings, was a delightful and transformative time for me. This red-haired, green-eyed woman made me forget I was ever a peasant boy, bonded to lowly servanthood, fated to a life-long struggle of proving my worth to superiors. I became a man, able to face whatever the world offered, inspired by the incredible woman who loved me. At last, Father McDowell's aims became reality—my spirit slipped all remaining traces of man's-imposed bondage—I became free.

One Sunday evening in late February, I was walking back to the seminary from my student preaching at a neighborhood church. Three men stepped in front of me.

"You Lanny McDowell?"

"I am, Sir, I . . ." I never finished before one man rushed and hit me in the chest. The blow was hard. I fell flat on my back. Before I could roll over to escape, another man kicked me in my ribs. My breath exploded from me. The first grabbed my hair and jerked my head back. A knife appeared in his hand; its blade soon pressed against my throat.

"Stay away from our sister," the brute said, "or you're a dead man. Do you understand? We know all about you, Scotsman. No stinking bondservant is going to touch her. We'll not warn you again."

The brute yanked the cross medallion, which identified me as a student of McIntyre Seminary, from around my neck. The chain broke and jerked my neck hard; I felt it might have broken a bone.

"Don't think you can hide behind the pulpit either; you're fit for nothing but a slave."

As the brute with the knife stepped back, the second man, a contemptible toad of a man, kicked me again in the ribs so hard I could not breathe. As I lay on the road, gasping for air, the men hurried away into the darkness. Only two men accosted me that night, but I was certain there was another, a younger man, standing back and watching. I recognized no faces, though they had identified themselves as Keevah's brothers.

I had to warn her that they were in Boston. No doubt, if they knew where she lived, they would abduct her back home to Portland. I couldn't let that happen. It took me a while to run to the house where she roomed. The old cobbler heard my knock and opened the door to see me doubled over, struggling to catch my breath from running such a great distance with painful ribs. He called his wife.

They both knew Keevah's and my stories. We may as well have been their own. They hustled me into their parlor. She sat me down and wetted a towel to comfort me while he labored up the stairs to fetch Keevah.

"I don't think they know where I live," Keevah said. "I write a good friend, my father's housekeeper, at her home. She keeps an eye on them for me. I trust her. She lets me know what they're up to, at least as best as she can. I don't know how they knew you were here unless Una showed them some of your letters. They could have tracked you down from the schools you attended—the same way I did. Somehow, they know we are seeing each other. That is troublesome."

"Ach, 'tis more than troublesome," the old cobbler said in thick German. "'Tis dangerous for Lanny here. Keevah, they must know where you live too. You must move to another home soon. We can help. Our friends from the old country live on the other side of your school. They speak English, but not so good as us. They are good people. They will keep you and tell nobody. Yah, that is best for you."

"We can still meet at the Wassermanns," Keevah said.

"Yah, we know the Wassermanns too. They are good people. You can meet there, but your brothers know where Lanny lives. They are probably watching him, or they have somebody else watching for them."

The old cobbler put his pipe in his mouth, then after a stern glance from his wife, laid it aside. "Lanny, you must be careful when you leave the seminary so nobody can know you are going to see Keevah. And, when you leave the Wassermanns, you must go to other houses to look like you are visiting other people—like a young preacher would do. We will arrange with some friends so you will have houses to visit. That way, you both can be safe."

It was a full month before the McIntyre staff permitted me outside the church or seminary grounds. I relied on another student to carry a message explaining all to Keevah. No one doubted my story of the assault or robbery of the McIntyre medallion, but I was unable to explain why it took so long for me to return to the seminary. No one believed I could have been unconscious for so long a time or taken so long to recover.

On the other hand, no one could prove otherwise, so based on my previous good record, they reinstated me as a pulpit-supply preacher. That allowed me to preach at smaller churches which had no preacher or when their pastor was unavailable. They also gave me permission to leave the seminary on Monday evenings.

Keevah's and my next meeting at the Wassermann's was joyous indeed. She surprised me with a Bible in which she had written of her love for me and her wishes that the Lord would watch over both of us. The old cobbler had convinced her that, though advertised as a pocket version, the Bible was too large to carry in a man's inside coat pocket. To solve that problem, he made a leather pouch a man could strap under his coat. Keevah accepted that idea because it would also keep the Bible and her message from any prying eyes of the seminary staff. I thought it a grand idea.

For extra precaution against the staff spotting the pouch and reading Keevah's message, I wore it under my shirt, strapped to my chest.

Being with each other after the long absence, Keevah's gift, along with the fear of her brothers, pushed our emotions too high. We shared each other in love that night.

I reasoned afterward, as the old cobbler had suggested, that her brothers did have someone watching me. The German's plan for me to visit other houses after seeing Keevah failed. They must have learned which homes I visited, and although I changed my order of visits, after a time, they guessed correctly.

Shortly after leaving the second house one evening, the brothers intercepted me. The brute, the one who had pushed me down before and threatened me with his knife, rushed me.

This time, I was prepared. Timing a swing of my stout walking stick with precision, I hit him above his left ear the second he lunged within my range. He went down with a loud grunt. The toady brother, caught by surprise, was late in starting his rush. I had time to set myself and gauge my swing for his head as well. He anticipated and threw his arm up in defense. The stick hit his arm with enough force to break a bone had not his jacket shielded it. The stick bounced upward, but I hung on. The man cried out in pain, grabbing for his injured arm as he went to his knees.

As I attempted to gain control of my stick, a hard blow to the back of my head caused me to pitch forward and lose my footing. I don't remember hitting the ground. In seconds, my hands were lashed behind me, and my feet tied so tightly I couldn't move. A heavy gag over my mouth kept me from yelling for help. Someone grabbed me by the shoulder and flipped me face up.

The toad nursed his sore arm as he kneeled over the unmoving brute. His curses and threats were louder than I could have yelled without the gag, but he was moving his arm—it wasn't broken.

"Shut up! You trying to wake everybody? Carry him if you must. We need to get out of here."

Only then did I see the man speaking. He was much younger than the other two but a good four inches taller than me. He looked stout enough to manhandle me with ease. I was certain he was the third man whom I saw watching when the others assaulted me before.

Brute struggled to stand. With Toad's help, he made it to his feet. His curses told me he was close to regaining his full wits.

The younger man jerked me to my feet, put a heavy rope around my neck, and tightened the noose so that it scraped skin everywhere it touched. Then, he removed the lashings on my feet.

"You walk when and where I tell you, or I'll let him cut your heart out. Believe me—he'll do it. Quiet, you two," he hissed at the two injured and angry stragglers as he steered me toward a dark alley.

In the alley, they tossed me into the bed of a wagon, threw some canvas over me, and prodded the horse into a jarring trot. The canvas and sides of the wagon prevented me from seeing anything, but I could hear them arguing.

I recognized Brute's voice from before when he threatened me with the knife. He and Toad wanted to kill me and get it over. He was enraged and insisted they stay with their plan. It was what I deserved. Toad agreed, but the younger man refused. He claimed to have a better idea.

In my predicament, with little chance of escape, I could only wonder how brothers could do this to one of their own family. I could never have hurt Bridget, the sister I loved, or even Blaire and Mairi, the sisters who hated me. It would be inhuman, but I had no doubt they were serious and would do exactly as they threatened. Would Keevah ever know the truth of my disappearance or what her brothers had done? I prayed for her as I had never prayed before.

When the wheels stopped bouncing over cobblestones and the rattling of the wagon ceased, I could hear voices of other men. Some were singing or attempting to sing. Others were arguing, laughing, or conversing. Occasionally, the shrill laughter of a woman cut through the din. I could only reason that they had stopped at some place of drunken entertainment.

"Stay with him. I'll be back," the young man said. "And keep your hands off; he's no good to us hurt."

Both Brute and Toad voiced their displeasure at the change in plans. I think it angered them that their younger brother had usurped the authority due older brothers. He had canceled their plans and then had the gall to order them to watch me when he left.

My hopes that they would comply died when they ripped the canvas away.

"Look what we have here," Brute sneered. "Scottish vermin lying here dirtying up our wagon."

"No," Toad said, "he's too pretty to be a Scot. His face needs rearranged."

The first blow caught me above my left cheekbone. The next came before I could even think. I could feel the skin over my eyebrow split as flashes of light filled my head. A kick to my chin snapped my head back so hard it bounced off the wagon bed. Even as dazed as I was, I was aware of the rope noose burning the skin from my neck. A final blow to my mouth and nose so stunned me I barely felt the vicious kick bounce off the Bible still strapped to my chest. Choking and gagging on my own blood, I struggled to get enough breath in me to stay alive.

When I felt a boot against my foot, I kicked with first one foot and then the other at where I thought the man's knees would be. My first kick glanced to the side, the second made solid contact. It was enough to cause the man to lose his balance. A heavy thud and recoil of the wagon accompanied his loud cry of pain. He must have fallen on the wagon sidewall before toppling to the ground.

I tried to get up. I couldn't even get to my knees. I was helpless, my hands still bound and the rope still around my neck. Both men began pummeling me with fists and kicks. Had the younger brother not come back, I am certain they would have beaten me to death.

The young man's angry shouts and curses stopped the onslaught but not the bleeding. I was able to roll to the side and spit enough blood to clear my throat. Sucking air into my bursting lungs brought me back enough that I could hear. Even so, I was too dazed to make out most of the conversation, subdued in volume, if not in fury.

"We agreed on undamaged property." A cool, indifferent voice broke into the fracas. "If he's not fit to work, we have no deal."

"It's just his pretty face," Brute said. "A few bruises and cuts won't hurt a thing. He's Scottish anyway; he won't be worth a rotten belayin' pin to anybody."

"Shut up," the younger brother said. "I'll handle this."

Someone lifted a lantern near me. In the dim light, I could see nothing but blackish blood on the wagon bed where I lay. The lantern moved away.

"You stop that bleeding," the cool voice said, no longer indifferent. "Take him to the *Adele*. Get him aboard and below decks. I'll have the ship's surgeon from the *Sibylle* come look at him. If he says the man is fit, I'll pay you then—not before."

"Those are merchant ships," the younger man said. "They don't have surgeons on board."

"True, but they have a midshipman, a jack-tar, or someone who does the job of surgeon. I trust the man from the *Sibylle*. If he says a man can work, he can work."

The voices faded for a few minutes, then the brothers came back, wrapped my head, and gave me water to spit the blood from my mouth. After more arguing among the men, the wagon started moving again. It was only a brief time before it stopped.

In the dark, they stood me up and marched me up a gangway and aboard a ship. With the rough rope still around my neck and something jabbing me in the back—no doubt a knife or pistol, I stumbled down a companionway and a steep ship's ladder. Without a word, one of them shoved me into the forehold. I fell and lay in that cramped space in the lowest part of the ship, which must have had the poorest air circulation of any place invented by man. After several hours, three men, one of whom I judged from his air of authority to be a ship's officer and two others wearing seaman's clothing, opened the door.

While one held a lamp, another seaman untied me and gestured for me to walk into an open part of the hold amidst supplies for an upcoming voyage. I was able to do so with only minor hurting despite sore and cramped muscles. One of the seamen, speaking English with a strong French accent, relayed the officer's commands. I moved my arms and legs and, as instructed, stooped over to pick up a keg of supplies from the deck.

"He's fit," the man said without further examination. "Clean him up and take care of that cut over his eye."

Speaking French, the officer told the seaman to do as the man said and move me back into the hold. He reminded the seaman to clamp a leg iron on me. Mixed relief and anger followed my realization that these men were shanghaiing me into service aboard a French merchant ship. Protest would be useless, and the large-bore flintlock pistol one of the seamen held persuaded me to cooperate. At least I would live to see Keevah again. All I had to do was jump ship at the first opportunity.

Shackled as we were in the pitch darkness of the tiny space, which served as the brig for the ship, it was impossible for me and two other men already there to avoid kicking or jostling each other as we shifted and stretched to fight off cramps. From the unintelligible groans of the other two men, it was obvious they were dead drunk when brought aboard. The lack of fresh air, the stench of drink, and unclean bodies made it difficult to breathe. It would do no good to call out. We were here for a reason—to be hidden until the ship cleared port and made open seas.

I was aware of the practice employed by ships needed to meet their crew requirements. Shanghaiing men for forced labor aboard ships was still common, even though England and the United States had signed a treaty after their war of 1812 to stop the practice of British warships impressing sailors from American merchantmen. Other nations, even American merchant ships, still followed the practice of shanghaiing and impressing men from land to fill their crew needs.

While attending schools in Boston, which had a busy harbor, I frequently heard and even took part in discussions of ships and seagoing customs. Among tales, facts, and rumors of facts, I'd heard that on some ships, shanghaied men not yet documented into the ships' log and who would not or could not serve disappeared with no record of ever being on the ship. I could not verify if the rumors were true or merely promulgated by the ship's officers to shanghaied men to accept their plight and serve willingly. Nevertheless, according to rumors, floggings and other cruel punishments to entice cooperation usually preceded a trip to the deep. I knew it to be dangerous and often deadly to resist.

I decided straightaway to learn and serve as best I could and wait for my chance. Jumping, or deserting ship, was a serious offense, but Keevah was the closest and most precious person in the world to me—I thought of her as family. I would wait and be ready. I would not desert her.

Hours later, scurrying sounds of preparing a ship for departure penetrated our dark prison. It was a relief when those sounds changed to that of the ship getting underway. Soon after, two men unshackled us and moved us into the crowded forehold. Someone tossed us portions of what might have been the crews' morning meal of cold mutton and soft tack. More hours passed before they led us into the officers' quarters.

Soon, the captain arrived. Speaking French, he told us we were part of the ship's crew and would serve as such. He reminded us that as ship's captain, he had complete authority over us. He never mentioned anything about choice. It was obvious why—we had none. He issued a short command to his first mate and left. The mate had two seamen with him, one of them armed with a brace of pistols in his belt. At his command, one of the crew, who spoke English quite poorly, handed each of us a hammock, an empty seabag, and one change of old and patched clothes. The mate then told us he would deduct the cost of the items from our pay. Neither of my two companions spoke French, and only one had an inkling of what was going on.

When the mate asked the English-speaking crewman if we understood, the seaman, with an arrogant display of authority, made a mess of things. Both of my companions protested. One, a brawny farm lad who knew nothing about sailing ships, burst into a fit of rage, demanding to be set ashore. The seaman pointed one of his cocked pistols at the man as if this was a common occurrence and a routine part of his job.

Rather than see bloodshed, I tried to explain to the angry man in English. The French mate saw no need for patience. Without a second thought, he ordered the seaman to put the man back in the tiny brig. To my other companion, he spoke in French, though his gestures made it clear that he too, could go back to the brig or go to work. Now was the time to decide. The man surrendered his defiance, though I saw the anger and hatred in his eyes. I'm certain each of the French crew saw the same. They showed no concern one way or the other. Nevertheless, the seaman kept his cocked pistol in his beefy hand.

The mate raised skeptical eyebrows when I spoke to him in French, asking if I might speak to the man now being shoved back to the brig. I said I might be able to prevent trouble as well as give him a crewmember.

"*Non*," he said in French, "the man will taste the consequences of his actions." He did concede that perhaps I could talk to him later. From his expression, I doubted that would happen.

Two of us spent that day and the next night shackled in that miserable brig with only a wooden bucket to relieve ourselves. The farm boy must have been condemned to some other part of the ship's hold more diabolical than ours. I never saw him again.

Someone threw scraps of food and old wine bottles of water to us—enough to keep us alive, I suppose. Other than a few sips of water, I partook of nothing. It was all I could do to control my anger and fear of what might happen to Keevah.

Thoughts of our separation threatened to overwhelm my mind and body. My Bible was still strapped to my chest, though I found no comfort in it. I could think of nothing other than the woman who had given it to me. Little did I know of the assurance that book, and the hand-written message in it, would bring later—in times of overwhelming loneliness—or of the trials because of it.

French Brig, *Adele*, 1823

On our second day at sea, we were marched back and forth along the windward rail for the better part of an hour. I assumed it was to keep us fit for future work. The overcast sky hid any sign of the sun. From the direction of the steady prevailing winds, I reckoned we were sailing south by east—not the ideal course to Europe, but on course to the many islands of the Caribbean Sea.

The boat, a two-masted brig, was larger than the *Muireann* which had brought me to America. I had always heard that the French were partial to fast boats. This brig, however, with her broad beam, was no racehorse. She was a merchantman, built to carry freight and a lot of it. Perhaps she intended to put in at another American port or continue southward to do business between the islands.

The end of the war between England and France had opened trade between Caribbean islands and a goods-hungry America to ships of many nations, including France. Manufactured goods from Europe and sugar, molasses, and rum from the islands were common cargo of such merchantmen. Some of those ships also smuggled slaves along with legitimate goods.

Laws enacted by America and most European nations, except France and Spain, prohibited the importing of slaves from Africa.

Nations with such laws exercised strict controls and inspections at most of their seaports to enforce those laws.

Known as the African Blockade, national navies, comprised mostly of English, with a few American ships, tried to interdict and seize slave ships on the high seas. Success of these efforts varied because the promise of huge profits encouraged slave ship captains to use fast ships and employ creative tactics to avoid capture.

Demands for sugar by both America and Europe fed the burgeoning and labor-intensive sugar industry throughout the Caribbean. The laborers necessary for this large industry consisted of Negro slaves either imported from Africa or slaves shuttled back and forth from southern American states. Shipping new slaves from the Caribbean Islands to America was illegal, but nevertheless a thriving business—a way to add higher profits to legitimate trade.

I wondered what type of trade this southbound ship was involved in. With a sinking stomach, I realized I could find myself in the vile business of trading in human lives. Keevah had strong feelings about slavery, which she referred to as an abomination. I, too opposed it, partly from my Biblical perspective of Christ setting us free from the imposed slavery of sin so that we could become willing and loving servants to Him. But I also suspected my opposition to slavery came in part from my experience of being a bonded servant to another man. I had tasted that demeaning relationship, which I did not choose and from which I could not escape. The thought of forcing any man or woman into slavery was repulsive.

On our third day at sea, my fellow captive and I, or pressman as shanghaied sailors were called, were halfway through our forced march around the deck when a lookout's cry from the crow's-nest far above the deck alerted the entire crew.

"Sails abaft, port quarter."

A ship behind and to our left had been sighted. I was surprised that no order came to hustle us below deck. After watching the boat through his spyglass, the first mate told the crew that she was closing fast. I could not judge her speed with my naked eye, but it was obvious she was flying more sail than our brig could carry.

Neither the captain nor the crew appeared concerned. I was not worried about privateers, as I had heard no reports of their activity this close to the American coast. Nevertheless, I felt a strange unease about the entire affair.

A couple of hours later, after she had closed a great deal of the distance between us, the captain himself examined the ship through his spyglass. Word spread throughout the crew that she was French; I relaxed. At the command to reduce sail, however, my disquiet returned in force. We had been on deck far longer than had ever been permitted before, with no effort made to move us below. We were still in plain sight of anyone on an approaching ship. It was obvious my shanghaied shipmate and I were here to witness or be part of the coming events. My gut cringed as the ship drew closer, and my suspicions about my fate grew. Gun ports along her sides confirmed she was a warship.

France was a signatory to the treaty with America and England prohibiting impressment of sailors into service from each other's ships. Warships of both England and France were in desperate need of men, and nothing prohibited them from impressing sailors from merchant ships of their own nations. My gut was telling me I would see this happen in a short time.

Both ships hove-to, making only enough headway for steerage, while a longboat from the warship ferried several sailors and officers to our boat. After formalities between our freighter captain and the naval officers concluded, the first mate signaled a sailor with a pistol to march us over to him and the warship officers.

The poor fellow with me had no idea of the ensuing conversation as it was in French. I, however, heard the warship officer asking if we were capable seamen volunteering for our country's service. Even as he spoke, his eyes coldly scanned us over as if shopping for cattle.

The brig's captain said we had come on board three days ago and hadn't been put to work yet. "This one," he said, pointing to me, "knows ships."

"How so?" the officer asked.

"I watch him during his daily exercises on deck. I've been judging men for many years. I can tell if a man knows a thing or two about sailing ships by the way he observes and carries himself on deck. Moreover, he may be useful to you; my first mate tells me he speaks fluent French."

"A Frenchman!"

"He speaks French, yes, with a Scottish—"

The officer interrupted the man's near-treasonous statement with a loud slap on his sword scabbard. He glared at the freighter's captain.

"He is a Frenchman! He will serve his country on a French ship of war. You teach the other fellow to sail. We will consider him at our next rendezvous."

Thus, in days, I became not a Boston student of religious studies, looking forward to a future with the woman I loved, but a seaman aboard the *Médée*, a French Navy warship, and condemned to months or years of brutal service on the high seas. Once again, what I treasured most was stolen from me.

I vowed this bondage would not hold me from the woman that, after so many years, I could again believe in as family.

CHAPTER 6

Henrysville, Indian Territory of the United States, 1850

Despite Hesed's wondrous water, the move to her house from Doctor Kendrick's treatment room was painful and exhausting. Ciara and Hesed stood on each side to steady me while Jack, the barber, and three other men carried and jostled me on a hard and unforgiving litter. Jack said it once served as the door to an abandoned house near the edge of town. It took more of Hesed's water to subdue the pain.

I awoke to the soft light of an oil lamp illuminating the drowsy Indian woman sitting by my bed.

"You have been asleep for a long time," she said. "It'll be daybreak soon. How do you feel?" Her dog-tired voice revealed she had been with me for hours. Even as badly as I hurt, I was relieved to see her.

"Hesed . . . like I've been run over by a lumber wagon."

"I see your sense of humor survived." Her grin started and then faded. "Or have you forgotten that a lumber wagon did run over you or at least dump its load on you?"

"Do I have a hangover? Or is it that water of yours?"

"Guilty as charged. But, if I hadn't given it to you, your leg would hurt much worse."

"I know. Thank you for helping. Hesed, I apologize for yesterday. It was clumsy of me to ask about things that are none of my business."

"We made a deal—my story for yours—*Dadanetselá.*"

"Yes, but I should not have brought up painful memories . . . and tears."

"Grayhawk, those memories are with me every day of my life. I don't often talk about them, and I certainly don't let my emotions get the best of me. I promise I'll do better."

"Don't promise any such thing. There is nothing wrong with tears or crying. They can help the healing."

Her dark eyes questioned mine for a quiet moment. She must not have expected that.

"Spoken like . . ." Her murmur faded. "Thank you. And, speaking of healing, I will be gone the rest of today. I'm going to take a nap and ride out to talk to Jeremiah Bearstriker about your leg. Ciara will bring your meals. Be nice to her! After all, she is a pregnant lady."

I nodded in acknowledgment as Hesed departed. After she left, I closed my eyes. Her words prompted me to wonder if she sensed my feelings of foreboding about Ciara. Did Ciara herself discern the same?

I awoke again to a soft knock on the bedroom door. At my invitation, Ciara entered with lunch. As if reading my mind, she inquired only as to how I felt and made no mention of her question about my not becoming a preacher—her question that caused me so much distress at her last visit. In a few minutes, she left me alone again.

Jeremiah Bearstriker was unlike any medical doctor, including any military surgeon I have ever seen. After perfunctory introductions and inquiries as to how my leg felt, he sat for long minutes studying my foot and leg, never speaking, touching me, or asking me to move a muscle.

After many minutes, he lifted my leg with gentle care, raising it a few inches above the feather mattress and held it in both hands. Were it not for the tenderness and persistent ache, I would have felt little additional pain. As it was, almost imperceptible movements of his fingers gave me the impression he was probing—exploring everything between skin and bone. I was grateful for his gentleness.

As he studied my injury, I studied him. Short, stout, and from the muscles rippling in his bare forearms, I judged him to be strong. His dark complexion, heavy jaw, and hawk-like nose confirmed his Indian heritage. Deep-set eyes, as dark as I'd ever seen, concealed his every thought and emotion from me, but his demeanor revealed his uniqueness among men. An air of humble confidence filled the room from his very presence. My initial apprehensions faded.

After a half-hour of silent study, he shared his diagnosis.

"I think one of the two bones in your lower leg is broken above your ankle. It is not separated but with considerable displacement. I suspect a jagged break. If not reset, it will take a long and painful time to heal, and I doubt you will ever walk on it again. A great deal of the swelling and pain is from occasional movement of the bone every time you move your leg and from extensive bruising of muscles, spraining of ligaments, and stretching of your Achilles tendon.

"If you were a horse, it wouldn't be necessary, but we might be inclined to shoot you anyway."

When I didn't respond, he looked me in the eye with the same stoic look he had for my leg. "Hesed told me your sense of humor hadn't been killed off. Perhaps she was mistaken. That was a joke."

"Sorry. You caught me off guard; I wasn't expecting humor."

"No offense. Your leg is not as bad as I expected; the bone is not shattered. Your healing will still be long and painful. We must first get the swelling and fever out before resetting and splinting your leg from ankle to thigh to prevent further movement of the bone. We will cool your leg with wet cloths for two or three days. When we reset the break, Hesed can give you something to help with the pain. It will take two of us to do what needs to be done."

"Thank you."

"You are welcome." Bearstriker rose to leave. "Hesed tells me you speak Cherokee and are familiar with many of our customs. She also says you are reluctant to tell how you came by our language. I'll not ask, but perhaps someday you will tell her. She can tell me."

"Perhaps . . . someday."

Although Jeremiah Bearstriker and Hesed Bluefeather were quite different in appearance, he reminded me of her modest yet self-assured ability to do whatever needed to be done. It was clear why the people of Georgia would have welcomed him to stay.

After Bearstriker left, Ciara entered the room with a large basin, a pitcher of water, and towels thrown over her shoulder. Bearstriker hadn't wasted time in giving her instructions. She intended to start my treatments immediately.

"Where is Hesed?" I asked.

"She wanted to make a short detour from Bearstriker's place . . . to see friends." Ciara glanced at me as she began to soak the towels in the water. She interrupted her work, placed her hands on her hips, and turned directly to me with a raised eyebrow and a roguish grin.

"Why? Do you prefer her to me?"

I felt my forehead furrow at such a direct and brash question.

"Of course you do," she said. "I would too if I were you. She is gentle, kind, compassionate, and patient, among other virtues a lady should have. Me? Not so much. Here, let me put these wet towels on your leg. Doctor's orders. Cool water, right out of the well; it will help take the fever out."

Contrary to what Ciara said, her manner in placing the wet towels on my leg did reveal gentleness I didn't expect. I would have preferred rough and uncaring treatment fit for the image I had and wanted to keep of her. Gentle was too much like Keevah.

"Thank you, that does feel better," I said.

"I'll be back soon to put fresh towels on. Bearstriker's orders are to keep them moist and cool and to change them frequently." She left the room without another word.

Alone again, I laid back and gazed out the one window at my left. All I could see when lying on the bed was sky and a lower fork of a large cottonwood tree in what I assumed was Hesed's backyard. Even so, it was much better than the odd window in the doctor's house constantly reminding me of a jail cell. Pain in my leg, the cooling towels, and the compulsory patience needed for healing brought back the memory of Bearstriker as he left the room.

Before stepping out, the man paused at the door and gave me a subtle but commanding nod and grunt before leaving. The moment the door closed, I became certain I had unwittingly agreed to tell him my story. It was too late now; I had been drawn into another

Dadanetselá. Both Ciara and Bearstriker would hear of everything I said.

Ciara's trap was closing tighter. The thought brought bad memories—too much like impressment into the French Navy.

***

French warship *Médée,* 1823

The 18-gun *Médée,* of which I became a shanghaied crewmember, was among the oldest and smallest corvettes still in service in the French Navy. I learned from one of the older crew that sixteen of her original eighteen 9-pound cannons had been replaced by twelve powerful and lighter, but shorter-range, 16-pound carronades, leaving her with two of the heavy long-range cannons mounted in her bow.

Reducing the weight of her armament helped her attain remarkable speed for her size but made her useless in any naval engagement with larger ships of any nation. Larger and newer French frigates carried at least forty guns of heavier caliber. Most English and American ships were more heavily armed than French ships.

At her age and with limited room for supplies, she was not a ship of the line, but she was still a commissioned warship of the French Navy. Corvettes served well for coastal patrol or harbor defense but were not suited for long deployment at sea unless as scouts for a large fleet that could supply them. I thought it unusual she was in the western hemisphere, far from the waters of France.

Why she was here and the reason for her unusual armament would become obvious soon enough.

The first lesson I learned had nothing to do with the ship. It was about authority. All the officers were aristocrats. The crew were not. Forgetting could have dire consequences for any crewman. Indeed, officers were expected to constantly remind us of their superior standing and consequent authority over us.

Officers communed with each other in what I thought exaggerated Christian and civil terms, never so to crewmen. Officers were gentlemen. Crewmen were beasts of burden whose sole purpose was to perform duties needed to sail and to fight. Except for the need for hands for labor, crewmen were expendable.

This relationship, often reinforced by brutal discipline, formed the model to some degree in the navies of most nations. Some captains and officers practiced it to a greater or lesser degree than others, but aboard the *Médée,* it was adhered to the extreme. I witnessed the broken spirit and sense of loneliness and isolation among numerous crewmen. Younger men, some still in their teens, and men aboard not of their own choosing, like me, were the most vulnerable.

It also fostered a vicious struggle among the crew to establish an unofficial but near-tyrannical hierarchy below decks. All men, despite their station in life, need a sense of worth and a degree of respect. Some are willing to use force to get it.

Captains and officers were aware of such social structures but often chose not to interfere because they served to keep the men in line. It was often risky for lower rank and less experienced officers to interfere in the crew's affairs. Officers on the *Médée* seldom entered the fo'c'sle.

Such a command style, if practiced by Captain Johannson, would never have allowed the friendship I witnessed between him and Bo aboard the *Muireann*. Never would it have allowed my friendship with Keevah to blossom and grow.

I became part of the landsmen squad under the direction of an older sailor who hated what he felt was a degrading assignment. The landsman classification meant we were unfit for working aloft in the rigging. Most men in the squad either had been shanghaied or had volunteered to serve in the navy rather than face time in prison for misdoings on land. None of them had previous seafaring experience.

We landsmen, though scorned and ridiculed by the seamen, were fortunate in one regard—we were required to keep our feet on deck rather than work in the rigging. And stay alive until we learn how to climb and work aloft safely.

It was not easy work—scrubbing decks to hauling on lines to hoisting or trimming sails, and never allowed time to rest. We were the lowest rank of the crew even though we often performed backbreaking tasks. The hard work and cruel harassment of both officers and seamen did provide motivation to learn sufficient skills to be promoted from the landsman to the ordinary seaman class.

I soon saw and felt firsthand the brutality and intimidation of the *tyran de l'gaillard*, the group of sailors who ruled the fo'c'sle in the deliberate absence of any officer. The leader of the group of thugs was a violent bull of a man named Gaston. He ruled his half-dozen followers by intimidation, proven cruelty, and physical power. While they supported him and reported any infractions of their despotic rules, I suspected any one of them would be happy to slit Gaston's throat while he slept—if his deed could propel the blade wielder into the position of *tryan*.

Without realizing I was breaking any rule, I drew Gaston's attention by responding to an *Aspirant's* questions about the English language. The young *Aspirant*, equivalent to a midshipman in the English navy, was a boy in age. He learned I spoke both English and French, so he approached me as I was busy scrubbing the deck. He asked me a few questions in his desire to improve his English. Our conversation was short, but one of the *tyran de l'gaillard* thugs reported it to Gaston.

To prevent any relationship from developing between an officer and me, Gaston invited me into the *galliard*. We landsmen were never considered the equal of the seamen, or even a real part of the crew. As a result, we were never allowed into the seamen's berthing area without permission; we berthed on the gun deck with our hammocks strung between the guns. An invitation into the quarters of the real seamen meant trouble. I expected the worse. It didn't take long.

Only a few of the *tyran de l'gaillard* were there. Not a one spoke to me. Indifferent gestures guided me to Gaston, sitting on the only wooden keg in the *gaillard*. His relaxed demeanor appeared non-threatening; in fact, a slight smile put me at ease. I approached, hoping for nothing worse than a scolding. He gestured me to come closer.

I was midstride when it came. He was too fast for me. In one fluid motion, he rose and swung. His fist caught me square in the mouth. I fell hard to the deck. Gaston stood peering down at me, fury masking every other feature of his face.

All the pent-up rage at being shanghaied from Keevah, beaten by her brothers, and being treated as a dog by officers and seamen alike erupted within me. Fear of Gaston and his thugs vanished. Fueled further by the laughter and derision of the men watching, I found the strength to spring to my feet.

My fist caught him in the face with the hardest blow I could muster. He backtracked in astonishment as my flurry of punches pounded him. The keg on which he had so arrogantly enthroned himself now proved his undoing.

Tripping over it, he fell to the deck. Like an enraged cat, he sprang to his feet. Blood poured from his nose; one of my punches had connected well. His face contorted in black hatred as he raised his fists and edged toward me—stalking his prey.

I awoke on the surgeon's table. A narrow slit of the one eyelid I could open allowed me to see the surgeon staring back at me. He soon blocked my vision by placing wet cloths over my face.

"You were stupid," he said. "He could have killed you; he has wasted men before."

"You must admit, he has guts," a voice penetrated my head.

"In place of brains," another scoffed.

It took me a few seconds to recognize the *aspirants* speaking. I wondered why they were here before remembering this was their usual berthing area—unless taken over as the action station for the surgeon. Their making light of my suffering would have angered me had I any steam left. I felt drained of energy and emotion. Gaston had thoroughly beaten me.

The surgeon released me to duty in two days, but it was weeks before my headaches and occasional blurred vision went away. His only prescription for those ailments was to lie still and cover my eyes with a wet cloth when off-watch. Not one of the *aspirants* or officers said a word about the incident, at least in my hearing. Nor did Gaston's men reveal how he came by his slightly blackened eye.

My landsmen crewmates each offered a helping hand with my work—when hidden from sight of Gaston's men. By three weeks, I was pulling full duty, even doing some tasks above deck in the rigging. Although I had taken a thrashing from Gaston, I sensed lower-level officers and several of the crew giving me a level of respect a landsman should never assume. I worried Gaston would sense it too. His response would not be good.

The *Médée* spent the next month patrolling the waters around the island of Hispaniola, looking for former slaves trying to flee from the destitution resulting from the destruction of the French sugar plantations. Negros on the island were free since their 12-year revolution gained their independence in 1803.

Working the vast sugarcane fields and production plants had been their livelihood before the revolution. The defeat of the French plantation managers had cost the new government their previous French markets for their sugar. Now, the only way many of them could survive was to submit to the almost slave-like discipline in the struggling Negro-run, government-owned plantations. Jobless men and women, who had been former workers had no options but to try to eke out a living from the tiny parcels of land allotted to them.

French gunboats such as the *Médée* apprehended any ship or small boat suspected of helping escapees flee their merciless conditions. Any Negros without ironclad documentation or aboard vessels the captain of the French gunship deemed unseaworthy were taken to French-owned islands and offered jobs in those French sugar plantations. No option but to accept the work was available.

Thus, the French Navy, though pretending to suppress the trade of slaves from Africa, acted in their grand humanitarian gesture to rescue Negros onboard allegedly unfit vessels from the hazards of the open sea. At the same time, they succeeded in maintaining the workforce for the profitable French sugar industry.

Many of the crew whispered objections among themselves concerning our actions. Gaston's men quickly squelched any contrary or moral opinions reaching them. I understood then why the *tyran de l'gaillard* and his minions were such an asset to the *Médée's* declared wartime mission. Morals and emotions, when challenged on a mission such as ours, could easily divert men from their assignments. Gaston and his men served not only to ensure a working crew but also to prevent the crew from polarizing into political factions and possible mutiny.

Within the crew, however, throttled opinions fostered silent and festering resentment.

Henrysville, Indian Territories of the United States, 1850

Bearstriker was true to his word. After a few days, the fever and swelling in my leg diminished. Satisfied enough to proceed with his plan, he called Hesed into the room. After the Indian woman had given me a drink of her water, she rolled a cloth into a tight roll and handed it to me.

"Put this in your mouth, like a dog chewing a bone, and clench down on it. Bite hard when it hurts. It will help."

Bearstriker said nothing. He knew I had seen it done before—his nod said it all.

Hesed was more compassionate. She placed a hand on my shoulder and fixed her eyes on mine.

"Ready?" she whispered.

I nodded. Her gentle grip on my shoulder faded into a comforting touch as she slid her hand down my arm and gave my fingers a lingering squeeze. Then, she moved toward the foot of my bed. The two of them went to work.

The pain was extreme—it felt as though they were twisting and pulling every nerve in my body out through my lower leg. Either Hesed's water took over, or I passed out.

I remember waking to throbbing pain. My leg, from hip to ankle, lay bound with cloth strips around several narrow splints; I could not move it in the slightest. This time, Ciara was sitting by my bed.

"How are you doing?" She placed a hand on my shoulder, drawing my attention to her as she examined my face.

"Like I've been run over by a lumber wagon."

"You said the same thing to Hesed yesterday. I take it you aren't seeing any improvement, at least not immediately."

"You told me she was kind and gentle—couldn't prove it by me."

"She did what she had to."

"I know. I didn't mean what I said. Despite everything we have done to her, she remains kind to everyone, white and Indian alike. I know though I can't understand."

Without expression on her face, Ciara looked square at me for a long moment. "You know more about Cherokees and the Territories than you're admitting, don't you? And your name, Grayhawk, sounds more Indian than Scottish. Why? What are you not telling us?"

"Not telling?" I felt my scowl grow. "Rather presumptive, don't you think?"

"You're right. Let me change the subject then. A few days ago, you asked me several pointed and perceptive questions about this town, the army sergeant, and my presence here. I will tell you. Sergeant Kirby is with a U.S. Army detachment bivouacked nearby to protect travelers and wagon trains as they pass through the territories. Unfortunately, military presence is necessary because a few isolated groups of Indians resent the intrusion of whites and try to keep them out by force.

"Anyway, this part of the territories is the northern of two parts set aside for Cherokees. Other parts are for other tribes, most of which were forcibly moved here by the government. Some of these tribes, including the Cherokees, are civilized, even by white standards. There are, however, some individuals who greatly resent their shameful treatment by the—"

"I know exactly how they feel!"

Ciara's jaw dropped. She sat silent, stunned by my outburst.

I pushed back on the pillows and resolved not to take my wrath out on her. "I apologize; I'm sorry I shouted."

"I accept. You seem quite passionate about the issue."

"It's personal . . . from long ago."

"It's personal for me too," she said. "And it's not only from long ago; it's right here and now—today."

I snapped my head around to face her directly. The movement caused me to wince from the pain in my chest. She gave no indication she noticed but continued without missing a beat.

"And now, your second question. What am I doing here, and what is this town doing here? It's a long story, but it started twenty years ago when The Indian Removal Act was passed by Congress.

President Andrew Jackson signed it into law in 1830. Since then, Federal and State governments have treated the Indians horribly. And, Mr. Grayhawk, I don't believe it's going to get any better."

"Mrs. Franklin, that doesn't explain why you and this town are encroaching on Indian land." I clamped my jaws, knowing my building anger shouldn't be directed at her.

"I do hope you'll understand better when I finish. First, we don't need to be so formal, and at the conclusion of our conversation, I hope we can be friends or at least cordial acquaintances."

I nodded; I had been out of place in resurrecting the formality she sought to erase.

"Very well," she said. "I'll continue. Take this town for example. The Cherokee tribal leader Henry Monacheke founded it, along with relatives and friends. At one time, the population was exclusively Cherokee. Today, it is less than eighty percent Indian. The rest are whites who have moved in—like me. Motivation for whites varies from greed for land to honest and dishonest business opportunities. Most of the white people here have a true desire to help the Indians create a respectable and fruitful life for themselves—despite current public opinion and government policies."

I looked hard at her and raised an eyebrow.

"Perhaps if you keep my friend, Hesed, in mind as I tell my story, you will understand."

"Hesed is the reason you are here?"

"Partly, but it's bigger than her . . . bigger than this entire town. Think back a few years . . . a few tens, or even a couple hundred years. Whites have taken from the Indians whatever and whenever they wanted. This latest congressional act has displaced entire tribes, Cherokees, Creeks, Seminoles, Chickasaws, and others from lands white people wanted. At least, this time, they set aside land for them, this Indian Territory, so the Indians could farm, hunt, and at least survive on it. Some of it is good land—which is why the whites want it now. Many are already settling on it, though by law, it's supposed to be Indian land.

"Even today, people in Washington are debating how to resolve the very problem they created. My husband is there right now—

trying to protect the rights of the Indians. History has shown it's a losing battle. What voting citizens want, the government will soon give them. Do you know some of the solutions the people who want this land are proposing?

"Currently, the most probable is to reduce the size of the Territories and crowd all the Indians into it. Do you remember the first day we spoke? I told you this land will soon become the Territory of Kansas. Soon after, it will become the State of Kansas. There is already talk and plans to make that happen. Where will the land for Kansas come from? Much of it will come from right here—the Indian Territories.

"My husband writes me powerful people in Washington are proposing all land north of the 37th parallel become U.S. territory. Some of the lands currently set aside for Indians, including the land we are on right now, will be taken away from the Indians—this town and lands north, east, and west included. All the Indians here and other tribes, including Hesed, will be forcibly relocated again.

"And it won't stop there. Other U.S. Territories, and eventually, new states will take from the Territories until there is nothing left. Then, what about the Indians? Some of those people who want land have proposed several solutions. Washington has suggestions too.

"One popular proposal is to set aside small reservations on undesirable land elsewhere and have the government feed and care for them—like cattle. Another is to let the Indians who are already here keep a parcel of land in the Territory to live on and farm, but only if they renounce all ties and allegiances to their tribes and heritage. In other words, betray and abandon their culture and all but their immediate families.

"Even if some Indians agreed, how long do you think it would take before they'd lose their land to some rich land dealers with high-powered attorneys or political maneuvering by the government to appease land-hungry voters? By the way, that very thing has already happened in some states."

"You're not telling me anything I don't already know, Ciara." Pent-up bitterness gushed like a geyser, scalding anyone within range. "I've seen it!"

Ciara almost choked. Wide-eyed, while still maintaining her composure, she studied me for a few moments before calmly voicing her question. "Have you been involved before . . . with these Indians . . . with other Indians?"

I looked away and clenched my jaw. It was none of her business.

An edge of cold steel glinted in her composed words. "In Indian removal?"

"Yes, if you must know." I glared at the ceiling; it didn't help. After a few moments of silence, in a strained voice I didn't even recognize as my own, I muttered, "I saw it coming . . . tried to stop it . . . I couldn't. I abandoned my . . ."

Ciara sat for a long time, never saying a word. When I couldn't stand the silence any longer, I turned to her. The tip of her nose was red, and her eyes too moist. She couldn't know, but she may as well have slugged me in the gut; Keevah looked the same way whenever her emotions got the best of her. I couldn't speak to apologize. I felt every bit as bad as she.

"Are you. . ." Ciara spoke gently, not at all like a persistent newspaper reporter, "Looking for someone, Mr. Grayhawk . . . for someone here in the Territories?"

Following a long pause, I shrugged my shoulders despite the discomfort it caused.

"I'm not sure what I'm doing anymore. Searching for something—a dream, a ghost, a scrap of hope. I know I can't stop until I find . . . something." I looked up at the red-haired woman, so unlike my Keevah, yet so very much like her, and muttered the terrible truth I had never been able to voice before. "I don't even know if they're still alive."

Closing my eyes, I tried to remove any emotion from my face. When I could speak, my words came strained.

"Please, I want to be alone."

I couldn't tell what Ciara murmured. I soon heard the door to my room close.

She didn't come back until she brought in a late evening meal of beef stew. My initial suspicion was confirmed; the Indian woman had again prepared my food. It went untouched.

Staring at the food Hesed had prepared for me, I tried to construct in my mind the image of her face and hands as if she were sitting beside me. The best I could do was an incomplete picture. Impressions of her kindness were more vivid to me than details of her face or body—except for her tears as she told me about her mother. My clumsy questioning had resurrected horrors of years ago, forcing her to relive her tragedies and losses. What kind of friend was I—to repay kindness with cruelty?

It seems I have had that problem for years. It was a long night; sleep never came. Every time I started to doze, the memories of man's brutality to man made me wonder if I had been forever branded with the same venomous behavior I witnessed aboard those French warships.

CHAPTER 7

French Warship *Médée,* 1824

I sat cross-legged on the *Médée's* gun deck with my back against a carronade, staring at my untouched evening meal. My thoughts of Boston vanished as one of my men eased himself down beside me. Against my will, I focused on my present situation. He was the smallest man on the *Médée*, but his strength, agility, and willingness to perform any task asked of him made him the best man on my crew. I doubted he had much formal education, but he observed well—never missing much, if anything. Graying temples and weathered face betrayed he was not a young man. Even so, I thought him a good sailor and often wondered why he was in my squad.

"Gaston hates you. You fought back and embarrassed him, and now, you've been promoted to squad leader. He will kill you."

"Askira, those are the most words I have heard from you. You are Japanese, yet you speak English quite well."

"I speak English, Manchu, some Spanish, and fluent French as well as my native tongue. They don't know that, nor do they realize I learn a lot by being silent."

"How did you end up on this boat?"

"Wrong place, wrong time. Same as you, and like you, I do not intend to stay—unless I misread you."

I nodded. "You read right."

"Then, if you intend to leave this boat alive, you will have to fight and kill Gaston."

"You know I can't beat him. All I can do now is to avoid him."

"You don't have that option. He will trap you at his convenience, and his men will testify you started the fight. Trust me; he will make sure they do. Lanny, he is bigger, stronger, and faster than you, and he is a fighter. He lives by aggression and intimidation and has his reputation to maintain. He can't let you get away with what you did."

"So, what choices do I have?"

"You have to fight." He paused while I looked down to wrestle with the truth of his words and then shook his head when I looked back at him. "You don't know how to fight, so I will teach you."

"You said he is bigger, stronger, and faster than me. No matter how much you teach me, I can't match him."

"Lanny, I have been traveling the world most of my adult life and have served in the armies of three nations. I have known men like him in all of them. They all intimidate by brute force, yet they all have weaknesses. I expect I too will have to face Gaston, so I have studied him, how he fights, and how he can be defeated."

"I could never do that."

"No, you couldn't, nor do you have time to learn everything I could teach. So, we will focus on his weaknesses. I will teach you how to defeat them. Before we start, you need to understand you must be aggressive. Take the fight to him at your first opening, and never stop. If you retreat, you will lose. Protect your head and keep your balance. Above all, keep your wits about you . . . panic, and you play into his hands . . . and you die."

Before I could grasp it all, he said, "Are you ready to learn to fight . . . to live?"

My hopes of seeing Keevah again began to glimmer within me. If I could defeat or even survive Gaston, I had a chance. It was a long shot—my only shot.

"I am ready."

We chose times and places for my training where Gaston's men would not see us. My squad soon learned of our activities. Not only were they silent about it, they posted lookouts to alert us if needed. My work had quickened my reflexes and hardened me, but I was no match for Askira's combat moves. I realized how little I knew about fighting. No one noticed or cared about the new bruises appearing on my body almost daily.

Askira drilled me relentlessly and refused to let my apparent lack of progress discourage me. He pounded the point home every time we met, that there would be no rules. I was not preparing for a fight—I was preparing to fight for my life.

"Gaston will not use a knife or weapon because his power draws from his reputation with his fists. Use of anything else would weaken his power. His fists are his weapons; they are formidable, but they are also his weakness. You will exploit his weakness."

Exhausted at the end of every training session, I had no trouble falling asleep with my ever-increasing hope of living through this conflict—to see Keevah again.

Those hopes came close to dying when leaving Hispaniola waters for similar duties near the Windward Islands, the easternmost of the West Indies. Shortly after sunrise, the cry "Sails ahead, five points to port" alerted every man on deck. We immediately took up the chase. Within two hours, the captain said she appeared to be two-masted, probably a brig of the type commonly used to transport goods and people throughout the islands and the American coast. He ordered stunsails aloft for more speed.

Two hours of pursuit put us within distance to see, with the naked eye, she was indeed a brig flying the United States flag. She had hoisted more sail, including topgallants and stunsails, at the ends of her main yardarms with intent to outrun our corvette.

She might have been successful but for the lightening of the *Médée* by discarding her long-range guns in favor of the lighter, shorter-range, but deadly carronades. Even with the brig's extra sail, the *Médée* was closing well.

"All hands to gun stations."

The order refocused our attention to our mission. Discussions of the brig's lines and fine sailing qualities ceased. Our mission was to board and inspect this brig's cargo for human slaves. We knew what to do. We had done it before.

The carronades, capable of firing sixteen-pound balls, were loaded instead with chain shot, two heavy balls connected with six feet of heavy chain. When fired, the two balls rotated through the air with the chain between them. The effect was to cut a six-foot swath through an opponent's masts and rigging, destroying their sails or dismasting them without damaging the hull. A dismasted ship was helpless and easy prey for boarding parties. A quick surrender was the usual and preferred result.

Once within range, our captain ordered a course change and brought our two long-range, bow-mounted cannons to bear. He ordered a shot well forward of the bow of the brig to convey our intentions. We had returned to pursuit when a cloud of white smoke erupted from the stern of the brig. Within seconds, another cloud appeared. The first shot raised a plume of seawater well ahead of us. The second whistled over our heads, but its plume erupted far to starboard.

"Good lord, sir, she's shooting at us." The amazed cry from the lieutenant reached to the foremost man on the gun deck.

Only those of us near the captain's command position on the poop deck heard his calm response. "We are clearly within his range, but his firing was poorly timed and off-target. Unless I am mistaken, which I doubt, such poor gunnery is an indication of a less-than-disciplined crew, probably amateurs. Stay your course and make ready the carronades."

His orders made my stomach drop. We had stopped and boarded other ships, but for the first time in my experience, we were closing on an armed adversary who was willing to fight.

The brig continued its sporadic firing upon us as we closed on her. No shots came closer than one that put a hole in our starboard stunsail. Within the hour, our captain maneuvered to put us abeam and slightly ahead of the brig. Two cannons amidships of the brig now opened fire. Their accuracy was no better than the stern guns had been.

"I believe she's carrying only six, maybe eight guns, sir," the Lieutenant said.

"To warn off predator ships. She's no match for us."

"Shall we carry the fight to her, sir?"

"She's on her fastest point of sail now. Any course change will slow her. Douse the stunsails; we can keep pace with her without them, and they reduce our maneuverability."

"Aye, sir," the lieutenant said. "When we get the stunsails in, the landsmen on the port guns will report to position, and all carronades will be ready. Why doesn't she strike her colors, sir? She can see we are a warship. She doesn't stand a chance. Are they fools?"

"Fools, yes," the captain said. "Fools to get into a business which can earn them years in an American or British prison if they end up in the hands of those governments. You notice they are trying to shoot high—to dismast us rather than sink us. They could still outrun us if we lose a mast. They are willing to fight against odds for their freedom."

I stood forward of the mainmast to direct my squad in handling the sheets and halyards for the stunsails. The lieutenant strode toward me.

"McDowell," he said, "this will be your first action. Most of your men know what to do—they've done it before. You stay out of the way of the gun crews and make sure your new men follow the orders of the gun captains. You will answer for them."

"Aye, sir."

Within twenty minutes, the stunsails were down, and their yardarm extensions were removed. The *Médée* changed course to bring her closer to the brig.

The second lieutenant, serving as gunner, and commanding all the gun captains, signaled the lieutenant when he was satisfied with the range. Shots from the brig continued to splash off target, most of them beyond us as they tried in vain to dismast us.

"We are in range, sir."

"Bring us broadside."

"Aye, sir."

Blood surged through my veins, and my breath quickened at the subtle course change. Gun captains made a quick check of their guns and crews. Not one corrective order was necessary.

"Straight away," the gunner yelled.

Again, the *Médée's* course changed to hold her broadside to the brig.

The gunnery shouted his countdown to the gun crews as the *Médée* rolled with the sea swells. He timed his orders for the guns to fire as they rose with the roll of the ship. The rise of the guns would cause the chain shot to fly high and strike the masts or tear out the rigging, effectively disabling the ship. It would also minimize injury to the crew and passengers. There was no reward for dead or injured slaves. Plantation managers would pay only for people who could begin work immediately.

As the carronades thundered and spewed flame and smoke at the brig, her two cannons roared back in near unison.

One 16-pound ball from the brig shredded the bottom third of our main lower topsail, destroying all its running rigging. The other struck between the number one and number two port guns. Hull fragments and splinters erupted into the gun deck and crew. The ball carried through the boat, smashing into the number two starboard gun before falling to the deck, crushing a man's foot as it bounced to rest against the carriage for the number three port gun. I was watching at the time, but it all happened so fast that my mind couldn't comprehend it all.

The ball and flying hull fragments severely injured two men, including one of my landsmen. Flying splinters cut or impaled themselves in another four men.

"McDowell, get those men to the surgeon, yelled the gunner.

Blood was already running on the deck before four of my squad, and I could move the worst of the injured. The gunner barked more orders, and someone threw buckets of sand to prevent the gun deck from becoming slippery with blood.

We carried the two men struck by the ball into the surgeon's station first.

He glanced at the two. "Put them over there; can't you see they're dead?"

Men whose injuries would allow them to return to duty were treated first. The man with the crushed foot was last. The two young *aspirants* helped him onto the table, which they had transformed from a dining table into a surgeon's operating table. Someone had the presence of mind to apply a kerchief tourniquet below the injured man's knee while he was still lying on the gun deck. The surgeon released and then retightened it when blood began spurting from the man's mangled foot.

"You two," the surgeon pointed to me and another man, "Stay and help."

An ear-splitting roar jarred every joint and bone in my body. The force of it slammed my ears and chest from all directions. The entire boat shuddered in recoil from the shock. Hearing and feeling the firing of the carronades when on the gun deck was bad enough. Down below, it was the sound of hell itself. It drowned out the surgeon's last words, but his gesture to my other two men made it clear they were returning to action on the guns.

Two *aspirants*, the man from my squad who had helped move the injured, and I held the poor man to the table until he fainted from the pain of having his mangled foot sawed off. It was impossible to tell if the cup of rum offered him before the operation had any effect other than to tell him what was going to happen. It was a grisly business. I thanked God no other wounded needed such treatment.

The brig struck her colors after our second barrage toppled her foremast.

The *Médée* escorted the crippled ship back to Guadeloupe, as the first lieutenant said, "To repatriate her Negro passengers to their French plantations." Local and French authorities apprehended her mixed crew of English, American, and Spanish. We would never learn of their fates. Our officers celebrated their sizable reward while our dead were buried, and our crippled crewman was left on the island for medical treatment—where little was available. The other injured men resumed duties as their injuries allowed.

The *Médée* was a warship, supposedly performing service for the greater good of France. As a part of the ship's crew, I was involved in some of the vilest treatment of human beings I ever imagined. Keevah's Bible and my hope in the Lord were my only grasp on sanity during the five days anchored off Guadeloupe for repairs from the battle.

I longed for my red-haired friend. Would she still want me again if she knew? As for me, I doubted my shame would let me face her.

Repaired and resupplied, the *Médée* again set sail southward for the Windward Islands. Our mission this time was to patrol the waters between the island of French Martinique and the active slave center at French Guiana.

Askira's mind proved to be as disciplined as his body. Once at sea, his constant demands for my training gave me little opportunity for self-pity. Our clandestine exercises became more intense and more painful for me. At times, in anger or frustration, I tried but was never able to hurt Askira. Even so, my confidence in my abilities grew, though it was obvious I could never reach the level of fighting skill of my tutor.

His teaching emphasis changed as my skills improved. While continuing to critique and improve my techniques, he focused increasingly on my mental approach to the fight. Any distraction or lack of attention drew quick and severe criticism. If I fell for a feint during our mock fights, he would remind me in forceful terms Gaston could kill me. Yet, at the end of every session, Askira reminded me how far I had come, and he was pushing me hard to save my life. Were it not for my realization and his continued reinforcement of it, I would have hated the man. Instead, I revered him.

During the *Médée's* patrols around our assigned islands, we passed several French-flagged ships. We neither challenged nor boarded any of them. Our officers remained silent about our lack of action. No crewmember dared question why—we all knew those ships were conveying slaves to work the French-owned sugar plantations on the islands. Further distaste of our mission and the men in command grew in many of the crew.

Gaston's band became more watchful, often breaking up gatherings of sailors or listening to conversations among the crew. I watched many crew members withdraw, speaking in hushed voices only to those they trusted. Gaston was no fool. It seemed he could smell discontent as if it were a rotten infection spreading throughout the ship. His aim was to keep a lid on it.

He chose his time wisely. The *Médée* had lain hove-to under a sweltering sun for three days on the open sea, waiting for the supply ship, which was supposed to have been there when we arrived. Everyone onboard knew without a supply ship; we would be on half rations until we could reach Martinique, ten days if the winds held. Temperaments were under trial on our ship, which already had wide conflicts of loyalty to purpose. Division of ranks could soon follow. The specter of protest, uprising, and even mutiny was high.

In whispers, several of us expressed concerns Gaston would send a message to the crew.

I was getting off the first dogwatch one evening when two of his men approached me. There was no invitation this time. They escorted me into the fo'c'sle, where Gaston and another of his men waited. Aside from the five of us, no one else was there. Usually, the fo'c'sle would be busy with a couple dozen men.

Gaston sat on the same wooden keg as during my first visit. There was no fake smile on his face this time. Instead, I saw a poorly repressed snarl of hatred. His men crowded me close to him and then stepped away.

Gaston, with one hand behind his back, stood. With no pretense of conversation, he brought his hidden hand out and showed Keevah's Bible. He or one of his men had searched through my rolled-up hammock and seabag, where I kept the Bible while I was on watch.

"That is mine!" I shouted.

"Wrong, McDowell," he sneered. "Whatever you have is mine—if I want it, and I want this note from your woman."

He opened my Bible to the fly page, looked me straight in the face and ripped out Keevah's love note. Flinging my Bible to his left. He wadded the single page with one hand and threw it to his right without ever taking his eyes off me.

Despite my rage, Askira's reminders to keep my wits about me exploded into my mind. I ignored the Bible and my precious note thrown to distract me.

He stepped toward me. I smelled an attack. His right fist was already beginning its powerhouse hook to scramble my brains and end the fight with one blow.

Instead of stepping back in retreat as he expected, I darted in close to his body, forcing him to shorten his swing and lose much of its power.

With one continuous motion, I grabbed his shirt collar with my left hand and yanked it down with all my strength. Despite his repulsive hate-filled breath, I kept my face within inches of his. My attack with my right fist was already underway.

His shortened hook caused his fist to miss behind my head. My lunge toward him gave me the momentum to strike his face with the power of every muscle in my body. The heel of my upward-striking hand caught him on the bottom of his nose.

My momentum and continued thrust snapped his head back even as his forward drive carried him into me. I had already struck when his rock-hard biceps hit my shoulder and knocked me off balance. His weight threatened to take me off my feet. Askira's drills taught me to recover.

Unable to regain his own balance, Gaston staggered backward before falling heavily to his knees. His right arm, still around my shoulder, pulled me down until I bent almost double.

Askira had trained me from our first day to keep my feet. Desperation helped me free myself and regain my stance.

Instead of continuing my attack, I made a mistake and stepped back. Realizing my error, I moved in to strike his head again while he was immobile.

Blood began gushing from his nose. His glazed eyes tried to find me as he attempted to get off his knees. I paused mid-strike. This was clearly a damaged man relying on fighter's instinct alone to survive.

Horrified at what I'd done, I watched him fail. His eyes rolled back into his head as he wobbled from side to side. A few seconds later, he toppled heavily to the deck.

I spun toward two of his men who stood closest to me.

"That will be all," thundered the first lieutenant. He burst into the fo'c'sle with the ship's captain of marines, followed by four of his marines. Each marine held a musket at the ready.

"You," he ordered one of the marines. "Get the surgeon. Put him on that bench," he said to the others.

"Get this place cleaned up," the first lieutenant pointed at two of Gaston's men. "You stop his bleeding," he directed the remaining sailor.

"To the brig with this man!" he bellowed and pointed to me.

The captain of marines gestured for me to move.

"Sir—"

"Now!"

There would be no explaining. Two marines escorted me to a cramped corner of the hold, defined as the brig by rusty strap-iron walls. The marines snapped the padlock shut without a word and left me in the dark.

Not too many months ago, I had started my adult sea-faring life under similar circumstances—locked in a dank corner of a ship's hold in the dark. What would Keevah think of me now?

Hours later, the light of a lantern moved toward me through the dark hold of the ship. The same marines who had put me here unlocked the brig and told me to come with them. I soon found myself in the officers' quarters with the first lieutenant, the master of arms, and the captain of marines.

"You are fortunate, McDowell," the first lieutenant said. "You almost killed a man."

"He is alive?"

"Very much alive, though you have laid him up for some time. If his rage and hatred don't kill him, he will survive. That blow . . . you intended to kill him, didn't you . . . to break his nose and drive the bones into his brain. Askira trained you, didn't he?"

I slowly nodded.

"Yes or no, McDowell," he bellowed. "An officer of the French navy asked you a question!"

"Yes, sir."

"Don't think we don't know who he is and what he is capable of. And don't think we don't know what is going on in our own ship. We are not stupid."

"Yes, sir."

"You and Askira have had good reports until now, aside from your earlier affair with Gaston. We have no desire to lose your service. Gaston, however, benefits this ship in other ways. Consequently, both you and Askira will be transferred to the first French warship we encounter—if they will have you. You are relieved of your duties and confined to the brig to avoid further confrontation between you and Gaston until a transfer is completed. The captain of marines will determine your exercise rights."

I forced myself to acknowledge. "Yes, sir."

The first lieutenant stared wide-eyed with raising brows.

"You obviously don't know how fortunate you are, McDowell. He could have killed you—or we could have punished you so severely you would wish he had killed you." He flicked a hand at the door. "Dismissed. Get out of my sight."

I spent the next fourteen days confined as the *Médée* slogged toward Martinique in light winds. The entire crew was on half rations because of the nonexistent supply ship. I hardly noticed due to my mercurial state of mind—rejoicing I was alive and yet seething at my unjust punishment for saving my own life.

The captain of marines and his squad proved their dislike of Gaston by allowing me ample time to exercise and to talk with my former crew, now led by Askira. My men assured me a seaman, who hated Gaston as much as we did, found my bible and returned it to them. They would keep it safe for me. Keevah's note was never found.

I did learn some French board games with the marines as we passed time together.

French Warship *Illyrienne*, 1826

The French frigate, *Illyrienne*, lay at anchor in the harbor at Martinique when we arrived. Within hours of our arrival, the first lieutenant kept his word and offered Askira and me to his counterpart on the ship. Every French naval vessel at sea was short-handed and would be delighted to take on extra hands. The deal, agreed to before anyone on the frigate laid eyes upon us, took effect within the hour.

A 58-gun ship of the line, she dwarfed the *Médée*. Her mission was not to intercede in slave transport but to serve as a deterrent to other nations against interfering with the activities of the smaller French gunboats. Those gunboats, like the *Médée*, served French national interest by keeping the slave trade working for the profitable sugar industry.

The *Illyrienne* was waiting for a replacement to relieve her of her West Indies tour. With her stores full, most of her crew had nothing to do but spend idle hours onboard or partake of the onshore pleasures a French-run paradise island offered.

My relief of getting off the *Médée* and away from the man who wanted to kill me was short-lived. After a brief introduction to the ship and receiving our assignments, my group leader told me as soon as our replacement arrived, we would set sail for France for refitting, and then sail to the coast of Africa. Our mission would be to assist in the international efforts, spearheaded by England, to intercede with the illegal shipping of slaves from the African continent and return those Negros to Africa. America also had ships serving in the anti-slave blockade, but they were active in the mid-Atlantic, the Caribbean, and along the American coasts.

I almost choked at the hypocrisy. Under relentless diplomatic pressure from England, the French government agreed to provide a naval vessel to support the blockade of Africa. As a crewmember of the *Illyrienne*, I would pretend to stop the export of slaves while protecting French slave ships from the British navy. We all knew France and Spain were not official signatories to treaties with England, and most of the slaves taken from Africa continued to be in vessels flying French, Portuguese, or Spanish flags.

America still relied heavily on slave labor but no longer depended on importation of new slaves from Africa. Slaves in America married, raised families, and, in large part, their children replenished the supply of slaves, all at a terrible cost to those shattered families. Smuggling additional slaves from the active French trade in the Caribbean met the needs of expanding markets in the growing America.

It did allow America to acquiesce to England's pressure and support the English African Blockade. It also justified putting warships in place to prevent aggressive French slavers from preying on American slaves to feed the needs of their profitable sugar enterprises.

It was all a cruel game—with human lives as pawns.

Officers on this new ship had the same problem as those on the *Médée;* many of the crew saw the evil the same as I. However, this captain and his lieutenants did not rely on a power structure within the crew to keep order. The ship's captain of marines was a zealous supporter of France's reliance on slave labor. He trusted his well-trained force of handpicked marines to maintain control. They did so effectively—often with gusto.

Not yet accomplished as an ordinary seaman, I, nevertheless, found myself serving as such. I was surprised to see Negros onboard serving as landsmen, as I had served on the *Médée*.

On our second day at sea, when the crew went through gunnery practice, I was astonished to see those same Negros serving as gun crews for six of our 58 guns. Indeed, every one of those same gun crews had a Negro gun captain who oversaw the team's actions and actual firing of the weapon. A shipmate's answer to my question helped clear up my confusion—but was of no help in my understanding of man's inhumanity to man.

"They are slaves."

My despair deepened at finding myself forced to engage in an activity that I despised and relying on the very slaves I was dehumanizing to protect me as I performed it.

"We may be farther from home, McDowell, but there will still be opportunities for escape. You may yet see your Keevah again." Sensing my despair, Askira slid down to sit beside me as he had done by the carronade carriage on the *Médée* and tried to help me through my gloom.

"I am not of your faith," he said, "but I do know you must continue to believe. Trust your God. He will provide. He will see you through this. I have seen it happen before."

I looked into my friend's eyes, trying to see where his faith lay. "Who is your god, Askira?"

"I have no god . . . and I have many gods. I have been to places, seen the faiths of many peoples, and have learned much. I choose from various faiths as I feel the need or the call."

"That is not God's way."

"That is not the way of your god, young one," he smiled gently as he spoke. "But man has many gods he can call on. Come, we don't want to be caught sitting idle, even if the ship is."

Askira and I found ways to keep ourselves busy even when we were off watch and relieved from our duties. The three-masted frigate, *Illyrienne*, was a true ship-of-the-line and, as such, made a pretense of outfitting all crew in uniforms—a leftover from their Emperor Napoleon's days. For ordinary seamen, the uniform consisted of canvas trousers and a blue and white striped shirt with a red kerchief. New crewmen were not issued new uniforms but were given the uniforms of senior crewmen, who in turn, were given new uniforms. The new uniforms they received were only less worn than the ones they handed down. Mending uniforms and repairing worn-out hammocks kept us busy for several days.

Three weeks after Askira and I came aboard, the *Illyrienne's* replacement arrived. We completed our final preparations for departure during the two days of pompous formalities between the captains and officers of the two ships. At sunrise of the third day, we set sail for the navy yard at Rochefort, France, and a brief shore respite for the crew.

After three weeks in Rochefort, re-armed, refitted, and resupplied, the *Illyrienne* set sail for the west coast of Africa and her new mission.

The next year was an endless ordeal of heavy-handed discipline by officers bent on confirming their aristocratic superiority. The captain of marines and his men made no effort to conceal their intent to ferret out anyone who might have negative thoughts about the command or mission of the *Illyrienne*.

Many of the crew relished the thought of pursuing and capturing ships of other nations since few of them were armed, and even fewer fired at us. If slavers carried cannons, it was to protect themselves from pirates. They were not prepared to battle armed and manned warships.

We chased phantom ships along the slave coast of Africa, often ignoring cries from the crow's-nest. Other times, any man on deck or aloft in the rigging could see sails fleeing from us. Only those officers who possessed spyglasses could see what flag those ships were flying, but in such cases, everyone on board knew they were French. Twice, we encountered British warships returning captured Spanish slave ships to the African ports from which they had departed.

On another occasion, a captured ship flew the French flag. Whether by custom or treaty, I did not know, the British ship placed her prize and her crew in our custody. Our marines escorted the slaver's captain and first mate into the *Illyrienne* officers' quarters as if they were guests.

Soon after, one of our lieutenants selected a dozen seamen, including me, to prepare to board the slaver vessel with him. An *aspirant* and a detachment of marines filled out his boarding party. The armed marines would relish their assignment to quell any thoughts of mutiny by the boarding party or resistance by the original crew of the captured ship.

The *Illyrienne* escorted us as we sailed back to *Gorée* Island, the port she had left. I shall never be able to erase the memory of the sounds and smells of hundreds of distraught human beings bound and crammed into the hold of a ship without proper means of sanitation.

Returning these Negros to the same people who put them on the slave ship was of the highest hypocrisy. They would most likely be on another ship for a stealthy nighttime departure to the French Guiana slave center within the week. We did live up to the letter of the international blockade agreement, however, and served the economic fortunes of France in the process.

It made me sick to my stomach.

Aboard the *Illyrienne*, I daily watched misgivings of our duplicity grow into disgust among a large number of the crew. Revulsion with oneself, with no way to escape it, led to despair. Those men affected most spoke little to their crewmates, lest the ever-present and increasingly aggressive marines should hear. Isolation from everyone on board was the safest way to preserve one's body and sanity. Loneliness, even when in cramped quarters with more than two hundred men, was preferable to being part of a crew who saw no evil in their actions. The cost of such thinking was high.

One young seaman, whom I knew only as *Luc*, had been voicing his distress to the few of us he trusted. He approached me one evening after we came off the second dogwatch. Most of our watchmates had retired for the evening to catch what sleep they could before their next watch. I stood at the forward waist-rail, watching the sun dip behind the horizon, wondering and fearing what Keevah would think of me if she knew.

Like most of the crew, *Luc* thought me a man of the cloth. Like them, it made little difference to him how I had come to serve on a warship. Men came from many walks, some not so respected, before joining a ship's crew. It was best not to query unless a man offered information. This young sailor had been on the crew with me as we sailed the slave ship back to *Gorée* Island. The experience had clearly shaken him. In desperation, the tortured lad came to me for solace.

In hushed voices, we talked of many things: home, family, and God. To escape the attention of any zealous marine, we avoided saying words to convey our true thoughts, each hoping the other understood our hidden meanings. I tried to convince him with veiled words God sees a man's heart and understands more than we can ever hope to. More importantly, He forgives all those who trust Him. Such is our Lord's desire. *Luc* left more at ease, but still troubled. I prayed he could find the peace he sought.

Near the end of my next watch, the captain of marines, with two of his armed men, approached me. In full view of every man on deck, and without explanation, his men shackled my hands behind my back. At bayonet point, the two eager marines escorted me below decks and shoved me into the ship's brig.

After hours had passed, the same marines took me to the captain's cabin where the captain, the first lieutenant, the captain of marines, and the ship's bos'n awaited me. Without so much as a glance upward, the captain read the charges of insubordination and the sentence of nine lashes.

"Bos'n, you know your duty." With a flick of his hand reserved for a bothersome insect, he dismissed us.

At the start of the next day's midday watch, before the morning watch crew went below, orders rang out to muster all hands on deck. With military formality, four marines, two ahead and two behind, marched me to the waist deck.

"Seize him up," the bos'n ordered.

Two marines pulled my shirt off before spreading my arms and lashing my wrists to the mainmast shrouds. Ropes around each ankle pulled my legs apart until I stood spread eagle. My bare back lay exposed to the entire crew on deck and vulnerable to the whip. I was helpless to do anything to protect myself.

A marine with a bayonet-attached musket prodded *Luc* forward until he stood within my view. As I watched, the bos'n, handed the shaken lad a cat-o-nine-tails.

I turned my face away and stared at the open sea.

"You strike the first blow," the bos'n said. "Strike hard. If I think you are easy on him, you will both receive his full punishment. And I will not be easy on you."

Lapping of waves at the water line and the creaking of the ship's rigging were the only sounds entering my ears. Not a sound came from the men assembled to witness the event, meant to crush any ideas they may have about disobedience to their superiors. There was little joy for any of them to see a shipmate flogged.

I closed my eyes, tightened my body to withstand the coming blow, and waited.

The explosion of pain shot through my body like a bolt of lightning. My gasp echoed back to me from my shipmates. I was barely aware of the bos'n taking the whip from *Luc*, but my mind registered the first lieutenant's command to keep *Luc* at my side— to make certain he would see every lash and taste the cost of my and his presumed offense.

The pain of each blow was so great I lost count. I tried to suffer my punishment in silence, but somewhere along the way, I could not contain my cry. "Oh, Jesus, oh Lord Jesus".

The captain's bellow, though sounding distant and muffled, made his message clear.

"Don't you beg for mercy from Jesus Christ; you are on my ship now. Jesus can't help you here. If you want mercy, you beg it from me! I sentence you to three more lashes for your insolence."

I remembered each of those last three lashes. Each one scarred not only my flesh but burned my very soul as if the devil himself wielded the whip. Yet, I bore up under those blows better than any before. The captain's words, though arrogant beyond measure, served the opposite of what he intended; his words fortified my faith. Under that whip, I resolved to help *Luc* claim the peace Jesus offers. No more hidden meanings this time—I would tell him straight.

"Take him below to the surgeon," the bos'n sneered.

I don't remember the marines untying me, though I recall fragments of struggling down the steep companionway steps. Pain spared me from the surgeon's work. He claimed I was unconscious the entire time as he closed several slashes and spread his healing salve on my welts.

A flogged man was supposed to receive 24 hours to recover before returning to duty. I received less. At early morning, two marines rousted me and marched me to the main deck. When I arrived at the spot meant for me, close to a shrouded body laid out on a plank, the captain recited the customary words for burial at sea. Two sailors lifted one end of the plank. The body slid over the side. Sounds of the sea slapping against the hull of the warship on which he died, cloaked the splash of his body. The echoes of a man's last testimony of his time on this earth went unheard, even to his shipmates.

"Return to duty," the bos'n said and walked away.

I stood, unable to move, staring at the now-closed rail gate through which the body had passed.

"Who was he?" I muttered.

"*Luc*," a sailor said. "He hanged himself last night."

CHAPTER 8

Henrysville, Indian Territory of the United States, 1850

Hesed studied my face without saying a word. Even after all these years, *Luc* still bothered me. I didn't want to say more about it. I broke eye contact with her.

"I can see talking about that sailor upsets you," she said. "So, I won't pursue it anymore . . . except to suggest you not blame yourself for what other men did."

"I know. I keep trying to convince myself."

"It's difficult to win an argument against yourself, isn't it? I know—I've tried."

"Have you ever won?"

"No, I've quit trying because it will never change anything. Even when I win the logical side, I lose the emotional side. I need to accept what happened and move on. One can't change the past."

"What was your argument? If I may . . .?"

She paused and studied my eyes as if to judge if she should trust that part of her soul with me.

"My mother . . . on the trail," she said softly. "What I did, what I didn't do, what I could have done, or could not have done. I don't have any answers; I don't know if I ever will. I can only trust the Lord to forgive me, and love me, and be with me through this life."

"He has already forgiven you, Hesed, and He has always loved you."

"I know; it's what keeps me going. What about you, Grayhawk? Has the Lord forgiven you too?"

"Yes." I mumbled, "of course."

"I know He has," she said softly. "Perhaps what I really meant to ask is . . . have you forgiven yourself?"

She waited for me to speak. When I said nothing, she gently placed her hand over mine.

"Talk to me, Grayhawk; I will listen."

I remained silent for a long moment and then nodded. I needed time. Memories flooded back—memories I had tried for years to kill, that I never wanted to think about again. But I did trust Hesed.

French Warship *Illyrienne*, 1828

Most of the crew celebrated at the word we were returning to France. It meant weeks of refurbishing and restocking while the ship lay idle at the Rocheport naval base. Any duty away from Africa and slave ships would be welcome, and there would be time for entertainment ashore.

The news brought me no joy. Tortured by nightmares of *Luc*, I was able to grab only snatches of undisturbed sleep while off-watch. I would never know if the lad understood the meaning of my cryptic words—ambiguous because of my fear of the consequences men might exact on me.

Had he taken his life in desperation, not believing God could see him through his trial? Or had he hanged himself because of the single whiplash he inflicted on me, the very person he confided in for help? I never had the chance to tell him I did not blame him for that blow or for any role he might have had in my flogging.

While on-watch, I found myself performing like a numbed beast of burden trained to perform assigned tasks. Nevertheless, I was grateful for the diversion the work provided. My sanity survived because of those duties and Keevah's Bible, but my tormented mind slipped deeper into depression.

I began to think less of *Luc* and worry more about my own relationship with God. I felt a great chasm was growing between us. My welts and cuts healed, but the ache in my soul remained an open wound, refusing to mend. I spent many sleepless hours wondering why.

The image of a dying seabird I had once seen, with wings too weak to lift her out of her death spiral into hungry seas, haunted me whenever I did manage to sleep. Had I failed God so badly to cause

Him to turn His back on me? Would I ever feel hope again, or had God, like the strength in that seabird's wings, left me for all eternity—when I needed Him most?

Askira forced me to keep training in my fighting skills. My pleas and demands for privacy met with his dogged insistence to train. I wanted to brood in solitude and silence at my misfortune. When I refused to fight, he attacked me. Forced to defend myself, I began to hate him.

***

Refitted and resupplied, the *Illyrienne* was two days out of Rocheport before word came down, that we were headed back to the Caribbean. Askira made the most of the news to get my spirits up. It helped some. Now, I had at least had a reason, however weak, to allow a glimpse of hope—I would be closer to America and Keevah. But also to Gaston.

Askira's training, our fighting, and my hatred of him grew more intense during the weeks we sailed from Rocheport naval yard to the West Indies Island of Martinique—to the same harbor we had sailed from two and a half years before. Yet, after weeks of his aggression, I began to realize I was becoming adept at both defending myself and in carrying the attack to him. As my confidence began to return, so did my self-respect and my gratitude for Askira. Once again, my Japanese shipmate saved me—at least my sanity, if not my life.

No sooner than the *Illyrienne's* hold was filled with supplies from the yard in Martinique than my former ship, the *Médée,* sailed into port. The next day, longboats began ferrying her crew to my ship and to the frigate, which had relieved us from Caribbean duty. Word spread both larger frigates would remain in the Caribbean to protect France's interests in the West Indies. Some of the smaller gunships like the *Médée* would be taken out of service, at least for a time.

Keeping two of her 58-gun frigates in these waters meant France was having trouble protecting the slave trade for her sugar plantations. We soon found out the Americans were getting tired of French gunboats capturing their ships and diverting American slaves to French-owned plantations. The Americans also had a growing market for new slaves to fill the expanding economy in the western stretches of their country. Since America had passed laws prohibiting importing slaves from Africa, they had to find them elsewhere. French slaves were an ideal solution.

French gunboats, committed as they were to protect their own slave trade, presented American slavers with a problem. To solve the challenge, the Americans had taken to arming several fast ships with sufficient weapons and trained crews to defeat the gunboats at long range—beyond reach of the devastating carronades.

Strategists in the French navy knew it was one thing to defeat a small gunship carrying short-range weapons—another to defeat an armed ship-of-the-line. The two French 58-gun warships now in these waters could defeat any of the American gunboats. They meant to put an end to American piracy.

An hour before we took part of the crew from the *Médée* on board, we learned most of her crewmembers would join existing squads within the current command. Two additional squads, under the command of the *Médée's* lieutenant, who was now serving as third lieutenant on the *Illyrienne*, and one of his *aspirants,* would take the rest of the gunboat crew. Askira and I would lead those squads.

I, and most the crew of the *Illyrienne*, watched as almost forty men came aboard. Gaston's face turned hard with hatred when he saw me. I saw something else in his narrowing eyes. I saw fear—a kind of wariness a predator has for certain prey—prey with teeth, which can kill.

"Gaston is angry." The former lieutenant from the *Médée* stepped beside me. "He has lost his power and authority. He's been disgraced in front of the entire crew. Your being here rubs his face in it. He will be more dangerous than before. I tried to have him transferred to the other ship. Those officers want nothing to do with him—neither do I, but he will muster to either you or to Askira's squad."

"Assign him to me, sir."

"You can handle him?"

"I'll have a better chance with him in my squad, sir, than in any other."

"I'll have no fighting or killing in my command. The two of you had better work things out . . . or you will both lose. Do I make myself clear?"

"Aye, sir. I will convince him his survival depends on my continued good health and happiness."

"See that you do." The lieutenant turned and strode away.

My unspoken prayers that my impulsive decision would not be my undoing may have yielded results. Gaston's hatred of me never diminished over the following months, but he did try to conceal it from my eyes, if not from others.'

He no doubt knew his former shipmates from the *Médée* hated him as much as he hated me. His former gang abandoned him the instant he lost his position of *tryan*. He was friendless and alone in a crew of more than 200 men. The few times I stood up for his rights to other crewmen may have convinced him he needed my favors and what little influence I had as a squad leader—or it may have been my reputation as Askira's fighting partner that kept him at bay. Whatever the reason, we both accepted an unspoken, though cautious, truce.

The American pirates, as they liked to call themselves, proved to be as cunning as they were greedy. Money flowed in the Caribbean slave trade. They knew how to get it. Too many times during the next ten months, the pirates either out-foxed or out-sailed us. Their armed gunboats were fast and maneuverable. They were protecting or serving as decoys for their slower slave ships. Their constant harassing kept us from searching for their slave ships.

Most often, there were no winners to our skirmishes. The Americans were content to divert us from our intended prey with a small but accurate broadside and then shadow us while staying out of range of our guns. Seldom were we able to defeat and capture one of their ships, and even less often did we capture an American slave ship.

The American Navy also had ships in these waters to enforce their law against importing slaves from Africa and to stop another type of pirates who were capturing and holding American merchant vessels for ransom. Their navy would offer no help to France in dealing with pirates flying the American flag. As far as the American navy was concerned, pirates could interfere with the French slave trade at will.

Our officers suspected the American navy went so far as to equip and train the slave pirates in gunnery. Their pirate gunboats' accuracy and rapid reloading resembled both the American and English navies.

Against this strategy, our powerful 58-gun French frigates could not close with our nimble enemy and fight our kind of battle. Instead, we suffered minor damages with few casualties at each encounter. Over the course of months, those few added up to many. I witnessed numerous lives and limbs lost. The ever-growing stains on the surgeon's table told the grim story.

Then, we learned of an audacious plan to sail into the Cuban waters near Santiago, Cuba. Strict Spanish laws required all non-Spanish flagged vessels to bring slaves into Havana. There, the Spanish levied heavy taxes on both the ships and the slaves.

To avoid those taxes, rogue captains from any nation sought other ports to deliver their cargoes. A large supply of new slaves, more than Spanish ships could provide, was critical to support the island's booming sugar industry, so Spanish authorities turned a capricious eye to the illicit trade. It could be profitable for those in the right places.

Our fleet commanders felt their warships could convince any Cuba-bound slave ship to divert to French-owned islands. The slavers could still make a profit and could avoid a costly encounter with the Spanish Navy, which would escort slave ships of any nation to the tax-collectors in Havana.

In addition, many free Haitian Negros, not realizing they would become slaves again, were sailing into Santiago to escape the brutal demands and treatment by their own Negro government. Our officers told us these slave ships and refugee boats were excellent opportunities for France, and we could do it without confronting American ships.

***

Cuba, 1829

To replenish our water supply before sailing into action, the *Illyrienne* dropped anchor in a stream-fed cove two days sail east of Santiago. Following orders, Askira and I prepared our squads for the unpleasant chore of making numerous runs to fill all our water casks. In any navy, lowest ranking crews always catch the dirtiest and hardest work—especially if it is non-sea related.

"This is our time," Askira whispered as we oversaw our crews lowering the longboats. "You are going to see your Keevah again."

After the two boats were in the water, our squads boarded and took on as many empty water casks as we could hold. It would take many more trips to bring the full and heavier casks back to the ship. After delivering its load of full casks to the ship, the longboat would return with more empty casks. With good timing, we could make this work in our favor.

At least, we thought so until four musket and pistol-armed marines boarded—two in each longboat.

I shot a glance to Askira. His clenched jaw and measured nod said once his feet touched Cuban soil, he was not returning to any French warship. Marines, any number of them, were not going to stop him. I nodded my like intent.

Filling the ship's water casks from a small stream, moving the weight over a rocky ledge to the beach, and then lifting the heavy casks into the longboats was hard work. After the water was loaded, came the backbreaking task of rowing the laden boats back to the *Illyrienne*. Seamen from other squads spelled our men for rowing duties every two hours.

Askira and I stayed without relief—our duty, as lowest-ranking squad leaders, was to direct the task. We saw it as our opportunity to escape. Jumping ship is an offense punishable by death by hanging in any navy. We didn't intend to be caught.

After three hours, two marines assigned shore duty—impatient to be back aboard the *Illyrienne*—climbed into the boat ferrying fresh water to the ship. This was their way of getting replacements, and it was our way of getting away.

I whistled to draw the remaining two marines' attention.

"This pool is getting muddy. We need clean water." Gesturing to Askira, I said, "We're going upstream to see what we can find."

"No," the marine nearest me commanded. "You stay with me." He turned to the other marine and gestured in the direction of our crews. "Keep an eye on them."

"You don't leave my sight." He swung his musket in our direction. "I'll go with you."

Exactly what we hoped he'd say.

I led us along the sand and gravel streambed, which at times was many times wider than its current ribbon of clear water. This stream, which meandered from one side of its bed to the other, must at times, carry vast quantities of water with the power to scour all vegetation and soil from its path. Sand and dirt were washed away, while larger gravel and rocks remained at its passing.

Thankful we were not here at a time of flooding, I made a pretense of looking for a spot deep enough for our men to fill the ship's casks. After several sharp turns around large boulders, I stopped and looked back to see if we were out of sight of the other men.

It had already happened, and I hadn't heard a sound. The marine lay face-up in the gravel. Askira had his musket and was already stripping him of his pistol and ammunition cases. The man never moved. I don't know if he was dead or unconscious. Askira never told me; I never asked. He handed me the pistol without saying a word and nodded upstream. We ran.

Keeping close to the stream and the ample vegetation growing beside it, we kept ourselves concealed from anyone following. Less dense vegetation on either side of the streambed's lush growth offered less concealment to hide a man. Most of the scrub brush on the surrounding hills stood no higher than a man's waist. Occasional trees I did not recognize would reach upward ten or twelve feet, but their lower limbs would not hide us from the *Illyrienne's* marines, soon to be searching for us. The tortuous path along the stream and its well-watered growth was our way to get away unseen.

We ran for several hundred yards before stopping to catch our breath. I hadn't expected the land to rise so rapidly, but we were already well above the mast height of our ship. Were it not for

Askira's relentless conditioning of the past months, the hard exertion would have left me gasping for air. After a few moments, we were ready to start again.

"Wait," Askira said. "Get in the brush. Someone is almost on us."

In a few seconds, I heard the scurrying footsteps Askira had been listening for all along. As they approached, the sounds of labored breathing accompanied them. Both of us stayed hidden, waiting for the man to show himself. Before rounding the last boulder, he stopped for a few seconds to catch his breath. In a moment, Gaston barged into full view with eyes directed down, choosing his steps among the rocks.

We stepped out from our concealment. The sounds of cocking our weapons froze Gaston in his tracks. Like a startled deer, he jerked his head up. Those huge hands, which had fought and killed other men and had tried to kill me, crept out, palms open to above his shoulders.

"Don't shoot," he gasped. "Let me come . . . I want to come with you."

Askira and I trained our weapons on him. Neither of us spoke.

"Let me come." He stopped to suck air. "I'm a dead man on that ship . . . without you, McDowell . . . You know that . . . They all hate my guts . . . Please."

"You'll have to keep up," I said. "We will not be caught."

Askira lowered the hammer of his musket. "We are both armed and capable, Gaston, and I will not hesitate. Mind yourself. Let's get moving."

For hours, we followed the streambed. Our shoes, meant for working on wet decks, offered little support in gravel and rocks. When we stopped, it was for short minutes. I did note Gaston, though breathing hard, kept up. Before dusk, we climbed a hill, hopeful of getting a glimpse of the sea and the *Illyrienne*. Askira topped the crest of the hill before either Gaston or me. His smile, one of the few I had ever seen on him, told the story. I looked where he pointed and saw our former ship under full sail, miles from where we had anchored.

Our shouts of joy would have alerted anyone of our presence; no one answered. We had made it! Not one of us cared if our former officers and shipmates, as well as the nation of France, considered us marked men—deserters from her National Navy, deserving of nothing but hanging from a yardarm.

We turned our faces to the north. Through the branches of the now plentiful trees, we could see green hills ahead of us. Through them, lay our path to freedom.

"Those are mere foothills," Askira said. "Beyond them lie the mountains—the *Sierra Maestra*; they will be hard; they are rugged."

I shot him a quick glance. "You know their name?"

"I have been on this island before. Where do you think I learned to speak Spanish? Let's get moving. We need shelter and rest. Where we are going will not be easy."

His warnings meant little to me—they were my way to Keevah.

Askira appeared to need little sleep. His strict discipline of his body may have affected all his natural functions. He had us climbing at first light, following the stream as it twisted through ever-steepening hills. The broad valley by the sea, where we started, deepened into a narrow ravine as its once-rambling waters first burbled and then tumbled into a narrow torrent in its haste to join the sea.

My two companions proved adept at living off the land by snaring birds and different kinds of squirrel-like rats. Even snakes and lizards were not safe if we saw them. Edible fruits and berries were rare but welcome whenever we could find them. My academic past and seminary studies left me ignorant about how to survive in a foreign wilderness. Gaston fit in well, never hesitating to pull his share of the load. Mindful of his past, Askira and I took turns standing watch during the night rather than trust our lives to him. The former *tyran de l'gaillard* accepted his fate without complaint or argument.

Our need to stay close to water and find food forced a tortuous route up the mountains. Our shoes, meant for working on a ship's deck, soon wore out, so we fashioned footwear of rat skins. Thin and untanned as those skins were, they soon wore through and needed replacing.

Most sailors go barefoot much of the time while on deck, so our feet had toughened to a certain degree—to wood decks, not to mountain rocks. Nevertheless, we soon found it faster, though more painful, to go barefoot rather than take the time to make shoes out of animal skins. In time, our feet toughened to where we could wear sandals of wood attached to our feet with straps of skins. Gaston had a knack for fashioning our footwear with the short-bladed knife every sailor carries with him. We each had our knives but no other tools with us.

After four weeks of travel, our stream, now nothing more than a trickle, vanished into a few thin seeps of moisture along the sides of a series of shallow rock outcroppings. This water moistened what little soil existed there and allowed thin brush and grasses to grow. A couple hundred feet up the mountain from the seeps, green growth ended in dry mountain rocks where only deep-rooted trees could survive.

"We need to go back to where we can get water," Askira said, "and fill every skin we have. From there, we will climb the ridge and look for another stream."

It took us ten water-rationed days of hard climbing before we crested the last of an endless string of ridges. Before us lay even higher mountains in our path.

I sank on a boulder, staring at them without saying a word.

"The heart of the *Sierra Maestra*," Askira said. "We will not be going there."

Gaston plopped down beside me. "We're not finished yet, McDowell. Those mountains are green with trees. There must be water somewhere. We'll find it."

"We'll find it in that direction." Askira pointed to the west, where a small gulley began to carve its way down the side of the ridge. I guessed the distance at a mile or more.

"Follow it with your eyes. It leads to a canyon, and the canyon opens into a big valley. That is a major drainage. There will be water somewhere in the canyon. Let's move down this ridge and camp. We could use the rest."

We continued to conserve our tiny supply of water, but we did eat the last of the smoked and dried rat. The meat consisted of no more than a few bites for each of us. It was tough and stringy, but to my risen spirits, it was a feast. That night, I dreamed of Keevah.

Three days later, hungry and thirsty, we did find water, as Askira said we would. The next day, Askira shot a wild goat with the marine's musket. We rested, feasted on goat meat smoked over a tiny fire, and rejoiced the entire day.

Though the terrain was rugged and thick with trees and undergrowth, we moved without trouble. The tiny rivulet we first encountered grew to a bubbling brook and then to a rushing stream with deep holes and cascading waterfalls. With fishhooks and a line fashioned from goat bone, gut, and sinew, Askira caught fish—a welcome diversion from smoked goat meat. Berries were abundant along the streambed.

Within a week, our stream joined others to become a small river as we entered a flat valley. Our diet improved to include fish, berries, roots, and an occasional large rodent-like animal none of us could identify. Not long after, we stopped using the musket—after we stumbled upon remnants of an old campfire and footprints in the mud along the river.

"When in Cuba before," Askira said, "I heard about large sugar plantations in a central valley in the mountains. We might be in that valley or one like it. The Spanish run the plantations with thousands of Negro slaves. They will not be pleased to see us."

We took Askira's words to heart and followed his orders to scout well before moving. Several times, we saw groups of two or three armed men we assumed were hunters. We took pains to conceal ourselves; it would not go well if they discovered us. Our clothing, tattered and torn as it was, would still identify us as sailors from a French warship—not welcome on Spanish domain.

After spotting four armed men goading along a single file of six Negros tied to each other with ropes around their necks, we realized the type of game the hunters were pursuing.

"We're walking right into a Spanish plantation," Askira said. "This valley must be filled with them."

Gaston offered one of his few suggestions. "We need to backtrack into the mountains again, skirt this valley, and find another way to the north coast."

Askira nodded. "Let's fill our water skins and get out of here. It'll be best if we stay on the high ground away from the river or any streams. Runaway slaves will need water; the Spanish will look for them where there is water."

We spent the next two weeks finding our way while avoiding any contact with people. The sight of those six men lashed together like livestock bothered all of us. It was a stark reminder of what we had been a part of for the past years and months. A frequent topic of our evening discussions was whether the campfire and tracks we had first seen belonged to a runaway slave. None of us voiced even a guarded hope for his fate.

Traveling these mountains proved even more tedious than before. Now, we had to watch for people. Anyone, regardless of color or nationality, could prove our undoing. Our occasional trips to get water often took an entire day. Cautious scouting to ensure we wouldn't be spotted was routine. Three weeks of following the river found us again in an ever-narrowing steep-sided gorge. This time, we trailed it from high in the surrounding hills, which made the going harder.

"Those clouds mean trouble," Gaston said as we prepared to go to the river for water. "We're in for a bad storm. The wind is already increasing. Let's get our water and get back into the mountains to find shelter—not just from rain, but from wind. It's going to be a big blow."

I had noticed him several times during the previous day as he checked the sky and the capricious winds. Now, I had an uneasy feeling he knew what he was talking about.

"I saw it like this four years ago. We weathered the worst storm I'd ever seen in the harbor in Saint-Martin, a harbor protected on all sides by land. Even so, we lost two corvettes to that blasted wind; ripped the sails right off, and they were furled tight too. It'll be bad. We need shelter."

CHAPTER 9

Henrysville, Indian Territories of the United States, 1850

Hesed remained quiet while I finished both my story and the meal she brought. After removing the empty dish, she spoke.

"Ciara and I saw those terrible scars on your back when we wrapped your chest. I know her well. She's a strong woman, and she's seen a lot, but that shook her. She mentioned it again last night. I've seldom seen her so troubled by anything."

"It's something I've tried to forget."

"I need to tell her what happened and why because she'll never forget it. She'll always wonder what you did to cause that."

My frown and reticence didn't deter her.

She stared at me in silence till I gave a begrudging mumble.

"Thank you," she said. "Let me change the subject a bit, and I say this with kindness and respect. Please correct me if I'm wrong, but you seem to have something against Ciara. I've known her a long time, and I don't think she has a mean bone in her body. In fact, she's a kind and generous person. She can be direct and determined at times, but you must remember she is trying to run a newspaper. I think she's doing a good job of it too."

"What do you mean . . . run a newspaper? She said she was a reporter."

"She is, but she's more. She owns the newspaper, Grayhawk."

"A woman, so young—owning and running a newspaper"?

"Lock, stock, and barrel. Her husband bought the property and some of the equipment because it's almost impossible for a young woman to obtain financial credit on the frontier. He put everything in her name, and she has paid every cent due on it."

"It seems a risky proposition with him being gone so much of the time."

"It is all hers, her dream, her passion, her quest. He stands behind her all the way."

"Her quest? What is she searching for?"

"Not so much searching as in pursuing her calling, running her race, striving to make a difference. She may be facing formidable odds, but she has two clear objectives to her work."

"She's not jousting at windmills, is she? Many journalists do, you know."

"No, Sir." Hesed's eyes flared for a few seconds. Cold steel glinted in her words, though she spoke quietly. "She is not jousting at windmills. She is jousting at rampant evils in our nation and here in the territories as well. She knows exactly what they are, and she will know when we have won or lost. She is not a Don Quixote."

Her eyes showed fight if I wanted it, though her manner remained calm. I had seen western Indians employ similar patience while fires of war raged within. They could bide their time, as could she in defending her friend.

"Hesed, my comment was out of line. I am sorry. It was not my intent to demean her in any way. I was trying to say I hope she is not spending her energy fighting ghosts or insignificant causes."

The fight faded from her eyes. I was thankful; I did not want war with this woman.

"Neither issue is trivial," she said, "although they do intertwine, I will tell you of one of them. The other, she wants to discuss with you directly."

"And which will you discuss?"

She paused and glanced downward. I sensed a looming confession. Her shoulders drooped, and her lips tightened to bare both revulsion and shame. I resolved to withhold judgment on anything she would tell.

"Ciara abhors slavery. She realizes she cannot change the entire nation, but she believes she can, and she is determined to change the situation here."

"Here? In this town . . . why here?"

"Not only in Henrysville but throughout a large part of this region. She can explain her reasons."

"Hesed, I don't mean to pry, but this seems important to you too. Why?"

"I am a Cherokee. We have been trying for years to be civilized. But how can we call ourselves civilized when we enslave Negros?"

"Ah . . . the white man's curse."

"No, it's not only the white man's curse. All through history and around the world, people have enslaved others. We used to enslave Indians from other tribes. Then we started enslaving other people, Negros, with the excuse if whites did it, it must be right. It isn't right, and it never was."

"Not all whites practice or believe in slavery, Hesed."

"I know, and not all Indians do either. Even here in the territories, we have heated divisions on slavery, the same as people in the States do. Do you know eight years ago, a group of Negro slaves owned by Cherokees revolted and tried to escape to Mexico? On their way, they picked up slaves from the Creeks and Choctaw tribes. Some of them were killed or captured early, but others made it all the way to Texas.

"It is a sad commentary on our supposed civilization that a posse of Indians, numbering over a hundred, hunted them down. Cherokee, Creek, and Choctaw, all of them Indians, captured and returned those Negros to their owners. The posse hanged five slaves for killing two slave hunters. Some of the fallout was the Cherokee nation enacted stricter laws to control slaves, expelled all free Negros from their territory, and set up a company to catch runaway slaves. And we call this civilization?

"This is what Ciara is fighting, and I am committed to her side of the battle. She can tell you more . . . if you will let her."

She rose. "I've overstayed my time. I must get back. One of us will bring your meal this evening."

I hoped Hesed, instead of Ciara, would return. The thought was growing in me that it was not hostility I felt toward Ciara but fear.

What would her constant reminders of Keevah do to me? Grief had once reduced me to a pit so deep in the past I had cried out to God to let me die. Loneliness and despair had reduced me to a hollow shell. I was all too familiar with the ache of emptiness that at times, was unbearable. I could not live through such agony again. Was it my fear Ciara would put me back into another black pit of grief and regret and return me to the brink of destruction?

And the root of my unease? Was I afraid of dying alone—without family—without loving or being loved? Did Ciara expose an unknown fear residing deep in my very bones?

Hesed left me wondering what she thought of me after learning of my involvement in the slave trade. I wanted her, not Ciara, to come this evening. She already knew some of my sordid past, but she also needed to know about Elijah and Anna.

She did bring me my meal that evening as I'd hoped. She sat in the chair as if expecting me to continue my story. To tell what I wanted her to know, I'd also have to share more about my desertion from the French warship and my flight through Cuba. As I ate, I began telling my tale as I remembered it.

Cuba, 1829

After Gaston's warning of the storm, we hurried to fill our water skins and returned to the hills. We soon saw a rock overhang and what looked like it might be a cave. I crawled under the rock and into the hole. The faint odor of stale campfire filled my nostrils. I assumed my own smoke-tainted clothing in such close quarters was the source.

"Stop! Move no farther!"

The accent of the deep male voice was pure King's English. My blood ran cold. The English were like hounds pursuing their game, and we slavers were no more than the foxes for their self-righteous sport. To some hounds, national boundaries and sovereignty of nations made little difference when it came to sport . . . or collecting bounty money.

"One more step, and I'll strike. You'll never touch her—not while I'm alive."

Whoever the speaker, he was protecting someone; he may not be pursuing slavers after all. I played my hunch.

"I don't want to touch anyone. My companions and I are looking for shelter. A big storm is coming."

"Who are you?" the voice demanded.

"I'm an American; I was shanghaied onto a French warship. I'm trying to get back to America."

"Are you alone? How many others? Who are they?"

"One Japanese, one Frenchmen; both are like me, trying to get home again."

"Stay where you are. I'm going to light a torch. If you are not what you say, you are as good as dead."

"We are wearing French naval uniforms. We have no other clothes." I started to pull the pistol from my waistband, then thought better of it. The first sight of a weapon could cause the man to strike. Better to show no hint of aggression.

Sparks from a flint appeared yards distance from where the man spoke. There was someone with him—maybe the female he mentioned. After a few seconds, a tiny glow from a torch revealed the gaunt face of a young Negro woman. The bud of flame soon grew, sending fingers of light flickering throughout the entire cave. Torchlight soon undraped the lean frame of a tall Negro man who held a stout club of a tree branch over my head.

"May we share your shelter?" I said, raising both hands in a gesture of goodwill.

"You may come in." Her voice, weak and trembling, reached from the back of the cave. She spoke in the same manner of English as he had.

I shifted my attention from the man to the woman. Even in the flickering of the torch, it was clear she was wearing dirty and ragged men's clothing—much too large for her. What struck me, though, were her eyes. Sunken in a face thin and drawn from too much fear and deprivation, they burned with the quiet defiance of a fighter. She reminded me of stories I'd heard of new slaves starving themselves to death rather than submitting to a life of degrading servitude.

"You will do as she says, but don't move a muscle until you've handed over that pistol."

Though thin, the Negro's long arms and broad shoulders hinted at a stature at least a head taller than any of us. I handed the pistol to him. "The Japanese man has a musket too," I said. "We took them from a French Marine as we were escaping. We mean you no harm."

"I will determine that. You stay as you are and have your man pass the musket to you. Once you have it, you pass it to me." He cocked the pistol and pointed it at my head. "Understand this, sir, the lady and I will both fight and die rather than be forced into slavery. Now, please do as I say."

In the flickering light, I noticed scars on the man's ankles, dried scabs on one and the other wrapped in a blood-soaked rag no doubt torn from the tail of the woman's too-large shirt.

"Are you runaway slaves?"

"No. We are escaped captives. We are not slaves. We never will be." He brought the muzzle of the pistol closer to my head. "Get the musket in here."

I shouted back to Askira, explaining the situation to him. He passed the musket to me without argument. I passed it to the Negro. It was useless anyway; a glance confirmed Askira had removed the firing cap. The man didn't seem to notice; he laid it aside.

"Tell the Japanese man to come in." Then, nodding his head toward the far wall, he said, "Then, you both move over there."

After Askira entered, we both crawled over and sat with our backs to the wall. I was surprised when Gaston crept in. The man I had known before would have abandoned us the very moment we found ourselves in trouble. Outside the cave, he was free and unencumbered. He had made no commitments to us; he owed us nothing. Loyalty to no man but himself had always been his nature, yet he chose to risk his freedom and his life by staying with Askira and me, two men he had hated while aboard ship.

Perhaps it was the threat of the storm, but I thought not. He would have had enough time to find other shelter had he decided to leave us. No, these past many weeks of hardship had forged a bond among the three of us. He chose to honor that bond like a man. I marveled at the change in him.

"I am *Ikuseghan*." The man said, still pointing the pistol at us. "This young lady is *Akinlana*. You can surmise how we came to be here. Yes, I saw you take note of the shackle scars on my legs. She has scars too, on one leg instead of two. The slavers' courtesy, I suppose, to the gentler sex. Would you care to tell us your names and how you came to be here?"

Each of us, in turn, told our names and nationalities and confirmed the story of our escape and flight.

"And how did you come to be on a French warship in these waters? Were you all shanghaied as Mr. McDowell claims he was?"

"I was shanghaied in London by an English privateer," Askira said. "Within a week, they sold me to a French warship. Three months later, I was transferred to a Corvette, a small French warship. I met Lanny there. That is the name we know him by."

"Very well. We will do likewise. And you, Mr. Gaston?"

"I joined the navy."

"The French navy?"

"Yes, the French navy," Gaston struggled with his English. "I am French. I had no idea what I would be getting into. I had no job, no future; it was a way to eat and survive."

His words may have been true, but every man onboard the *Médée* or the *Illyrienne* avoided talk of Gaston's past for fear of retaliation. I suspected more pressing motivations were at play to get him in the navy and out of France.

Ikuseghan turned the pistol toward me. "And now, Lanny, even in this poor light, it appears you have something strapped to your chest, under your arm. Would you surrender it, please?"

"That's his Bible," Gaston said. "He's a preacher—a real preacher. You don't need to take it from him."

"It's alright, Gaston," I said. "I trust he will return it."

I pulled my ragged shirt off and unbuckled the leather pouch Keevah's shoemaker friend had given me. I handed over the pouch containing Keevah's gift.

"Thanks to a negligent Spanish guard," Askira said, "we have water and some of their cured goat meat outside. We will share what we have. Please let us weather the storm here in this shelter with you."

"You are welcome to stay, and your food will be appreciated. *Akinlana* needs rest and nourishment right now . . . we both do." After satisfying himself my pouch contained no weapons, he returned it to me.

"Askira, will you fetch your supplies? Lanny, I have no reason not to believe your stories, but my commitment to protect *Akinlana* requires I keep your pistol for the time being. I assume the reloading supplies are in the pouch Askira carries on his belt. I will need to keep it also, or at least enough for several reloads of this pistol. As I see it, if you are captured, you will face a courtroom trial. If we are captured, we will hang without a trial or face a life of slavery. I have sworn to her that will not happen—not while I am alive. I hope you understand."

"I understand, but with one correction: if the English capture us, we will face prison; if the French capture us, we will hang as deserters. If the Spanish capture us, they will return us to the French and the gallows. As for the pistol, I carried it to lighten Askira's load, I have never fired one in my life."

"Nor have I," *Ikuseghan* said.

"Askira knows how to fire and reload it," I said. "He can teach you. Considering your situation, it may be wise for you to learn."

Ikuseghan pointed the pistol away from me, released the hammer, and turned the weapon over in his hands as if studying it before laying it on the ground next to the musket. He turned to Askira as the Japanese man reentered with our supplies. "May I give *Akinlana* some of your water"?

I watched him give the woman a drink and care for her wounds. She was even smaller and thinner than I thought at first; I guessed not much more than five feet tall. After caring for her, he drank some water himself.

Askira cut the goat meat and handed a piece to each person; the piece for the woman, he handed to *Ikuseghan*. After delivering the woman's share, the Negro returned, sat by me, and started chewing the stringy meat.

"Tell me," I said. "How did you two English-speaking people ever get caught in this slavery trade?"

Ikuseghan looked back at the woman for a moment before answering. "Because we are Negro. We were both workers at an English missionary hospital in Nigeria. In fact, the missionary orphanage was our life, our home since we were infants. We've been told we speak with the King's English accent. That is the language spoken by the missionaries; they are English. We speak several regional African dialects; however, English is our first language."

"You were taken from a missionary hospital?"

"Not exactly. We were with a group delivering medical supplies to remote villages. Some Arab and Portuguese slavers, no doubt with some inside help, set up a trap in one of those villages. I can't imagine they were targeting missionary aid teams, but when we walked in, they took advantage of the situation. Two young missionaries and one guide lost their lives trying to protect us; they were white. The rest of us were Negro."

"Didn't your English language make any difference?"

"*Akinlana* and I were the only ones who spoke English, but they didn't care. In fact, on the slave ship, they told me our English would bring a higher price for us and more profit for them. But enough about us; what about you? Gaston said you are a preacher. Is that true?"

"I was a seminary student in Boston when I was shanghaied. It was my final year. I had plans to marry after I completed my studies and received my certificate."

"*Akinlana* and I had planned to wed too. We've been talking about it since we were twelve; we've known each other all our lives. We were best friends. We still are. Now, we're trying to stay alive . . . and free."

"What do you think your chances are of getting off this island? There are Spanish and Cuban slaveholders and military on both coasts; they patrol inland too—mostly around the plantations."

Ikuseghan dropped his gaze to the ground. Shaking his head, he looked up and turned his palms up in futility. I turned to Askira. Our eyes met for several long seconds before he answered my silent query with a nod.

"*Ikuseghan*." I struggled to pronounce the African's name. "You must understand; we are fugitives too; we cannot guarantee anything. You and your lady are welcome to travel with us. We have been successful in staying free so far; we are becoming familiar with their tactics. Askira is our guide; he has been in Cuba before. We are going to the north coast where we will obtain a boat . . . somehow, and sail to the United States. And, like you, we will not be captured . . . by anyone."

"I must talk to *Akinlana*. It is her decision as well as mine."

"One other stipulation," I stopped his movement. "You have heard how badly we butcher your names with our mispronunciations. May I suggest we call you Elijah? He was a man of God who, at one time also fled for his life from evil people. And may we call your lady, Anna, the Greek version of a Hebrew name for one who is gracious, one who gives? These are names we can remember and pronounce."

Ikuseghan laughed. I was certain he hadn't done it in months.

"You may call us those names. I know of Elijah's trials well, and Anna is truly gracious. You are quite perceptive. Your selections of names compliment both of us. Now I must discuss your offer with *Akinlana* . . . excuse me, with Anna."

After a few moments of quiet discussion with Anna, Elijah returned. "We will go with you. We have no other options; we don't know where to go or even where we are at this moment. I ask you to let me keep the pistol; it is for Anna. It would be horrible for her if . . ."

"You may have to kill men with it," Askira said. "Are you prepared to do that?"

"I know what is at stake for all of us." Elijah looked at his opened palms as if searching for stains of men's blood on them. After a moment, he looked Askira in the eye. "I have devoted a great deal of thought and prayer to that possibility during those weeks on their evil boat. Lately, with the threat to both of us, especially Anna, I have made my peace with what I must do. I am prepared to kill—or die—if necessary."

Askira nodded. "Keep the pistol. Let us hope you do neither."

Gaston proved correct in his forecast. I had never seen or heard anything like the winds and rain that swept over us for most of the day. Afterward, downed trees, water spewing down every gully, and ever-present mud made travel difficult. There was water everywhere; none of it fit to drink. We cut our rations even further. I noticed Elijah giving portions of his to Anna, who was gaining strength. I suspected both had been without food for some time before we found them.

Near the end of the fourth day, Askira found and shot a stray goat. We spent the entire night and the next day searching for dry wood to keep the coals of a smoky fire burning to dry and smoke the meat. As weak as she was, Anna never hesitated to do her share of the work. Neither did she withdraw from her self-imposed duties of caring for Elijah's injured ankles. She always reserved a small portion of her drinking water to cleanse his still-open wound and sacrificed another strip from the tail of her shirt to replace the soiled wrappings on his ankle.

I watched Askira study Anna and Elijah. He seemed fascinated with their relationship and ritual of tending to each other's injuries. They always concluded with prayer, spoken too softly for us to make out the words. Occasionally, Elijah would ask to borrow my Bible to read to her. Their deep sense of peace at such times, despite our perilous situation, would put Askira into deep thought. I sensed his regard for them growing each time he witnessed their apparent peace under circumstances that were anything but.

Our travel during the following weeks was slow; though the storm-swelled streams were dwindling and clearing, water fit for drinking could again be found. We had been three days without food when Askira shot another of the large rodent-like animals we had eaten before. None of us knew what it was, but we made a meal of it.

Our cautious scouting ahead detected several groups of people, which we avoided by going back into the mountains. Goats were harder to find; farmers had rounded up most of the animals loosed by the storm. The occasional feral goats we did see were wary and difficult to approach. Each time, they outwitted Askira and kept out of range of his musket. Desperate for food, we decided to send Askira close to a farm to obtain food while the rest of us stayed hidden. Gaston asked to go.

Hours later, as Anna, Elijah, and I lay hidden under a rock outcropping near the top of a hill, we heard a musket shot in the distance. Elijah pushed Anna farther under the rock and positioned himself in front of her. Clenching his jaw, he pulled the pistol from his waistband. His eyes scoured the forest below in the direction of the shot before he turned toward me.

"You think that was ours . . . or someone after them?"

"One shot. Doesn't sound like a patrol after two m—"

The sound of a second shot muffled its way through the trees before I could finish my word. Before either of us could mutter another sound, a third shot told the story. It would take at least three men, each with a musket, to space three shots in such a short time. I glanced at Elijah. His stoic expression told me nothing. His eyes bored into the forest. Cocking of the pistol hammer was the only sound among us.

We stayed hidden until daybreak, as Askira had instructed before he left. After a few sips of water for breakfast and fearful of what we'd find, we crept down the hill, through the trees and brush, toward where we had heard the shots.

"Lanny." Askira poked his head from behind a tangle of brush, "Ssh. Quiet."

I motioned to Elijah and Anna to be silent. The three of us converged on Askira's hiding place.

"We are fine. We led them on a merry chase to keep them away from you. There must be a Spanish marine squadron stationed nearby. I'm sure they recognized our uniforms as French—probably think we're trying to steal slaves. They will return with more men. We must move . . . fast."

He looked at our two thin and half-starved companions. "We did get food before they saw us. We need to ration it. Gaston and I have already decided Elijah and Anna get double rations while we're on the move. We can't afford for them to become weak or lag behind."

Gaston nodded. Askira didn't give him time for anything else. The Japanese soldier was in command mode. "Elijah, keep your pistol dry. If the powder gets wet, it will fail you when you need it." He addressed us all, "Grab some bread and goat meat now. Eat as we move. Let's go."

Move we did. I was thankful we were in hill country instead of the mountains we had passed through. Even so, it was hard going. Like the rest of us, neither Elijah nor Anna had shoes, and though they were used to going barefoot, the hard pace took a toll on them. Resting or sleeping for only hours at a time, we traveled day and night, whenever there was moonlight or sufficient starlight to see.

In less than a week, we arrived near a fishing settlement on the coast and found an abandoned hut set back into a wooded hillside. It appeared to be a failed attempt at living and farming on too-rocky ground. It sufficed for us.

The next few days we spent in hiding and healing while Askira scouted the area. He reported most the people living along the shore were fishermen. Those who lived further inland eked out a living by both fishing and farming. The poor soil here was not suitable for growing sugarcane, and the people could not afford slaves even if they wanted them, which they did not. Except for a few freemen, there were no Negros, and seldom any searches by the Spanish for runaway slaves.

***

Lengthening shadows ushered Askira back to our refuge after his fourth day of exploring. He burst in with his Japanese version of an Irish jig. Our chuckles relieved the tension of days of anxious waiting.

"I have found," he sang out between hops and skips, "someone who will shelter and feed us."

He reminded me of a nervous squirrel I had once watched in Boston. After he finished his dance, unable to sit still, he fidgeted and paced, gushing about an old fisherman who, though uneducated, seemed well acquainted with iniquities practiced by his fellow men—especially those who were desecrating his homeland with their inhumanity this very day.

Askira told me later he thought the old man might have been involved in one or more of the failed attempts of Spanish-speaking countries to free themselves of Spanish rule. He never did tell me how he knew about those attempts, but he had said he'd been in Cuba before, and he had a good command of the Spanish language. I wondered how much his military background played into his knowledge of various revolts in some of those Central and South American countries.

To my knowledge, Cubans had not yet resorted to armed rebellion, and Askira had not mentioned any armed conflict. But even in Boston, before I was shanghaied, I had heard talk of Cubans expressing heated opinions against dictatorial Spanish rule. Now, I wondered if this man Askira had found had been one of those exhorting other Cubans to revolt.

Our Japanese friend's fervor infected us all with excitement. I couldn't, however, shake my concern of risk in trusting someone we had never met before and whom we knew little about.

Reservations about Askira's judgment and my guilt for not trusting my friend kept me conflicted about the wisdom of our next move. Nevertheless, I held my peace—he had never failed me before.

Under the cloak of darkness, Askira urged us to keep silent and follow his pace as he led us closer to the sounds of surf breaking upon the shore. A collective gasp escaped from most of us as a black apparition appeared before us. In a second or two, our alarm faded—it was but a ramshackle hut blocking out part of the star-studded skyline.

Before Askira could speak or knock, the door opened. Bathed in warm light, the white-haired fisherman he had spoken of held up a small oil lamp to illuminate us. Without a word, his gesture for us to enter restored my trust in my Japanese friend. We all crowded into the tiny room. The smell of the place, though faint, reminded me of the sea and fish markets along the Boston harbor; it reminded me of Keevah. A crushing yearning in my heart strengthened my resolve to see her again.

He offered the empty chair at the table to Anna. The rest of us turned the tops of a couple of equipment storage boxes into benches.

The old Cuban's thick, gnarled hands and fingers evidenced a long life of hard work with nets, ropes, and oars. Yet, his sun-bronzed and weathered face bespoke a gentleness of spirit despite his hard life. His eyes drew most of my attention. Masked by bushy brows and deep wrinkles born from years of squinting at reflected sunlight on the sea, they appeared milky. I felt for him—he must be almost blind. I wondered if he could still fish.

As Askira spoke of some of our recent trials, the man raised his bushy eyebrows. As he did, I could see pale and crystal-clear grey eyes underneath those brows. I exhaled long in relief, and thanks to my Lord—our new friend was not blind. Only inches taller than Anna, he must have weighed twice as much as she, all of him muscle and bone. Whatever his age, he could still work his trade.

In the other chair at the tiny table sat a wrinkled and aged Negro man. White hair lay curled close to his head, giving him the image of a babe in an old man's body. His stooped back and broken hands would have made any manual labor difficult at best.

Askira interpreted the fisherman's Spanish as the man introduced himself. "You can call me Raphael and call my friend here, Obasi. He was a slave in the Mountain Valley sugar mill, though he is a freeman now. He came to me after an accident in the mill injured his hands.

"Rather than house and feed slaves who can never work again, the plantation managers give them their freedom. Continuing to feed, clothe, and house him and others who can no longer work would be a drain on plantation profits. Setting them free to become burdens to their fellow Negros, or to fend for themselves is their answer. Obasi ended up here."

The old fisherman moved to the Negro man's side and placed a hand on his shoulder. "He still remembers his African name, Obasi. To me, that's who he is, Obasi—a grateful and willing helper . . . and he is my friend."

Obasi spoke Spanish in his soft baritone and then watched Askira interpret.

"He says we need new clothes, not sailors' uniforms—the Spanish will be sure to spot and arrest us in these clothes. For a good knife, like the ones we are wearing, he will get clothes for all of us."

More golden-toned words filled the hut.

"He says he can also get clothes to fit Anna."

I unbuckled my belt, pulled off my knife and sheath, and handed it to Askira. He offered it to Obasi. With effort, the old man wrested himself up from his chair, accepted the knife with a nod and a smile, and ambled out the door.

My gut cringed as I watched my knife go. A sailor is never without his knife; his life may depend on cutting himself free of tangled lines. A knife is essential for obtaining food for a man living off the land. A fugitive without a knife is defenseless in a country like this. I was all those, and I had given my knife away.

The old fisherman must have noticed my concern. He rummaged in a weathered wooden box at the foot of one of the two narrow cots and produced a knife. He pulled it from its worn and stained scabbard and gave it to me. I rolled it over in my hand. Clearly, its aged blade had outlived many handmade handles, such as the one now attached to it. I guessed the blade, when new, had been about six to eight inches long. Honed to sharpness too many times, it had narrowed near its middle, weakened, and broke, leaving only three inches of flat-tipped blade.

Still, it was better than nothing. I accepted it with one of the few Spanish words I knew, "*Gracias*."

Raphael grinned and nodded.

"We need a boat, Raphael," I said.

Askira interpreted.

"A boat with sails, big enough for all of us, with room enough for food and water."

The old fisherman nodded. He did not seem at all surprised at our request. He must have known we had few options.

"Fishermen around here don't have big boats anymore. The Spanish have taken them all to *Puerta Gordita*. People who run the plantations go there to drink, gamble, and play. They use the boats for parties or to go fishing."

"Do they have boats big enough for us there?"

"They have big enough boats, but you must know the sea is bigger."

"We know, Raphael," I said. "We have sailed this ocean in French warships. How far is this *Puerta Gordita*?"

Raphael nodded and grunted at Askira's interpretation.

"Around the point." The fisherman pointed a gnarled finger to the east. "Maybe a thousand *varas* . . . yards to you Americans. A reef extends from the point and makes a natural breakwater. Behind the reef is a small bay the Spanish have taken over. They don't permit us to fish close to it anymore."

Askira and I exchanged a glance.

Raphael's eyes bored first into mine and then into Askira's. In a moment, he said something in Spanish, his tone more in declaration than in question.

"*Si*," Askira responded to him directly before turning to us. "He knows we are going to steal a boat."

With closed eyes, Raphael turned his face to heaven and shook his head. After a second, he again faced us and nodded. "*Si . . . si.*" I wondered if he'd decided if he were one of us, he would do the same.

"Don't worry," I said. "We will be gone from your place. No one will know you told us anything."

"What about Obasi?" Gaston spoke for the first time. "He knows we were here."

Raphael answered Askira's interpretation. "Obasi and his friends, who are getting clothing for you, will never tell the Spanish anything; they hate them. You are not the first they have helped. You may stay here, but as you can see, I don't have room for all."

"No," I said. "We have enough space at the old hut."

"The Espinoza hut? The one by the woods? That is good. No one has lived there for years. There is nothing left for anyone to want. It is a safe place. Take this bread and dried fish; Obasi collected it from nearby families. Come back tomorrow night; you will have your clothes."

I cocked a querying eyebrow at Elijah and Anna. Meeting my look straight on, he nodded his head; she did the same. They may have been short of food and water when we found them. Neither was short of courage.

CHAPTER 10

Two days later, Askira and I, dressed in worn and patched peasant's clothing, lay hidden in the brush on a low hill overlooking *Puerta Gordita*. Our interest focused not on the one large building or the smaller barracks-looking building but on the six boats tied up alongside the roughhewn dock.

"You know boats," Askira said. "See anything you like?"

"Two are large enough. Both need major deck work to survive open seas. We don't have time for that." I was about to share my disappointment when I noticed a longer and better-constructed finger jutting off the dock. It had not drawn our attention—no boats lay alongside.

"Look, there's a long finger jutting to the left of the main dock," I said. "It looks made to moor two boats—no more. Maybe it's for plantation bosses. I think we should wait and see if anything bigger comes in later—maybe in a few days."

"We need more time to gather supplies and food anyway," Askira said. "Perhaps Raphael or Obasi can get us more information."

"Might save us from getting caught sneaking up here to spy on them."

Askira nodded and motioned for us to leave.

We never did learn which of our two Cuban friends had the confidants at *Puerta Gordita*. Whoever they were, they were good. We learned a retired army officer commanded the camp. His staff consisted of two assistants, a group of eight guards made up of thugs and former soldiers, a half dozen native Cubans, and four or five Negro slaves.

The guards, though responsible for camp security, focused most of their efforts on preventing petty theft by camp staff and dealing with anyone who had imbibed too much. Protecting the camp perimeter against intruders was boring duty—nothing ever happened. After all, who would want to intrude? The camp had nothing of value except its stores of liquor.

Personal knives and firearms were forbidden because of the fondness of drunks to fight. Locked gates secured the dock landing at night to prevent unauthorized access to the boats. At night, two guards stand watch outside the dock gate. It is unnecessary to walk the dock or inspect the boats at night.

We also learned a naval-type longboat and a Cuban sloop-rigged fishing boat were the only ones ever moored on the long finger. The Cuban boat had been an offshore fishing vessel before the Spanish seized her.

A high-level Spanish plantation director had taken a liking to the Cuban boat. He had ordered it pulled onto the beach two years ago to refurbish the hull. His workmen found shipworms had destroyed the hull planking and transom and weakened the keel itself. As a result, the entire hull, mast, and sole of the boat were new. The deck and cabin house were what remained of the original boat.

The man took great pride in his rebuild and laid his personal claim to the boat, limiting its use to himself and others at his invitation only. He even renamed her—*Sofia*, his wife's name. His second in command would return the boat to *Puerta Gordita* in one week.

When Askira and I asked Raphael about it, he said, "That boat will do you well if you know how to sail her."

"Anything in particular we should know?"

"Can't say. It's been a long time since I was on her; the Spanish have rebuilt her. She's heavy and slow in light air, but she loves weather. She can fly in a heavy wind; heard it said she can handle anything up to a *Huracán*—if her skipper manages her sails right. You be sure she has storm sails and plenty of ballast if you take her out. Can't say how she handles since she's been rebuilt."

Our informants were good; in a week, we got word the fishing boat had returned. Askira and I returned to get a look at it. Hidden on our hill, we watched Cubans and slaves remove unused provisions, scrub the decks and cabin house, and furl the sails.

"They are doing a good job," I said, "of getting her ready."

"For us," Askira said. "Let's get back. We need to get our provisions ready to move. We won't have much time to load everything on board when the time comes."

Within hours, Obasi and his friends staged our supplies near an abandoned and dilapidated fishing pier in a small inlet a mile up the coast from Raphael's hut. Well-used wooden kegs contained our food, which consisted of beans, rice, some root vegetables, dried and salted fish, and salted pork. They looked to be tight; I hoped they could withstand days of moisture and humidity on the open seas. Spanish-made water kegs, like store kegs but with metal banding, looked to be leak-proof, though several of them had additional rope bandings. I made a mental note to use these kegs first; the rope was there because of weakness.

I marveled at the sacrifices these fishermen and their families were making to provision us with these supplies—most of which had to come from their own boats and homes. I agreed with Askira when he suggested we give the musket and loading supplies to Raphael in exchange. We let Elijah keep the pistol, and a few reloads. If a warship from any nation caught us at sea, neither weapon would do us any good. The pistol would be for Elijah's Anna—if it were a Spanish or French warship or a slave ship of any nation.

With our plans made and our provisions ready, we waited for the first moonless night. Guided by a local fisherman who had a decent command of English, Askira and I made our way to the sandy shore halfway between the point and the *Puerta Gordita* dock.

The fisherman, who told us to call him Diego, looked to be a few years younger than Raphael. Though no taller than the older fisherman, his wiry frame and cat-like quickness provided testimony he was not one to trifle with. He said he used to fish the bay before the Spanish plantation owners took it over. Raphael backed his claim that he knew the *Puerta Gordita* bay and reef well—better than the Spanish did. I concluded his eagerness to help was his way to spite Spain. He made no secret of his hatred of Spanish rule.

We accepted his name, though we knew it to be false—he had to protect himself should the Spanish capture and question us.

"To reach the pier and the boat," Diego said, "we swim at least three hundred yards toward the far tip of the reef. When we get to the middle of the bay, we'll rest for a few minutes. Then, with the sea at our backs, we swim toward the dock. Use the guards' lamps as beacons to guide us."

Wooden fishing net floats, scorched black in cooking ovens to make them impossible for the guards to see in the dark water, would be our swimming aids. Each of us had two of them lashed to our chest. We could hold them under one arm and swim with the free arm.

"The reef is busy with sharks at night," Diego said. "If we make no unusual splashing noises, they won't bother us."

I couldn't help but wonder what sharks might consider an unusual noise—wouldn't they think it unusual for me to swim with them at night, regardless of how much or how little noise I made? Diego didn't seem concerned. Shirtless and wearing pants cut off above the knee, Askira and I followed him into the water.

The Cuban fisherman moved through the water like a fish. Despite his whispered cautions to us, both Askira and I struggled to match his silence. I thought we were halfway to the middle of the bay when we stopped to rest. He took the time to instruct us on how to manage the floats better. When we were ready to resume swimming, he dropped his bombshell.

"Don't panic if you see or feel a shark. They are curious and may swim close. Sometimes, they will even brush up against you. Don't splash or strike at them or try to swim away. It will agitate them and attract more sharks, and you can't outswim them. Let's go."

We swam far enough out in the bay to satisfy Diego, rested again, and started toward the pier and our target boat. Then, the sharks came. Diego sensed them, or one of them touched him.

"Sharks are swimming around us. Stay calm and remember what I told you."

A noticeable rush of water on my leg convinced me I was about to die. I don't know if Diego felt it too, or if he sensed my fear.

"Steady," he whispered. "They are swimming slowly. They are not agitated or excited, only curious. You will be fine."

No sooner had he spoken than Askira gasped. "It touched me."

"With its head," Diego asked, "body... tail?"

"Body, close to its tail... I think."

"Good. It wanted to see what you would do, what kind of big fish you are—or if you are a fish."

"I'm no fish—but I'm something it could eat."

"Yes, but you're not on its usual diet. Sharks can be picky eaters, same as people."

"Some of them."

"Right... some... sometimes," Diego softly admitted. "Let's cut the chatter. We're getting close enough for the guards to hear. Keep moving... ignore the sharks... they will leave."

I tried to match Diego's unruffled pace, but I could not ignore the sharks. I prayed they would leave, or at least not eat me. When one made a slow, gentle touch, moving a large part of its body along my thigh, fear paralyzed my arms and legs.

Even in the darkness, Diego somehow knew I froze. "Keep moving as if nothing happened," he whispered. "They are not sure what they want to do. We need to act as though we don't care about them. If they sense fear and think we are fleeing, we become prey. They will attack then."

I tried to control the fear within me and follow his guidance. Chance of death or injury from cannon and musket fire from hostile ships had stoked unease in me many times, but this was not unease—it was terror. Bullets and cannonballs are not alive—they have no teeth or eyes and no intent. They never wanted to eat me alive. Those inanimate objects did not trigger mankind's age-old response to beasts of prey or his inborn fear of them—these sharks did.

An unrelated yet rational thought interrupted my fear for a few seconds—how sad Keevah and I would never see each other again. In my mind, I was already as good as dead. The dread numbed my soul. I didn't know how to cope with it—except to follow this Cuban fisherman, do as he said... and pray.

"Stop," Diego whispered. "We will leave the floats here; we can't risk them knocking against the dock. We go in a single file. Askira, you lead. Stay under the dock close to the boat. Lanny, you follow .

.. Lanny, are you alright? Hey, the sharks are gone; they left us fifty *varas* back. You made it. You're safe. You hear my instructions? Like we planned."

I nodded before whispering, "Yes."

"Go," he said with a gentle push on my back.

We eased through the water to the pier and then beneath it to put us beside the boat we planned to steal. Diego soon joined us.

"We get out of the water here," he whispered. "I will go first, Lanny, you follow. I will help pull you up. We must be silent. Askira, you are last."

We crouched low on the dock until the water stopped dripping from our pants. Any unusual noises could give us away to the two guards who stood chatting while watching the dock landing. No one had business being on the dock at night. The guards had orders to see no one was.

When Diego was satisfied, we crept into position toward the guards. Askira and I stopped at our planned positions. Diego crept closer to the lanterns, concealing himself in the shadow cast by a dock post. When he arrived at one of the lanterns, he removed his hat, waved it in front of the lantern, and ducked down in the shadow of the post.

A few seconds later, a small fire erupted on the very hill from which Askira and I had spied on the camp. Another fire started about a hundred *varas* from the first. Both guards turned their attention to the fires. Rapid exclamations between them told us they had not seen anything like that before. We had seconds to act.

Askira swung around the gateposts to reach the side with the guards. Diego was already waiting for him with a short paddle he had picked up from somewhere. They attacked.

Askira took his man down without a sound. It all happened too fast for me. Diego swung his paddle against his man's head. The guard fell with a surprised grunt.

As planned, I boarded a nearby boat for ropes and pieces of sailcloth. The old and broken knife Raphael had given me was sharp—it worked well to cut away what I needed.

I tossed the ropes and canvas around the gate. Askira handed me one guard's musket. I pried the small gate lock open with it and then extinguished the lanterns as soon as my companions bound the guards. Diego's friends doused the fires on shore within seconds.

With both men gagged and tied, the three of us carried them down the long dock and deposited them in one of the larger boats moored there. We then moved to our target boat. Diego hoisted the mainsail while Askira and I released the mooring lines.

The ever-reliable evening offshore breeze filled the sail even before Diego had it half-hoisted. The boat started drifting as we tossed the last mooring line aboard. We pushed her away from the dock to avoid bumping the other boats and to provide steerage headway. At the last second, we jumped aboard.

"You take the tiller," Diego said to me. "I know this bay and the reef. I'll go to the bow to guide you. Watch me. Take her where I say and when I say. Askira, you handle the sails. You'll be busy because we will change our heading several times to get out of here."

We heard the lapping of water against the hull as our boat picked up speed. Not a sound of alarm came from the dock; our mission was successful—so far. With no fires onshore, any watching eyes would get not even a hint of anything going on in the camp or on the dock. No one would suspect anything until daylight or until the next change of guards.

"After we get out of the bay, we'll sail northwest to clear the shoal waters and reefs along this coast. This heading will also help set our sails to the wind. You have three or four hours to get to the old pier, load your supplies, and head for the open sea."

The boat may have been heavy and slow to start, but with steady wind in her sails, she picked up speed and glided through the water with ease. It was clear why the Spanish plantation director liked her. Diego himself was impressed with the short time it took us to sail to the half-fallen dock where the rest of our group was waiting with our stores.

"Something is wrong," Askira said. We all knew it even before we eased *Sophia* up to the dock. Elijah and two fishermen helped secure our mooring lines. Our companions and two other fishermen were gathered in a knot beside the pile of stores.

"Gaston has been shot," Elijah said. "Three Spaniards showed up around a half hour ago. They must have seen us and sneaked up to investigate. When they saw Anna and me, they started running and shouting at us. We are all sure they were going to arrest us—probably thought we were some of their slaves. Gaston grabbed the pistol and pointed it at them, yelling and motioning them to go away. When they didn't stop, he fired over their heads. Then, they started shooting and hit Gaston. We pulled him behind the supplies. I was able to reload the pistol. I fired at them—I'm sure I didn't hit anything. They left in a hurry."

"They will be back," Diego said, "with more men and muskets. You need to go."

He shouted commands to the Cuban fishermen. They started loading supplies without a wasted word or motion. I stayed on board and stashed supplies as the men handed them to me. Though knowing they were putting themselves in danger by helping us escape, not one of them offered to leave until they had the supplies and Gaston aboard. Although of Spanish blood, they were Cubans, and this was their land. Their hatred of Spain's dictatorial rule was a hot ember deep in their gut, ready to erupt at any provocation.

Sophia's sails filled with the offshore breeze as the fishermen helped her ease away from the old dock. As was her disposition, she took her time in picking up speed in the steady wind. We headed northeast to clear a few small coral heads before turning to the northnorthwest. Navigation duties fell to me; I had an introduction to the task when my old friend, Bo, and I plotted the brig *Muireann's* course on the deckhouse wall. I intended to put many miles between *Sophia* and the coast before daylight and before the Spanish at *Puerta Gordita* could begin searching for us. We guessed it would be at least two or three days before they could get word to any naval warships to look for us.

Sophia was no longer a working fishing boat. Her interior was now suited for pleasure cruising. Fittings for hammocks and well-appointed cabinets, built to hold enough amenities to please her Spanish masters, had replaced most of her storage for gear and fish. Aside from limited stowage for our supplies, the added hammocks for resting and sleeping suited us well.

Gaston now lay in one of those hammocks. Anna stayed below, trying to comfort him as she cleaned blood from his clothes and body. I feared for him. The musket ball had blasted a gaping wound along his side and opened his belly. We could do nothing for him except remove his shirt and jam it into the hole to stop the bleeding. Even had we been naval surgeons, we couldn't have sewn it together—there were only shreds of flesh left.

I prayed for his soul. I had seen too many men with abdominal wounds. His chances were not good, but we might not know for days. It would be terrible.

Sailing Yacht, *Sophia*, 1829

As we sailed north in the soft starlight of a moonless night, the massive form of Cuba faded before sinking below the star-filled horizon. The steady offshore breeze we were counting on to propel us gave way to variable puffs from the west and southwest. Rather than ask Askira to trim the sails for each puff, I chose to change *Sophia's* course to match the set of our sails to the wind. Though we did lose some speed at times, I was able, with the aid of stars, to stay close to our desired heading northward and away from the Spanish-held island.

We sailed in these unpredictable winds for another hour before the prevailing westerly winds filled in. With the steady wind filling her sails again and riding predictable wind-powered swells, our little boat settled into the rhythmic rocking chair motion of a sailboat in harmony with wind and sea.

It was anything but peaceful onboard. Gaston, who had risked himself to save Elijah and Anna, lay in pain, perhaps dying. The rest of us juggled tensions between our hopes Gaston would live, that we could escape, and our fears a slave or warship of any nation would spot and try to capture us. Though exhausted, no one slept except Askira. With iron-like discipline, he lay on one of the narrow benches the Spanish Plantation manager had added to each side of the cockpit and slept. The Cuban fishermen, who had built her, favored an open cockpit with plenty of room to maneuver. We preferred the Spanish benches.

Our navigation tools were limited to a battered compass, a Spanish-drawn chart of the waters near *Puerta Gordita*, and our hand-drawn chart of this part of the Caribbean. Before we left Raphael's, we had gathered around his tiny table to resurrect, from our collective memories, the seas and lands between us and Florida. It was crude and far from complete, for none of us had ever set foot on those islands. Some had seen charts or heard from other sailors about them. Our efforts at least offered some guidance for compass headings. With these meager tools and the promise of a few more nights of faint light to obscure our sails before the new moon appeared, we embarked on our flight to freedom.

And my return to Keevah.

When the eastern horizon showed pink, and I could no longer keep my eyes open, I rousted Askira. We changed places without a word. I stretched out on one of the narrow seats, wondering if I could ever rest in such circumstances.

Elijah awakened me midmorning with a breakfast of strong Cuban coffee and a piece of warmed salted pork. Sometime during the night, Anna, unable to keep her eyes open any longer, slipped into the hammock across from Gaston. In her stead, Elijah took over watching the injured man.

Askira motioned me to take the tiller as soon as I had finished my breakfast. He checked those in the cabin before coming back into the cockpit. He lay on a seat, stared at the sky, and said not a word.

"You alright?" I whispered.

His nod said he was. The set of his jaw said it was none of my business.

I checked our compass heading and made some minor tiller and sail adjustments to set a northwest course. *Sophia* settled into her new heading. With the steady winds in her sails, our boat would maintain her course without steering changes. All we needed to do was to make periodic checks of the compass to ensure no wind changes were pushing us off our planned course. I lashed the tiller in place, sat on the bench opposite Askira, and stared at him.

"They are of your faith," he whispered. "How do they do this?"

"Care for Gaston?"

"Yes—not only for Gaston—for anyone who has spent years in this slave business—him, you, me. We have been their enemy as much as the captain of the slave ship that brought them here."

"He did save them from the Spanish slave hunters."

"I know. I didn't expect that. But it doesn't explain why they are trying to save him—he was also protecting his own skin."

"They are doing the same as their God would do if He were here."

Askira paused a moment, thinking and shaking his head. "I don't understand. It's not natural."

"You are right, my friend. It's not natural—not for the natural man. It's from the supernatural. It's from God. Was it natural for two hunted and starving people to share their shelter from the storm with us—when we could have been their enemies? That was supernatural too—from God."

"I have heard your faith says to love your enemies. That makes no sense. I don't understand . . . I don't think I ever will."

"You will, my friend, in time—"

Askira jumped up and pointed to the west. "Sails—on the horizon."

We both stood.

"To the west-south-west," he said.

I climbed to the cabin top and grasped the mast for balance. Searching in the direction of his pointed finger, I was able to find the familiar shape of topsails in the distance.

"I can't make out if we are seeing one or more sails. Wish we had a spyglass."

"You think they can see us?"

"Not at this distance. Our mast is much shorter than theirs. They'll have a watch posted in their crow's-nest, but they'll be lower than their topsails. If they get closer, we'll drop our sails."

"And be dead in the water?"

"Yes, but harder to see. We could never outrun them; we must hide."

"Hide in the middle of an ocean?"

"Yes, in plain sight. We make ourselves hard to see. Our sails are huge flags—as theirs are to us. It's almost impossible to spot a bare mast unless you're right on it. Right now, we need to watch those sails to tell which way they are going. We can take turns watching, but don't lose sight of them."

"I'll get Anna; she has sharp eyes."

Anna came on deck at his call.

"Who are they?" she said after following my pointing to the horizon.

"Doesn't matter," I said. "We're dead if they catch us . . . at least some of us".

She understood. Her dark skin would keep her alive—until they tired of her—or sold her.

"Elijah." Her voice, though soft and respectful, carried a measure of urgency.

Askira moved to allow room for Elijah's leap into the cockpit.

For several long moments, the two escapees stared at the distant harbinger of disaster.

"Is there no way," Elijah asked, "we can outrun them?"

"No," I confirmed. "I doubt if they have seen us. We are seeing the sails at the tops of their masts. We're not as tall as they are, so we'll still be below their lookout's horizon."

"And what do we do," Askira queried, "to stay there?"

"We have two choices: douse the sails as low as we can get them to make us less noticeable. But Raphael told me the current all along this coast runs to the north and west. Without sails to power us against it, we could end up right in their laps. "I hope your second choice is better."

"We leave our sails up, we come about for two hundred and sixty degrees and sail east by east-northeast, more than ninety degrees to where we are heading now."

"Straight back to Cuba?"

"No. Parallel to the coast. It's our best chance. We can't stay our current course; they'll have us for sure. Our hope is to stay as far from them as we can."

My companions stared at the threats on the horizon.

"If I were in command of this boat," I said softly. "I would change course to east by northeast right now."

All eyes turned to me as Askira spoke. "Lanny, you are already the captain of this boat. We all know it. Command is yours."

"Aye," Elijah murmured.

Anna nodded—unable to hide traces of terror behind pleading eyes.

"Very well. We're going to gybe to put the wind over our stern. Askira, you set the jib portside. Elijah, the boom will swing starboard as we change direction to bring our stern through the wind. Use this line to set the mainsail. Let it loose at first, and then I'll tell you to pull it in or let it out more to set the sail. Anna, you go below to see Gaston remains in his hammock when the boat heels. He'll know what is happening, but you may have to steady him . . . he can't do it himself."

I took a compass reading of the threatening sails so we could find them again and then checked my crew, the wind, and the waves. "Ready?" I pulled the tiller over. "Hard aweather she is."

A moment later, I breathed a silent "Thank you" to the Spanish plantation manager who had rebuilt the old fishing boat. She handled splendidly, even with a landsman manning the mainsail. "Thank you, crew. You did a fine job."

With the aid of the compass, Askira located the feared sails. "I'll keep my eye on them, Sir."

I looked askance at him.

He chuckled. "That's the way it is, Cap'n. You had better get used to it . . . Sir."

"Yes, Sir," Elijah said. "And a finer captain, I've never had."

We sailed away from the distant ship until the topsails were just visible above the horizon. When what appeared to be one sail became two, Askira took several sightings with the compass before declaring, "We're seeing two of her masts now. She's heading more to the north. Why the sudden course change?"

"She must be a warship," I said. "She could be patrolling her area."

"Or she may have spotted another ship to check out," Askira said.

"Or she's trying to evade someone pursuing her," I said. "At least she doesn't act like she saw us. We can change our course to the northeast for a couple of hours to get clear of her and then head back to the northwest. If we keep a good watch, we can spot her tall masts and sails long before she sees our short sails."

"Elijah," Askira said, "that is our job—to keep a lookout in all directions for even the tiniest hint of a sail or boat."

We sailed with the wind at our backs for two hours, making judgments of times by gut and sun—we had no timepieces among us. When we did turn again to the north, we saw nothing of any ships through the day and into the night.

On the next day, with the sun high in the sky, Anna came into the cockpit and announced Gaston was doing much worse. There was nothing she could do to comfort him. In fact, he was delirious much of the time, and although speaking and groaning, he seemed not to know she was there. His speech made no sense to her, and he fought off any attempt to cool his fever by placing wet clothes on his forehead. She had made the clothes from parts of his shirt which were not already soaked with blood.

Neither she nor anyone said more—we had all seen it before. By late afternoon, he became calm enough for Anna to again wash his face and place wet cloths on his forehead. He died before the sun dipped into the western horizon.

I studied the young African girl who had tried to comfort the dying man. Her quiet grief and teary eyes, which she tried to keep clear, made me think again of Askira's questions to me—why did she do this? How could she feel this way?

She was no fool. Even though Gaston had not been the person who captured and shipped slaves, he had protected the ships and persons of those who did. Yet, she, who was condemned to slavery by those same people, had cared for him and now grieved for his lost life. She knew who he was, what he had done, the kind of man he was.

Or perhaps she knew better than we—the man he had become.

The limited material we had onboard to suffice for a burial-at-sea shroud would be one of our spare sails—none of which we could afford to sacrifice. We would have to place him over the side without a shroud and hope he would slip under the waves because we had nothing to weigh him down. We decided to wait till darkness in case he did not sink—none of us wanted to see that.

The evening sunset was spectacular. It reminded me of the many sunsets Keevah and I watched from our perches aboard the brig *Muireann*. But it also caused me to wonder if I was the same man she had known and loved. How far had I drifted—from myself—from my God?

Anna moved close and sat beside me. "Will you say something over him? I brought your Bible and this oil lamp. I know we need the flame low now, but we can turn it up when you read."

I took the Bible into my lap and hung my head over it for a long moment. When I looked up, the tiny flame in the lamp must have caught the moisture in my eyes.

She placed a hand on my arm. "I am so sorry."

I said nothing. I cried not for Gaston but for me—for failing my Lord as I lived among so many men, witnessed their brutality to others over the past several years, and did nothing. For *Luc*, Gaston, and many others aboard the ships I had been on, I remained silent. What had Jesus done for us, and what had we done to each other? It was for my Lord, I cried.

What did He think of me now?

"Thank you, Anna; I won't need to read." I handed the Bible back. "I've seen far too many burials at sea. I know the naval service by heart."

At last light, we slipped him into the water. I said the prescribed words.

In muted melancholy, we sat as the sliver of moon traversed a good portion of the night sky. Hours later, Elijah and Anna retreated to hammocks in the cabin. Askira settled onto his customary cockpit seat. I stayed at the tiller for the first night watch. I doubted anyone slept.

I fought demons, knowing all along I was not worthy to speak the Lord's name or refer to eternal hope at a dead man's burial. Yet, my companions had expected it of me. Elijah and Anna's faith was whole, and Askira had been observing the fruits of their faith. Was I to wound my friends' faith or destroy any seed of belief Askira might have by further betraying my God in their view? For love of my Lord, I would do my best to help their faith remain strong and healthy. I would try to show Askira the way, even though I knew I was not fit to speak His name. Would God see me as a hypocrite for what I was doing? I was familiar with His view of hypocrites. I pleaded in silence most of the dark night for Jesus to forgive me.

Askira, the hardened warrior, tossed and turned as well. I didn't know what battles he waged. I hoped Jesus might be one of them. I didn't bother him, for I wouldn't know what to say or how to say it. That deepened my distress—for I once thought myself to be a preacher—a voice to men and women for my God.

Asksira took watch while it was still dark; we changed positions—him brooding at the tiller and me unable to rest on the cockpit seat. When the eastern horizon showed pink, Askira, seeing I was awake, spoke.

"Your God, he does not give comfort . . . peace?"

"Yes, Askira, He does."

"I don't see evidence of it. You are all grieving."

"Yes, we are grieving the death of a companion. But you mustn't judge God because we grieve. Grief is a part of life. God does not comfort in the manner of opium or alcohol—like many peoples around the world do. He does not dull the pain; He lets us feel it."

"Why? How is that comfort?"

"His comfort is His promise to each of us. He will walk with us in our pain. And He will get us through it. We need not fear despair. He lets us feel and grieve, so when we trust Him through the pain, we come out knowing and trusting Him even more. That helps us be stronger in our faith and closer to Him. Even when we grieve, we know He promised to be with us in our sadness, and we will possess eternal joy with him. His promise is comfort no man or substance can match. It also prepares us to share His comfort with others when they are hurting and grieving."

My Japanese friend went silent, contemplating my words. After a few moments without a sound from him, I wondered if I'd failed yet another man.

"Lanny, you are my friend; I know you well." He paused till I met his direct look. "I have seen you in deep grief after *Luc* died and after we buried Gaston. I ask this in kindness, my friend. Do you yourself believe . . . what you tell others to believe?"

Again, he waited, giving me time to respond. When I dropped my gaze to my feet, he spoke. "There is a common saying in my village in Japan. It translates to something like this; 'May a man live by his own counsel.'"

I continued staring at the floorboards of the cockpit. A few moments later, I raised my head and stared, eyes unfocused, at the vast emptiness beyond the horizon. I didn't know how to answer his question.

"It is not for me to know," he said gently. "It is for you, my friend, to think about . . . and decide."

CHAPTER 11

We sailed northwest for four days without seeing the sail of another boat. Often, during my waking hours, I wrestled with Askira's question. It would be hard to explain my angst to a non-believer; I would never be able to explain it to a believer.

Did the reasons for my distress lay in my failures to be what I believed God wanted me to be?

Keevah's gift of the piece of broken scrimshaw, still protected by the sweat-stained leather pouch in my pocket, had been my secret since the night Keevah's brothers shanghaied me. Askira knew I had it because I always laid it aside to prevent it from being broken during our training sessions. He never asked or knew what the pouch contained. I never told him, but now his question caused me to consider it.

The policy at the McIntyre Seminary was to abandon all personal treasures because they led to pride. Had they been right? Was pride in my own abilities and accomplishments and my failures to meet my expectations the reason for my alienation from God? Had my failures been bruises to my pride? Was this fragment of scrimshaw feeding a prideful arrogance in me? They at the seminary might have been correct.

I grasped the pouch and my precious scrimshaw in my hand and stared at it. After a time of painful reflection, I accepted what I must do and drew my arm back. I would rid myself of the source of pride and start restoring my relationship with God. I hated to let go of my one physical connection to Keevah, but I had to do this.

"I don't know what that is," Askira said, "But throwing it away won't solve your problem."

I stopped and stared at him.

He continued. "It is not the object in your hand but your mind that is tormenting you. To rid yourself of the problem, you must change yourself, not the thing—for you will always find another thing to take its place."

I knew he was right, but what was my problem? Shame? Pride? Remorse for what I had been doing seemed more of a problem than pride, for I could see nothing to be prideful about. Fear of men and what they might do to me was real at one time. But that had gone by the wayside when my flogging led to my resolve to tell *Luc* the truth and then to find I was too late. I prayed God would reveal my stumblings to me as my companions and I sailed this tiny boat toward America.

And sail we did. For fifteen days we evaded sails of any kind, often reversing several day's progress by our evasive actions. Not counting on the need to elude other ships, we thought we could make Florida in three weeks. Now, it became clear we had underestimated both our food and water stores. During several storms, we used our sails as rain catchers and were able to fill our empty water casks to the brim. *Sophia* was well equipped with fishing gear; we caught enough fish to supplement our dwindling stores of food. After exhausting our supply of cooking fuel, we resorted to soaking the rice and beans overnight and eating them uncooked, along with raw fish when we had any.

Despite the hardships, our determination to survive and reach America intensified. Askira, our resolute soldier of fortune, saw to that. I may have been the captain where sailing and navigation were concerned; he was the leader as far as crew morale was concerned. I was thankful.

During one watch, when Anna and I were alone in the cockpit, we talked long about Gaston. Her questions about his past, I answered fully, including details of his attempts to batter and kill me.

"He told me he respected you as much as any man he has ever known. He knew you had every reason and opportunity to allow other crewmen to exact their revenge on him, even to kill him, but you stopped them. You stood up for him—you kept him alive. You could have left him behind when you jumped ship or after he was shot; he knew you chose to take him with you and with us."

"It was the right thing to do, Anna."

"He said you are a true man of God."

My throat tightened. How could I tell her the truth?

"While I was with him in the cabin," she said, "before he became delirious, I shared the gospel of Jesus with him. He asked the Lord to forgive and accept him. I'm certain he was serious. I believe the Lord gave him peace before He took him, and He took him quickly instead of letting him linger for days."

I leaned my head back and closed my eyes. My clenched jaw and tightened throat made speech impossible. I nodded my understanding. When I looked at her, she nodded back with a faint smile, squeezed my arm, and went below to send Elijah up for his watch.

I had given her the name Anna upon my guess at her nature when she allowed us to seek shelter from the storm with them. The name fit—she was gracious. I wondered if this young African girl was one of the Lord's angels or if she was merely a human being acting the way God meant for humans to act.

I slept several hours straight that night for the first time in many weeks.

The next day, we ate the last small portions of rice Elijah had been rationing. We had no fish because sharks were now following our boat and devouring every one of our catches, leaving nothing but boney heads for us. To gain what nourishment the heads contained, all we could do was pick out and share any morsels of flesh the sharks left.

After two days of eating scraps of fish left by the sharks, we were able to bring in the front half of a skipjack. The tuna-like fish our Cuban friends called *bonito* is one of their favorite catches. A shark made a meal of the back half, leaving enough fish to fill all of us. Even raw, it was a banquet.

That evening, Askira took the first watch. I slept fitfully, not because of the fish in my belly but because gusty winds from the southeast had started replacing the steady westerly winds. Gusts became stronger and more variable through the night. Stars twinkled in clear skies around us except toward the south. The moon, as if unconcerned about our growing fears, bathed us with soft beams of its light. Those same moonbeams revealed a distant cloudbank filling the entire southwest to southeast horizon. Askira's and my hushed talk about the cloud, the unusual winds, and the confused waves roused Anna and Elijah.

All of us crowded into the cockpit. Flashes of lightning in the southern sky revealed Elijah's tightened lips and unmasked anxiety behind his often-stoic face. Anna's wide eyes were less successful in hiding her fear. I wondered what kind of weather they experienced on the ship from Africa—or if the storm in Cuba had frightened them more than I thought.

Throughout the day, Askira and I tried to downplay the meaning of the winds and waves to our non-sailor companions. They were not so naïve—or perhaps they sensed apprehension in us as well. We all knew *Sophia* was a sturdy boat, but she was small—not meant for handling severe storms at sea.

As for me, I was more fearful of the cloudbank to the south than our current sailing conditions. It blanketed most of the horizon with layers of long, stretched-out storm clouds. Behind and above those clouds was a single smear of grayish-white across the sky. As the evening sun set, the smear turned from gray to a deepening orange. After the sun had gone down for us, the high cloud continued its sunlit change toward red. Immense thunderheads announced their own presence by poking through the darkening smear into the lighter rays of sunlight. It was as beautiful as it was terrifying.

Elijah spoke. "It's a big storm. We should pray."

All of us bowed our heads, Askira too. I glanced to see if he would. Elijah spoke to God for all of us.

After our prayer, our Japanese soldier friend scrutinized Anna and Elijah for the next several minutes. They both appeared more calmed and trusting as I asked Anna to help secure everything in the boat. Elijah focused on his tasks in helping Askira change our cruising sails to smaller storm sails. Askira could contain his curiosity no longer.

"You trust your God so much—to remain calm in the face of what is about to happen to us? Do you think your prayers will cause Him to calm this storm?

"My friend," Elijah said. "We did not pray to God to stop the storm. We asked Him to get us through it—to calm us. You see, we are already safe. If we die in this storm, our souls are forever secure with our God. This storm, like this life, is temporary; He is eternal, and we will be with Him forever." He paused to glance at Anna and then at me before turning again to Askira. "This is true for all who trust in Jesus."

Askira remained silent, pondering what he had heard. I knew in his years of travels he had been a student of peoples and their religions. He must have heard versions of what Elijah had told him. Our current situation would allow him to grasp the full meaning of those words. I hoped he would see the truth in them.

During the night, the winds changed from southeast to east and increased, and we had to take down both sails. Stars and moon filled the cloudless sky above us, though, to our south, the skies were black. The monstrous cloudbank would soon blot out the moon altogether. Waves were gaining in height and ferocity. A towering wave overrunning our stern could swamp and capsize *Sophia* in an instant. To prevent that, I turned the boat to the east, and we threw out the boat's old storm anchor to keep the bow pointed into the oncoming wind and seas.

Steering was impossible in these conditions. A few minutes after the clouds blanked out the moon and stars above us, cold rain began falling. I lashed the tiller in place, doubling the ropes and tying them extra tight.

"This will keep her teeth into the wind for us. Let's go below."

We all crowded into the cabin and out of the weather. After many minutes of hearing nothing but the howling winds and pelting rain, Anna started singing hymns. Her voice, ringing through the storm's din, brought us all out of our slump. Elijah pitched in with his rich baritone. I followed. Askira didn't know the words, but with a genuine smile, he tapped out time with his foot.

Our reprieve didn't last. *Sophia's* bow shot upward as she rolled hard to port. We all crashed into the cabin sides and each other when the massive wave hit and again when the storm anchor tugged our bow down from the wave crest. Then, the lightning started. Despite our attempts to brace ourselves, the battering continued for hours. We did what we could to stop the bleeding from our numerous cuts and bruises, revealed to us by pain and the almost constant flashes of light through *Sophia's* tiny portholes.

When our tossing began to diminish, I thought the worst had passed. Steady dim light of morning offered encouragement as it began to seep through the portholes. The next wave, accompanied by a gust that heeled our boat almost flat, may have been the most wicked of the night. Above the roar of water passing by and over the boat, we heard a cannon-like crack, followed by several seconds of splintering wood.

"There goes our mast," Askira said as *Sophia* rebounded from the heavy impact of the tall pole falling back on her stern.

"This could be serious," I said. "Let's hope we still have a tiller and rudder."

Sophia was losing her battle.

Her mast had been attached to her keel. Those forces of wind and water, strong enough to dismast her, had stressed and broken that keel. Seams between boards of her hull, no longer held in place by an intact keel, now opened and closed with the waves. Water squirted into the boat through those flexing joints. Where her mast went through her cabin top, large cracks opened to allow rain and seawater to pour in. She was filling with water.

Sophia had no bilge pump; she was far too small for one. I grabbed two small collapsible canvas buckets of the type used for multiple purposes on almost every boat. Dumping their contents into a hammock, I shouted to Elijah and Anna, "Bail with these. Throw the water into the cockpit. It will drain out from there. We must keep her afloat!"

Without a wasted second, Elijah and Anna began bailing.

Askira and I climbed into the pitching and rolling cockpit to see if we could salvage our mast. It had shattered about four feet above the cabin top and fallen back on the boat. The forestay, the stout rigging rope from the tip of the bow to the top of the mast, had not parted. Instead, it had pulled its fittings from the bow decking planks, taking a splintered foot-long piece of decking with it.

Sophia now had a gaping hole in the bow decking. Sea water flooded into the boat through the hole and opened deck seams every time an oncoming sea washed over the bow. The entire forestay with its fitting was now trailing us in the angry seas. We had to deal with the shattered and useless mast before we could do anything about the hole in the deck.

Struggling against wind, blinding rain, and waves, we freed the intact boom from the mast and lashed it aside to keep from losing it to the sea. It took both of us to cut each of the stern and side stays of the mast. One would hold a section of the tarred rope taut while the other slashed away with a knife while fighting to keep our balance in the unpredictable pitching and rolling of the boat. We then wrestled to move one end of the mast to the side of the boat and then the other end before we were successful in rolling it over the side and into the sea. Without the weight of a useless mast, we would have a better chance of saving the boat.

I nodded silent agreement with Askira when he pointed to our tiller and rudder, undamaged and still lashed as I had left them hours ago. Now, we had to stop, or at least slow down, the sea from flowing into the boat from the bow opening. Dodging water from the bailing buckets, we reentered the cabin to search for materials to plug the hole.

A few bronze nails, a hammer, a sailmaker's fid, some needles, thread, a couple blocks, four large pieces of tarred canvas patches, and several sizes of wooden plugs were all the boat's meager repair kit contained. We could use the tarred patches and nails. After cutting a wide strip from one of the spare sails, we folded the sail strip over itself several times and made quick stitches in the corners to hold two of the tarred patches in place. The Spanish plantation director's navigation table yielded a board to keep the force of the breaking waves from ripping our jury-rigged patch to shreds. Once we gathered our material and worked out our plan, we went back out on the bucking and spray-lashed deck to make repairs.

I tied one of our salvaged rigging ropes around Askira's chest and to the stump of the broken mast.

"Whatever you do," I said, "don't get washed over the side. It will be next to impossible to pull you back into the boat."

"I'll be counting on you to get me back in. And do it while I'm still breathing—if you don't mind."

Inching forward and fighting heavy spray as the boat heaved and rolled with the waves, he made it to the bow. Despite his repeated efforts, the screaming wind and angry waves made it impossible for him to keep the patch over the hole. He needed help.

After tying a lifeline to my chest as I had to Askira, I tied the other end to the mast stump and began slithering on my belly to the bow. Even as low as I was, wind-whipped waves almost washed me away a couple of times. Only the short bulwark kept me from sliding overboard.

I reached the bow. Holding onto the bow gunwale with one hand, I used the other to hold a corner of the patch in place. Askira pounded the nail through it and into some still-sound deck planks. A jerk of his head in the direction of the next forward corner of the hole told me he was ready for the next nail. Again, with one hand, I tried to hold the canvas where he wanted it.

After battling dozens of waves and vicious wind gusts that almost snatched us for the hungry sea, we had the four corners secured. I then held the board over the centerline of the patch. After he nailed it in place, Askira used all but two of the remaining nails to fasten the edges of the patch to the deck. Our repairs would not be watertight but would reduce the flow of water to a trickle instead of a torrent.

Inching backward, we made it to the cockpit and yelled for Elijah to cut another long strip from the sail. He handed it out to us. We wrapped it multiple times around the mast and stuffed it into the cracks in the cabin top. Askira secured the end of the canvas strip to the deck with his remaining two nails. This repair, though temporary at best, would reduce the amount of rain and seawater pouring in through the damaged cabin top.

We both reentered the cabin. Elijah and Anna looked exhausted by their non-stop bailing of knee-deep water into the cockpit, where it would flow through the scuppers back into the sea. I told them their efforts saved the boat and all our lives. Anna answered with a razor-thin smile and tear-filled eyes as she collapsed her fatigued body into a waterlogged hammock. Askira took Elijah's bucket. Our two Africans' long stint of frantic bailing had taken all they had. Though not yet healthy from their month on the slave ship and near-starvation after their escape, they had given all they had.

Askira and I bailed until the water level, sloshing with every plunge and roll of the boat, was reduced to ankle-deep. The wind, still gusting, was weakening, but the storm-whipped sea continued to hurl the boat in violent attempts to destroy us. Satisfied our bailing had us well ahead of the intruding sea and dog-tired ourselves, we wedged our bodies into corners where the forward bulkhead met the cabin sidewalls. Ignoring the watery wreckage, the seas had made of everything in the cabin, we drifted from fitful naps to deep sleep.

I awoke to water sloshing on my chest. Rays from a soon-to-be-setting sun seeped through the tiny ports. For the first time, my Japanese soldier was oblivious to the world. I needed him. I woke him.

Elijah and Anna slept without a sound. We checked to see if they were alive and then started bailing again. It was easier this time because both the wind and water seemed to have abandoned their quest to put *Sophia* and her crew on the bottom of the sea.

The boat rode the remaining swells from the storm with predictable pitching and rolling, her bow still pointed into the less hostile and steadier wind, the old sea anchor and its line still holding. The sky overhead was clear, but to the distant southeast, massive clouds, some poking through the smear of the storm, reached toward the heavens.

Lightning flashes inside those towers turned them into short-lived but brilliant, multicolored displays of the storm's power. The storm had not carried us into its belly but had spit our little boat out of its way. I whispered thanks to my Lord for the miracle of it. It was a long time since I'd talked to Him.

Askira and I decided to wait until the seas calmed more and the wind slacked before rigging the boom to serve as a mast upon which we could attach a sail. We waited until the next morning. In the meantime, we bailed seawater and inventoried the haphazard and waterlogged contents of our boat. One water keg was still intact. Opened seams on the others made them useless. We tossed them overboard. One keg might get us to America or not; we had no idea where we were.

Darkness settled in while we bailed. Seawater and anything else that went into our buckets went overboard. After hours, the water level was at the floorboards. Too tired for anything else, we lay on those wet boards and joined our companions in sleep.

Morning came with the sea attempting to conceal the mayhem of yesterday. Confused swells from the east and smaller ones from the south were constant reminders the storm had almost taken us. Seawater, continuing to squirt into *Sophia* through the opened seams in the hull, still threatened to sink us. Elijah and Anna begin bailing again.

Askira and I used what remained of the mast rigging, along with some of *Sophia's* extra rope remaining onboard, to tie the boom upright to the stump of our former mast. Much shorter than the mast, it required us to cut away the bottom foot of a small jib sail. Nevertheless, it worked to give us ample headway for steerage toward our destination.

All the fishing lines and nets were gone—washed away or tossed overboard in our haste to bail sea from the boat. We were hungry and without food or a way to catch fish. Still, our spirits were high; we had drinking water, and we could live for some time without food. We had survived; we were able to keep our battered and broken boat afloat and were heading toward home—a home none of my companions knew—but still home.

Henrysville, Indian Territory of the United States, 1850

I finished telling Hesed of the storm. She looked at me much as Ciara had when she found out I had trained to be a minister—astonishment tempered with the revelation she had suspected something like that all along.

"I want to know more, but I need to tell you, Bearstriker wants you to wear a special boot to keep the bone in place till it heals. He wants you to start wearing it as soon as the swelling goes down."

"Where does one find such a boot?"

"He has already arranged for a bootmaker to make one for you."

She ignored my squinted eye and raised an eyebrow as if she had already made up my mind for me.

"His name is Enoli. He will be here in a couple of days to measure your foot and leg."

"Black Fox."

She showed no surprise I knew the meaning of his Cherokee name.

"He is going to measure my leg? What kind of boot is this?"

"You won't like it, but it will help your leg heal. It will be stiff and will go from toe to mid-thigh. Bearstriker says once he laces it on, you won't be able to move any part of your leg, except maybe your toes."

"I'm not sure I'll like that."

"Be thankful he's not one of those naval surgeons you've told me about. Grayhawk, he knows what he is doing. He makes saddles and repairs harnesses for the livery, as well as crafts boots, shoes, and moccasins of all types. This is your chance to walk again. Try it, won't you?"

I nodded consent.

"Fine. Now I must go; I have work to do for Ciara. Perhaps tomorrow, you will tell me what became of your companions."

I watched her leave without responding to her implied request. I had no problem telling parts of my life to her, but I worried how much more she wanted. She already knew much, and still, she wanted more. I had never shared with her or Ciara about what drove me all these years—neither of my want for Keevah and family nor of the loneliness without either. The closest I had come was the moment I told Ciara I was searching for someone. That slip came closer than I ever intended to, baring my safeguarded memories.

Perhaps I was hasty in agreeing to our *Dadanetselá*. Hesed's and Ciara's inquiries always seemed to quarry memories from the depths of those I had forgotten—or had banished. But I had agreed to our deal. I couldn't back out now.

I tried to recall details of our voyage home in the stolen Cuban yacht to help me fashion the rest of my story.

Sailing Yacht, *Sophia*, 1829

Sophia was a heavy boat. She needed ample sail area to catch enough wind to propel her. Our small, jury-rigged sail gave us steerage but only a few knots of headway—maybe fifty miles a day if we were lucky.

"The north star is higher in the sky than it was a few nights ago," Askira said softly. He lay on a cockpit seat as I manned the tiller. Instead of dividing the night into watches, we took turns napping and steering as it suited us—there were just the two of us sharing the helm during night watches.

"I've noticed too. We might be in the large current running northward, not far off the American coast. We need to make headway west if we hope to reach America. The storm has pushed us far off course; trying to navigate by dead reckoning is impossible now."

Our hand-drawn chart, which we now had to recall from memory, revealed our ignorance of the part of the world where we now found ourselves. Any expectations of land were based on my memory of the eastern coast of the United States. I didn't know how far away that coast was, and I didn't know how far north we had drifted.

Despite our efforts at rationing, our one remaining water cask was running low. Elijah rationed less each day. Distant storm clouds with dark columns of rain falling to the sea beneath them birthed hope we too, would soon taste fresh water. It would have to be soon.

Often, we sipped our stale rations over cracked lips and swollen tongues and watched a far-off deluge of life-giving rain waste into the sea. At such times, the sun beat down with unmerciful intensity on our part of the ocean. It was so unjust while we, at the same time, bailed bucketfuls of undrinkable seawater from our boat.

All we could do was continue slogging westward and hope.

The sun was nearing the western horizon on the day we drank our last rations of water. It had been a hot and cloudless day with no promise of rain. Anna came into the cockpit. Askira moved over to my side. Anna sat beside Elijah. He took her hand as both locked their gaze on me.

"Lanny," he said. "We don't know what the future holds for us—or even if we have a future. We put our trust in the Lord for that. We have told you our plans from long ago were to wed. We want to do that now—to exchange our vows before the Lord and before witnesses. Lanny, will you marry us . . . this very evening?"

"I'm not licensed . . . I have no authority—"

"We make our vows to God," Elijah said. "He is our authority. We want you to lead us in making those vows and to witness we make them before God."

Askira joined in. "You do have authority to conduct the ceremony—to do what they ask. You are the captain of this vessel—commissioned by the very people who entrusted their lives to you. I think that gives you more authority to lead them in their vows and declare them married than any vessel captain commissioned by mere men who sit in a safe office on dry land."

"Lanny, you are a man of God," Anna said softly. "We want a Christian wedding, and you . . . only you . . . to marry us . . . Please?"

I tried to hide the wrenching of my gut. Anna meant me no harm—she didn't know all my failures or how deep those hurts burned. My life these past few years showed me more of an alien to God than a man of His word. Yet, I couldn't let these people down—Elijah and Anna, devoted believers, and Askira, who for months had been witnessing their faith.

The taste of deceit sickened me, but I had to do what they asked. I might have failed God, but I could not contribute to my friends and companions becoming like me. I could not stain Elijah and Anna's faith or poison Askira's budding interest in God by revealing the hypocrisy of my life.

I led them in their ceremony and declared them husband and wife. And spent hours pleading for forgiveness for my charade from God—my God, who wasn't listening to me anymore. The loneliness of that night was the worst ever.

This was the third day we had been without water. Three tiny flying fish had landed in our boat the day before. Each of us had no more than a couple of mouthfuls of food and even less fluid from them. Everyone was weak. Thirst began to play tricks with our minds. Illusions tormented us. We saw rain that wasn't falling, land where there was none and dreamed of drinking water that didn't exist.

Askira and I had learned of the effects of lack of water from tales of other sailors. Many stories warned us of the poisoning of mind and body that drinking seawater would bring. It was a warning we passed on to each other. As a group, each of us took on the task of keeping each other encouraged and safe.

Anna had the worst of it. Her small body couldn't have contained much water when healthy. Without it, she suffered. Often, when her mind deluded her, Elijah would hold and rock her like a small child until she fell asleep. When lucid, however, she was the best of all of us in helping to sort out our deliriums from our reality.

Askira and I doubted she would last another day.

Drifting between muddled wakefulness and dreams of Keevah, I sat holding the tiller late into my night watch. Faint light from stars and a sliver of a new moon began playing tricks on my vision. An eerie image emerged from the darkness, stretching across part of the horizon in front of us. A moment later, my tired eyes would see nothing but hazy gloom. A few minutes later, the image would reappear, appearing stretched in both directions before again cloaking itself in a dark and mocking mist. It appeared several times before fading away.

I remember thinking I had experienced something like this before—a long grayish-white strip seeming to float just above the horizon of the sea. I couldn't remember when or where, or what it meant. I thought it might be a fogbank or another hallucination. Whatever it was, it wasn't real. It didn't matter anymore. I drifted back to my dreams.

Several gentle bounces of the boat interrupted the reveries of Keevah and me watching a sunset from the foredeck of the *Muireann*. In a few moments, the sounds of her bow wallowing through swells diminished. Gentle lapping of wavelets against her stern soon serenaded my ears. My sailor's sense of the boat's rhythmic rolling with the seas faded. Taking my hand from the tiller, I leaned forward to lay my drained body on the seat. It was comfortable with the boat steady. I slept.

The afternoon sun was nearing the western horizon when Askira's grip on my shoulder shook me awake.

"Lanny, there's land. We're maybe a hundred yards offshore. The boats full of water. I think we're sinking, or we've already sunk."

It took me a few minutes to gather my wits. "This must be America, but we're not moving. We're aground, maybe on a sandbar." I glanced into the cabin to see floodwaters lapping at the bottom of the hammocks where Elijah and Anna lay sleeping. Whatever we're on, it's opened the hull seams. We'll never be able to bail it now."

"Looks like the tide is coming in. Maybe it'll carry us ashore."

"It may lift us off the sandbar, but she's full of water; it's still coming in. She must be resting on the bottom. Sand is filling the cracks and slowing the leaks. When she's lifted off, she'll flood fast and sink again deeper next time. Better rouse Elijah and Anna. We're going to have to wade or swim."

"I hope Anna has the strength for it."

"Tie some rope around the water keg. It'll float. She can use it to keep herself afloat."

Askira studied our jury-rigged mast. "Let's cut the boom free; it'll float. We can all hang on to it to get us ashore. There's bound to be deeper water between this sandbar and the beach, and the tide is making it deeper by the minute. What say, Cap'n?"

"I'll hold; you cut; you have a good knife."

We cut the boom down from its jury-rigged role as mast, removed the sail, and tied ropes around the boom to serve as handholds. It would float and support us as we made our way to shore. Our noise woke both Anna and Elijah. They came on deck to help. Weakened as we were, it took all of us to push the pole over the side and into the water. I grabbed the compass and Keevah's Bible in its leather pouch and wrapped them with the one oiled foul-weather slicker left on the boat. Askira and Elijah rolled and tied the spare jib sail into a tight bundle.

After tying the pistol to his waist, Elijah went into the chest-deep water and then helped Anna in. Askira, with the sail bundle under one arm, joined them and positioned himself near one end of the boom. One final look at the boat convinced me there was nothing else to salvage. I eased myself over the side and into the water. Keeping my slicker-wrapped pouch above water, I worked my way to the opposite end of the boom from Askira.

After one last querying glance at my crew and a silent nod from each, I started them on our long trek from the boat to the shore. Askira was correct when he said there would be deeper water between the sandbar and the shore. We had to swim at least half the distance. Even with the incoming tide pushing the boom and us with it, it was exhausting for all of us. Anna's grip was failing.

Elijah helped her hang onto the rope handholds. When he became too tired, Askira moved into his place. I relieved Askira when he gestured for me. Between the two of us, we took turns between helping Anna and swimming to push the boom to shore. Exhausted, Elijah gripped the rope and continued kicking his feet with all the strength he could muster.

Askira seemed to make it his personal mission to assure our two half-starved Africans reached land safely. I agreed with him. They were part of our crew. Though weak ourselves, we would not forsake them.

Dusk settled in as we neared the sandy shore; the shallower water made it impossible to swim. Neither Anna nor Elijah could stand. Askira helped Anna to her feet, but she was too weak to wade. He carried her to shore as a father would carry a sleeping child to bed. In the meantime, I helped Elijah to his feet. With one of his arms around my shoulders, we tried to wade. Askira came back and put Elijah's other arm around his shoulder. The three of us staggered ashore and dropped into the sand beside Anna.

I awoke to a sliver of moon high in the western sky. Compelling my tired body to move, I stood to look around and assess our situation. Before us, an immense sand dune blocked any view of what lay beyond. Above the dune, a ragged horizon, outlined against the faint star-studded sky, meant trees. They must be several hundred feet away. Those trees might lead us to fresh water. What lay between the dune and the trees, I could not see.

Behind us, the unbroken ocean stretched to the horizon. Occasionally, the foam of a breaking wavelet would glow silvery for a few seconds as it caught light from the moon and stars. Otherwise, the sea was black. The tide was indeed moving the shadowy hulk of our boat toward shore. Her stern was still aground, but she was taking on seawater and heeling over fast. Her starboard side and bow slipped deeper into the water with each incoming wave.

She had carried us over untold miles of ocean, kept us safe during the worst storm any of us had ever seen, and deposited us on solid ground. Now, we were abandoning her to the relentless surf and shifting sands of the Atlantic Ocean. She was only a boat, but my gut sank as I watched her. Her plight resurrected my heartaches of lost family—my family. All gone. All but one—Keevah. It rekindled my vow to find her.

CHAPTER 12

Georgia, U.S.A. 1829

Careful not to disturb Elijah's or Anna's sleep, I woke Askira. We tried climbing the dune. Each step strained our exhausted muscles. We were too weak, and the evening moon and starlight too faint. The sliding sand under our feet carried us back with each step almost as far as we moved up the slope. Our efforts in getting off the boat and swimming to shore had stolen both our will and stamina. It would be useless to try the dune again without rest. We retreated to Anna and Elijah, helped them move above the high tide mark, and lay down with them in the sand. We slept.

With a parched mouth, I awoke to the morning sun well up in the eastern sky. We had to get fresh water soon or die on this beach—with water within reach. I crawled on my belly to Askira. As I touched his shoulder, I glanced at the dune. The wooden bucket lay no more than ten feet from where we lay. I crawled over to it. The bowl of a handcrafted wooden ladle lay submerged in clear water. I tasted the water.

"Fresh! It's fresh!"

My shout roused my companions.

"Take small sips at a time." Askira went into command mode. "Too much too fast can make you sick. It can even kill you. I've seen it happen."

No one doubted him; we all took turns sipping from the single ladle our benefactor had left in the bucket. Our Japanese soldier of fortune once again provided life-saving discipline. He allowed us to drink after we waited whatever time he determined. How he knew, none of us questioned.

By midday, with thirst quenched, Askira and I felt strong enough to build a shelter with the sail, boom, sand, and a few pieces of flotsam from the beach. It wasn't much, but it would shield weakening Anna from the sun. We then set out to explore our surroundings.

Whoever left the bucket of water for us took pains to brush over their tracks. They left no hint of which way to look for them. They might not want us to find them, but we had no choice. Without food and more water, we would die. Anna needed food now, and Elijah was not much stronger than she was. Whoever they were, they could help; we needed them.

"Be alert," Askira said as we approached the top of the dune. Sea oats and other tall grasses grew in increasing profusion the higher up the dune we climbed. "We don't know who they are. Leaving water but not offering help troubles me. It doesn't seem right. They may have reasons, but we must be wary."

Askira reached the top of the grass-topped dune and turned to watch me. With my last few exhausting steps, I joined him. Between some tall trees and us lay a marsh of grasses and shrubs. This lowland, at least a couple hundred feet wide, ran parallel to the dune.

On higher land at the far side of the marsh grew a profusion of some type of low-growing palm plant. Their wide, fan-shaped fronds hid everything beneath some massive trees, whose gnarly branches spread sideways at least as far as their other limbs reached skyward. I had never seen trees like these. They must have been the famous live oaks of the southern states. Long strands of grayish moss hung from most of the lower limbs. These trees had formed the ragged horizon we saw last night.

Askira and I stood amidst tall grasses at the top of the dune, trying to determine our next steps, when several Negro men stepped around some of the palm plants. We watched in silence as several more appeared until six men stood looking at us. They huddled together for a minute and then split into two groups and started working their way toward us. Each group picked their way through the grasses as if they knew where to step. Their paths would bring them to the dune with one group on either side of us.

"They all have something in their hands," Askira said. "I make out at least two axes and a shovel—things that could be weapons. We have a useless, water-logged pistol and no powder."

"They might be as fearful of us," I said, "as we are of them."

"True, but I think we should return to Anna and Elijah and stay with them. When these men are closer, they will see we need help and are not a threat to them."

The men watched our deliberate retreat, keeping a prudent distance from us as they followed. They did not appear to be hostile; neither did they look pleased to see us. Moreover, they all carried some sort of tool that could become a weapon—offensive or defensive as the need arose.

Elijah woke Anna when he saw us approaching.

"Slaves." One man, who appeared to be their leader, pointed at Elijah and Anna. "They have slaves."

Elijah groaned as he rose. Every man's grip changed his tool to a weapon.

"No," he stepped toward the speaker. "We are not slaves. We escaped on Cuba after being brought ashore from a slave ship. Look at our ankles. You can see where the shackles cut and tore our flesh."

Eyes glanced at the scars. Not a word was spoken; not a grip on a single weapon changed.

"These men found us. They rescued us, fed us, and brought us here with them. They saved our lives."

Silence.

"They brought us here on that small sailboat and shared their food and water with us. They are our friends and companions. This one is even a preacher of God's word." He pointed to me and then knelt and put an arm around Anna. "He has led Anna and me in our marriage vows before God.

"We are not their slaves. We are their friends."

The leader pointed to me and then to the pistol in Elijah's waistband. "You have a pistol. You must surrender it to me."

"It is not mine," I said. "It is his. You will have to ask him for it."

Without a word, Elijah offered his pistol, handle first, to the astonished man.

After a few hushed words with the two men beside him, the leader took the weapon and turned to us.

"Follow me," he said. The three men started back up the dune. The others stayed behind to follow us.

Elijah didn't have the strength to lift Anna. Askira moved in to take over. I stepped up to help. Two of the men motioned us away. They stood her up, and the more muscular man hoisted her upon his back. He carried her piggyback over the dune, through the marsh, and several hundred yards to a clearing where I counted eight huts of various sizes and degrees of simplicity.

Several women approached at the leader's call. Two of them took Anna to a hut and somehow assured Elijah they would take care of her. The leader led Askira and me to another hut and asked some women to give us food and water. "Wait here," he said. "I need to talk to your boy."

"He is not my boy; he is a man. He is not a slave; he never has been. He is free. His name is Elijah. He and his wife, Anna, are our friends and companions."

The leader looked hard at me before softening. "Eat and drink now," he said, "to get your health back. Elijah will be back with you soon."

The women brought us food and water. As we were eating, I caught Askira's eye. His slight nod said he too was aware of the two men with us. The women were feeding us. The men were detaining us.

Elijah did return to us after several hours. He looked exhausted. Within minutes of his return, Anna also rejoined us. They both showed their pleasure at seeing each other. We expected that, though Elijah's tight lips and furrowed brow set my gut on edge.

What is it?" I whispered after our guards left and Anna had gone into the community hut vacated for Askira and me. Elijah and Anna would later go to another hut—and to the privacy they deserved.

"They told me we've landed on a barrier island off the state of Georgia," Elijah said. "These people are runaway slaves. Some have been here for over twenty years, a few have joined them more recently. Seems when the Spanish owned Florida, they helped American-owned slaves escape as a way of harassing American squatters. The Spanish helped them settle on these islands, which were uninhabited at the time."

"The Spanish own slaves too," I said.

'Yes, but they would steal or set free American slaves to punish the Americans whom they considered trespassers. Now, the Spanish are gone, and the United States owns Florida. Americans consider these people and anyone who does not have iron-clad documentation as runaways."

Elijah paused and looked at Askira and me. "They are fearful of the two of you. You are the first whites who know about them. What you will do and who you will tell frightens them. You could cost them their freedom. They don't know what to do. Arguments range from trusting you and setting you free or silencing you forever."

"What about you and Anna?"

"We can stay with them or go. There are other groups like them on other islands. They will help us go to them if we choose."

"What will you do."

"Neither. I think it is a matter of time before whites find one of these groups. Every barrier island will be searched, and every one of these people will have to flee or be captured."

"You can't travel as free without documentation. You will be captured too."

"Anna and I will go with you as your slaves."

"No, Elijah! I will not have slaves, you know that."

"I know, but I do hope you will carry a bill of sale to prove you own us as your slaves until we can travel to a northern state. Once there, we can get a judge to grant us freedom—papers and all."

"And where do we obtain a bill of sale?"

"One of the men here told me how to get it. He knows a man who can forge the paper. He says he's done it before, and no one can tell it from a real one. It may take several weeks—someone must go to the mainland very carefully. And the man who does the forgery wants paid."

"We have no money."

"We don't, but the leader of these people has our pistol and our compass. He is a generous man; he has offered to use them to pay the forger."

I studied my friend. His loss of freedom was more severe than anything I had tasted—his resolve to regain it was greater. I saw no other way but to help him.

"I understand," Elijah said softly, "you want to go to a city called Boston in the north. May we go with you?"

"Askira told you?"

"Yes. He told me when we were at sea—he would not tell why—he said it was personal."

"I will tell you as we go. It seems to me you have planned this out well."

"With help from these men. But everyone on the island will be put at risk, so they all must agree with the plan, or it's no go. I haven't talked to Anna yet."

"Your plan has its dangers. Do you think Anna will agree to it?"

"I am sure she will. I learned long ago not to mistake Anna's diminutive size for a weak spirit. She holds the courage of a lioness in her small body."

"A lioness? Not a lion?"

"Most certainly. You see, Lanny, a lion has immense courage when he needs it. A lioness has the same courage when someone else needs it—her sisters or her cubs. Anna is a lioness; she gives of herself for others."

I knew Anna would agree—she would go to the ends of the earth with him.

After several more of Elijah's long talks with them, these people's view of Askira and me changed. They no longer considered us a threat to their freedom. Indeed, the leader and several others coached us on how to move through the country with Negros, none of the locals could recognize. As they told us where to go and which people to see, it became clear this was a frequent activity of theirs—helping other runaway slaves start on their long trek north to freedom.

⁎⁎⁎

We stayed with our island hosts for another two months. Except for the ever-present fear that whites would discover us and for my impatience to start north to find Keevah, it was a pleasant time of recuperation and regaining our weight and strength.

I noticed Askira and Elijah began spending more time together, often with half-hearted excuses of going fishing, crabbing, or beachcombing. Their reasons became clear one evening when Askira asked Anna and me to join them on the beach where we landed. There would be no fire because it might attract the attention of white fishermen. A waning half-moon would provide adequate light.

Askira spoke first. "Elijah and I have been discussing your God during our absences from the group. What he has told me is quite different from what I have learned about other religions. I am considering accepting your God as mine, but I want to hear your version of Jesus. Elijah tells me all Christians have a personal relationship with him, however my life has been far different from yours. How does he relate to each of you, and how do you think he can have a relationship with someone of my past?"

We talked late into the night. Anna's and Elijah's enthusiasm fueled most of the conversation. I backed them up for a while, but soon I found myself sharing that despite the horrible sins I had committed on the slave ships, Jesus still forgave me and paid my penalty with his death. My words to my friend convinced me of my own faith. I could now answer the question Askira posed to me after Gaston's death.

For the first time ever, I heard Askira speak in a voice choked with emotion. "I have seen and heard so much from each of you. I believe. . . I know . . . you are correct. I know I need Jesus as my God. I ask him to forgive me and accept me as His own.

"Lanny, will you baptize me in this ocean tonight—right now?"

"My honor."

The four of us rejoiced the rest of the night and slept late into the next morning. I thanked my God for forgiveness and slept without misgivings for the first time in a long time. Those night talks of Jesus' eternal love were as meaningful to me as they were to Askira.

My African companions were indeed God's missionaries, sent to help lead my Japanese friend to God and to help heal my own crushed spirit.

***

In late March, the time came for us to leave. Our friends supplied me with attire fitting of a local farm owner. Askira dressed as my foreman, with Elijah and Anna clothed as local slaves.

Supplied with food and disguises, we and our hosts set out at night to an adjacent island in an old fishing pram. During the next four nights, what appeared to me to be a well-planned and executed conveyor system transferred us to no less than six islands and at least four teams of rowers for the pram. We always spent daylight hours hidden in an island community of Negros or concealed in dense island growth.

We were well inland, far from the barrier islands, before we appeared in public. Our Negro hosts at the time wished us well amid numerous suggestions on when to travel and how to obtain what money we needed without raising suspicions.

Our forged bill of sale for my two slaves held up to several challenges, including one narrow decision by a community court in South Carolina. By then, I had stopped trying to pass myself off as a farmer and, with Keevah's Bible, had become an itinerant preacher instead.

Elijah's and Anna's eloquent speech and extensive biblical knowledge convinced the judge they had been long-time slaves of a preacher rather than field workers, as our challenger claimed. Even so, it was a reluctant decision. The judge accepted the evidence in his deliberations, though I thought he would have preferred to send my Negro friends out to work the fields for the rest of their lives.

Following the court session, a small group of people, both Negro and white, outfitted Elijah and Anna with clothing more fitting to a pastor's servants rather than as field slaves. These same people set about secreting us out of the county. For the next week, we did not see daylight until we entered the state of North Carolina. Numerous people helped us on our northward journey, though our escorts and guides sometimes asked us to split up into ones or twos. They always reunited us at the end of each trek.

Askira stayed with us all the way to New York, where I believe his urge for adventure and new worlds became too great. I believe he stayed with us until he was certain Elijah and Anna were well out of slave country. We parted close friends, hoping but not expecting to ever see each other again. When he bid us goodbye, it was one of the few times I saw him display deep emotion.

Six weeks after leaving North Carolina, we were welcomed at a tavern in a small community on the outskirts of Boston. We stepped inside as the cold wind and rain of a late nor'easter began pelting us. During the time we stayed there, Elijah and Anna became quite close to a free Negro couple who worked for the tavern owner. My companions even spent the nights in the home of their new friends.

The morning of my third day there, with the weather still blustering, I sat by the dining room fire with other stranded travelers. As I perused one of the small Boston newspapers, the proprietor approached me.

"Sir, I would like a word with you. Would you join me in my office?"

I nodded and rose to follow him. We entered his living quarters in the back of the building. His wife smiled and nodded toward three steaming cups of tea already on the kitchen table. The man and his wife sat and gestured toward an empty chair.

"Please."

I sat.

"My man, David, tells me you want to free your slaves."

I tried to hide my surprise.

"You need not worry. We understand and can help. He also tells me you saved their lives and brought them here all the way from Cuba."

I relaxed a bit. "We saved each other's lives, and yes, we traveled with them from Cuba. David told you all this?"

"Yes, you see, he, I, and our wives work with a lot of other people, both Negro and white, to help slaves escape and become freemen. Both David and his wife were once slaves. Now they are free, and helping others become free also."

"I know something about that," I said. "We could never have made it from Georgia without help. We are grateful."

"To be free, the proprietor said, "each of them will need to submit a petition to a judge constituted by the state. Judges have wide latitude in their requirements and judgments, but in all cases, you, as owner, must sign the petition stating your wish to release the person from your ownership and that you feel he or she is prepared to function as a free person."

"It's that simple?"

"Not quite. The judge we use is known as honest and thorough in his decisions. He will question the petitioner at length to assure himself the person has the knowledge and ability to make a living and meet the responsibilities of a free person."

"Seems demanding. Why do you use him"?

"His court is known and respected. Any Writ of Manumission he issues declaring the person free must stand up to challenges. And there may be challenges. There are slave hunters all through the northern states looking for Negros they can capture and return to slavery. There are also forgeries and even documents issued by people posing as judges. Fake papers are useless in court. In such cases, the holder of those papers may end up a slave again—or sometimes a slave for the first time.

"Challenges against Judge Williams' decisions have never been successful. Most slave hunters know that. Only the foolish will try to win a case against anyone holding papers from Williams' court. We can help prepare the petitions for your friends. To their advantage, they are well educated, fluent in English, and have jobs waiting for them."

"Jobs? What jobs?"

"Several benefactors fund a small school nearby for former slaves. Reading, writing, and some basic arithmetic are the school's goals. They need teachers. Your friends will be a great addition, and they are willing. With your recommendation and their qualifications, they will have no problem being declared free."

"I will do my part."

Seventeen days later, with their freedom confirmed, Elijah and Anna set about establishing a home and life for themselves as free Americans. I worked for the innkeeper until I could buy appropriate clothing for myself and pay for transportation to Portland, Maine.

Alone, I began my earnest search for Keevah.

※

Portland, Maine, U.S.A. 1830

A month later, at midmorning on a weekday, I knocked on the door of a home in Portland—the address to which I had addressed so many letters to Keevah. To avoid confrontation, I picked a time when I thought neither her father nor brothers would be home.

"This is the Ferguson residence," the short, gray-haired woman who answered the door said when she saw me. "I am Mrs. MacDermott, their housekeeper. May I help you?"

"Yes. I am Lansdale Grahame McDowell. I am trying to contact Keevah Ferguson."

The woman's face and rosy cheeks turned ashen as she stared at me. "H—How do you know Keevah?"

"We met on her father's boat, the *Muireann*, when we were children coming to America. Look." I pulled my broken scrimshaw from its leather pouch. "I have half of this scrimshaw one of the sailors carved for her. She may still have the other half. She will recognize it."

Her glance at the scrimshaw brought a quick gasp. "Oh dear . . . she's shown that to me so many times. We were told you were dead . . . and then told . . . oh dear Lord." Her hands wiped the air as if trying to erase her words, then clasped her cheeks.

"You'd better come in."

She sat me in a parlor chair and took another, facing me. Still shaken, she tried to feign composed conversation.

"I feel as if I know you . . . from all Keevah has told me. May I call you Lanny? She always referred to you by that name."

"Please do, but you are upset; something has happened. What is it? Where is Keevah?"

"May God help me, Lanny. I'm sorry if I seem rattled. When her brothers brought Keevah home from Boston, she was pregnant—with your child."

It was like standing next to the muzzle of a carronade on the warship *Médée*. The shock so addled my brain, I stood gaping at the woman, unable to make sense of what she said.

"The boys insisted you had been killed in a runaway carriage accident. Keevah never believed it for one moment. She believed you would come for her. She never stopped believing."

"Where is she now?"

"Her father was so angry he disowned her and forced her to marry a Norwegian blacksmith. I know his name, but I don't know where they are. He travels where there is work for him. When they left here, they were going to Ohio to work at the canal diggings. They use a lot of horses and mules; he would have work there."

"How do you know this?"

"Keevah wrote me, as she wrote me about you."

"What about the child."

"She bore a son. He is with her; she never told me his name."

"What is the blacksmith's name."

"Give me a moment, I'll get it for you."

She left me alone to face the awful truth about what I had done. I should have been there for Keevah. I should never have let any of this happen, never should have abandoned her when she needed me, never should have left her with child.

The woman, with her face swollen and eyes reddened, reentered the room.

"Here it is." She handed me a slip of paper with a name scrawled on it. "I am sorry for my scribbling; I am so shaken by all of this. His name is Andolf Hegdahl. Keevah stopped writing me when I moved into the house with the family—three years ago after my husband died."

"Thank you," I muttered.

"Lanny." Fresh tears appeared as the woman placed a hand on my arm. "Her name is Mrs. Hegdahl now. She has a family and a life. I am so sorry, so sorry for both of you."

I thanked her again and turned toward the door.

"Lanny, what are you going to do?"

"I don't know," I muttered and turned to leave.

"Wait," she cried between sobs. "There's more you should know."

I turned to face her again. She gestured to a chair. I sat.

"Kevin, the youngest of her three brothers, confessed to me . . . sometime after the wedding, you were not dead. There was no accident, but the two older brothers did intend to kill you. He convinced them—I think forced them—to sell you to a man who shanghaies men to serve as sailors. He said it was to save your life. He never wanted to kill you—or even hurt you."

"Where is this Kevin now?"

"I don't know. He and the other two wanted no part of each other. They bought his share of the business; he left."

"And her father?"

"He seemed to die inside every day after he disowned Keevah. He lost interest in the business, so the two older brothers took it over. He is upstairs right now—on his deathbed. I'm afraid he is grieving himself to death."

"I must go." I turned again to the door.

"Lanny, please . . . let God guide you whatever you do . . . and do it in love."

"I will. Thank you, Mrs. MacDermott, you've been helpful. I must make sure they are safe; I must."

"Then go . . . and Godspeed. Goodbye, Lanny."

"Goodbye."

I turned and walked down the flagstone path, pretending I knew what to do and where to go; I knew neither. I felt crushed—I had lost my Keevah, family, and future.

※

I stayed in Portland, searching for someone—anyone who might give me some information about the blacksmith. I found no one. At dusk, on my final day there, I questioned the owner of the last livery stable in town about any farriers he had used to shoe his horses. He knew nothing about the blacksmith I was looking for. As I left the livery, a man walked up beside me.

"I understand," he whispered, "you are asking about a Norwegian blacksmith who used to work hereabouts."

"Yes, I am. What can you tell me?"

"Follow me. I can take you to someone who knew him."

I followed him down a narrow street to a warehouse. The smell of ships, sea, and fish was strong. I reckoned we must be near the waterfront.

"He said he would meet you and talk to you inside."

Next to two large warehouse doors was a personnel door. I opened it and walked in. Except for a single coal oil lamp lighting the area around a cluttered desk, the building was dark. I strode toward the desk. What I could make out in the gloom was parts and supplies for sailing ships.

"Well!" The door slammed shut. I wheeled around to face the angry voice.

"So, you've been asking about our sister, you Scottish scum. I'm surprised you're alive, but you won't be for long for what you did to Keevah."

The brute was speaking and approaching fast, his hands clenched into fists. The toad stayed behind two paces, but he wielded something fiendish in his hand—no doubt a weapon of some kind.

This was an attack; Askira's training took over. I stepped into the brute's lunge and slashed at his throat with the back of my hand while blocking his heel with one foot. I misjudged in the dark. My hand hit low, but my trip worked. He fell back into the toad enough to delay the second brother's attack.

"Take that side," Brute snarled. "I'll take him from this side." He approached cautiously, like a cat cautious of being bitten by the rat it had cornered. My eyes had adjusted to the dark by now. I turned sideways to see both men.

Toad poised himself, preparing to attack. He stood three or four paces from me. I feigned a step toward him. He retreated. I wheeled about to put my strong hand toward Brute. My sudden movement prompted him to lunge at me while swinging with both fists. He was a bully but not a fighter. I danced away from his charge. He turned to pursue.

In a split second, he was off balance. I darted in and flattened his nose. Spinning to gain leg power, I placed an upward kick to his abdomen, placing my heel just below his rib cage. Gasping like a fish out of water, unable to breathe, he went down like a rock and lay motionless.

Toad stood frozen for a couple of seconds and then attempted a pathetic swing with a huge wrench. I stepped back to let the swing go wild. Then, I stepped in with a vicious upper cut to his chin. He fell to the floor and lay still.

With both the brothers beaten and motionless on the warehouse floor, I whispered thanks to Askira and walked to the door. Before leaving, I looked back in the dim light to see both men laying where they had fallen. My blows would have given neither of them serious injuries, so I shut the door behind me and walked away. Within minutes, I started making plans for my trek to the Ohio canal diggings.

More than one canal site required many workers. Confusion reigned when it came to looking for a specific person. Sometimes, worker camps moved as their canal sections were completed. Men often changed from digging crews to towpath or bridge-building crews.

Many workers came from local residents who saw an opportunity to supplement their income with short-term work. When a section of the canal was complete, they would collect their pay and go back to their farms or regular jobs. So many transient and temporary workers made it impossible to find or keep track of an individual worker or to find out where he might be on any given day.

While I was inquiring of a work crew using mules to pull their large scoop-like canal digger, one aged man, whom everyone called Ol' Smitty, approached me. He said he had worked as a muleskinner on the Erie canal even before the Ohio projects began. He knew most of the foremen and many of the crews on this phase of the canal workings, and he could help. I accepted his offer without question, though I told him I needed to contact Hegdahl about a family matter. I avoided mentioning Keevah or my son.

I never understood Ol' Smitty's reasons for hanging around. The old man didn't seem to have a regular job and was no longer able to do manual work. I suppose after so many years on these complex projects, he couldn't get canal construction out of his blood. I offered him an opportunity to do something meaningful again. He was eager to help.

In his enthusiasm to find my blacksmith, Hegdahl, Ol' Smitty traveled miles and spoke to hundreds of workers. Neither he nor I ever found anyone who could tell us anything about the man. I did find a talkative farrier who said many blacksmiths leave the canal diggings for higher-paying jobs working for the army or freight companies.

I left Ohio, heading east to follow the already-established Erie Canal to look for Hegdahl. He might work for any of the many freight companies in business along that busy canal network. Failing to find him anywhere along the canal left me discouraged, but there were still many freighters all along the Allegheny and Ohio Rivers. I decided to follow the Ohio to southern Ohio, then strike out for southern states before winter set in.

In late fall, I found myself alone in the mountains of Tennessee. My horse lost a shoe. A day later, he came up lame with a severe stone bruise on his right forefoot. My plans of making my way further south died. Now, I had to find a way to get my horse and myself through the winter.

Chapter 13

Henrysville, Indian Territory of the United States, 1850

I sat in the straight-backed chair reading and rereading recent and past copies of the Kansas Herald Hesed brought to me. My boot-encased leg, cushioned by a pillow, lay propped up on a footstool. Ciara's writing style was direct and informative. Subtle humor often popped up in stories of local happenings. It made interesting reading; she was skilled at her craft.

Her editorials confirmed my gut feeling she was not one to trifle with. Facts, sound logic, and inexhaustible hope conveyed a fierce love for her country and the people in it. Calls, sometimes written between the lines, for moral and spiritual leaders to step up for both Indian and whites appeared at opportune times. Her words also conveyed her determination slavery was not to be part of their future.

Hesed or Ciara would soon come with my breakfast. I hoped it would be Hesed. If I told either one of them about that winter in Tennessee and the next few years of my life, I would be getting close to exposing my darkest secrets—demons challenging my essence as a man. But I knew I had to tell something. Those two were too perceptive to overlook such a gap in my story. They couldn't know what I did during those years was the reason for me being in their life today. I would need discretion in sharing that part of my life.

Hesed poked her head in through the half-open door.

"You're beginning to look like a bear this morning. Breakfast will come after we get you looking human." She placed a leather box on the nightstand, unfolded the towel she carried under her arm, and draped it around my neck.

"I don't want a shave," I grumbled. "I'm beginning to like this beard."

"No, you don't." She silenced me by wrapping a hot, wet towel around my face. "You've been scratching like an old hound for the last two days."

She began building shaving lather in her mug as the hot moisture of the towel softened my beard. Satisfied with her lather, she removed the towel and started slathering my face with her brush, not giving me another chance to decline.

"I'd rather do this myself," I said between soap-covered lips.

"You can't do it without a mirror."

"I can, and I have. Let me do it."

"No. I want you looking good when this is over. Better to have someone who can see what they're doing."

"Hesed, I'm telling you; I'd rather do it myself."

"You've never done this before, have you?"

"Of course, I have. I often shave myself, and I've had barbers shave me thousands of times."

"I'm not talking about shaving."

"No? Then what are you talking about? I'm having a difficult time following you this morning, Hesed."

"I am saying you have never argued with an Indian before, at least not one holding a straight razor to your throat." The twinkle in her eye preceded the delightful grin I liked so much about her.

"I do believe you've persuaded me," I said with a chuckle. "It would be wise to concede at this time."

"I thought you'd see it my way."

"For the time being, of course."

Her response was a quick snort, telling me there wouldn't be another time—the issue was settled.

"Lift your chin; let's get this over with."

"I see you brought me a shirt too."

"You will have to wait till I get you shaved before you put it on. I just washed that shirt. No sense getting blood on it until we see how this goes."

She concentrated on her task. Her skill with the razor convinced me she'd shaved men many times. Finished, she wiped my face with first a damp and then a dry towel. Without another word, she cleaned the razor, brush, and shaving mug before placing her tools and shaving soap in the leather box. Satisfied with her work, she sat in the bedside chair and looked me in the eye for several silent moments.

"You haven't spoken for a while," she said softly. "Did I offend you with my remark about the razor? It was rather crude; I apologize."

"No offense. You are good at shaving a man. How did you learn?"

"Jack the barber taught me. Henrysville was the first place we stopped after the army released us."

"We . . . ?"

"At first, after my mother died, almost everyone was kind and helpful to me. But soon, their own problems became too great, and I found myself on my own. I needed someone—some help—so I attached myself to a family. They let me tag along, but when the army released us, they all moved on. I was a burden . . . another mouth to feed . . . and I didn't fit in with their lifestyle. I chose to stay here."

"You were thirteen years old. How did you expect to survive?"

"I begged. I had plenty of time to learn after my mother died. It didn't take me long to see Jack's barber shop was a center of activity for whites from the wagon trains, soldiers, and a few Indians needing a shave, so I started hanging around. Most ignored or were cautious of me at first, but some would throw me a little extra change.

"Jack is a generous man, and he has Cherokee blood in him. Anyway, he paid me to do some chores, like keeping the floor clean, carrying water or firewood; you name it—I did it. I even learned to strop his razors to his satisfaction. Before long, he allowed me to get his customers ready to shave. I would apply hot towels to their faces and brush shaving soap on their whiskers. Most accepted me.

"Jack was also our doctor and dentist, at least the closest thing we had to one. He sometimes asked me to help. He even let me sew up some smaller cuts and wounds. I could do the small or difficult ones better than he could. He wouldn't admit it to anyone else, but he knew I knew . . . and he would tell me so. Usually, our patients would give me a coin or two as a reward. Most of the Indians in town would also share what they could with me.

"One day, out of the blue, he asked me if I wanted to learn to shave. He taught me."

She laughed. "You should have heard the buzz around town when I shaved my first man—he was white. He was a soldier who knew me from previous visits to Jack. He was not worried, but most of the other whites in town thought he was crazy for letting an Indian girl put a razor to his throat. He did convince other soldiers to let me shave them. After a while, I had my own group of customers, including some of the white men who lived here. On occasion, I would get some white travelers and a few from the wagon trains. A couple of years later, Ciara and her mother came to town, and my entire world changed."

She stopped talking, studying me as she gathered and folded her towels.

"You are too quiet. Something is not right. What is it, Grayhawk?"

"Hesed . . .." She watched me in silence while I gathered my thoughts. "You are correct to say I've never done this before, at least the way you describe it, but I've had a Cherokee woman shave me many times. She loved to do it . . . she was my wife."

Hesed reminded me of a rabbit caught in the open, fearful the tiniest movement would betray her to the hungry hawk circling above. I couldn't leave her like that.

"A band of Cherokees in eastern Tennessee befriended me when I was down on my luck. My horse went lame, and I was afoot in unfamiliar country. I spent fall and winter with them, hunting, sharing the work, and living as a member of the group. One of their young women and I were attracted to each other. We married the next summer. A year later, we had Ester, our daughter. More Indians joined us, and within a couple years, our group had grown into a small settlement.

"Then, we heard of the Government's plan to remove all Indians, including Cherokees, and give their land to white settlers. I joined a group of my Cherokee friends to oppose the movement and present a legal case to the Government."

Hesed stared wide-eyed at me. "D—did you know of anyone else doing that?"

"Yes, we soon learned of a well-organized group in North Carolina. They were led by competent men and had been working on this far longer. My friends and I went to offer our resources and information to them."

Still wide-eyed, she leaned closer. "And you met some of them?"

"Yes, we traveled to North Carolina, but soon after arriving, I received some news and had to leave."

I watched the light fade from her eyes. "I may have met your father, Hesed, but I don't know . . . I don't remember. I am sorry."

She dropped her gaze for an instant. When she looked up, her expression was stoic Indian, her dark eyes impenetrable.

"The news . . . was bad, Hesed, . . . about family. I had to go."

"I understand," she said. "It would have been nice for you to have known him. Was your family alright?

She studied my face; I found no words.

"I see they were not. I am sorry I asked. It is none of my business."

Neither of us spoke for several minutes, each lost in private thoughts.

"I'll get your breakfast. Ciara needs me for the rest of the day." She rose to leave. "Thank you for telling me."

Had I been able, I would have run into the wilderness, raised my fists to the sky, kicked anything within reach, and screamed at God. Anger, frustration, and grief would have fueled my frenzy until I collapsed. It would not have helped. I could not deal with the reality of the person I had allowed myself to become. I would end up sobbing in the dirt for what I had done—for what I had lost.

I know, for I did it many times.

This time, I could do nothing but sit in this chair with one leg in a leather cocoon bound so tightly I couldn't move anything but my toes. This time, I had to deal with my emotions and the truth of leaving my wife and child defenseless while I chased a dream—my dream of finding Keevah, who was another man's wife, and my son, whom I didn't even know.

***

Ciara brought me a late dinner.

"I see my friend of many talents has given you a shave."

"The best I've had in a long time. You are correct when you say she has many talents. I'll have to add barber to her resume."

Ciara smiled and nodded. "She also made your dinner tonight. Looks like something special."

"She sometimes does," I said.

I examined the meal without touching it. Looking up, I asked, "Ciara, can you sit for a while?" I motioned to the rocking chair Hesed had brought into the room earlier.

She sat and gazed at me without saying a word. I sensed surprise in her eyes as well as pleasure.

"I know Hesed has told you everything she knows about me, But I didn't always tell her all the details. You've been good to me, and I don't want you to get any wrong impressions, so let me clarify some things.

"Yes, I have fallen into deep despair about some things that have happened to me and things I have done, but I have never forgotten or purposely turned away from God. It is true I have questioned my relationship with Him, all because of my weaknesses and failures to trust Him, never because of His lack of faithfulness to me. I still have a long way to go, but I am making progress, and I'm trusting Him to get me there. It's important to me that you know."

"I understand and never doubted you, but there are a few details on other things I'm not clear on. Mind if I ask some questions? And please eat your dinner while we talk."

She sat throughout our long question and answer session with her hands in her lap or shifting her weight and holding her swollen belly. I could see some of my answers caused her to squeeze her hands together so hard her knuckles turned white. Sometimes, her lips tightened, or her eyes became too moist, and the tip of her nose turned red.

Again, she reminded me too much of Keevah, but her noncommittal expression confused me. I couldn't read if she was sympathetic, judging, or forgiving me for my actions.

"Thank you for telling me more. Can I return the favor and answer any questions you might have of us?"

"I have been wondering how you and Hesed met and how the two of you ever got so close . . . if you don't mind?"

My usual hostility toward her had vanished. I felt relieved and relaxed with her for the first time since I had seen her. My realization of it came as a surprise; it felt good.

"When I was fifteen, some soldiers brought my mother and me to town to get supplies. We were part of a small group of wagons taking the Santa Fe Trail to Santa Fe, which was part of Mexico then. My papa was an entrepreneurial type and wanted to start a freighting business. Wherever his work took him, my mother and I went along.

"Unfortunately, we met with another wagon train, which had stopped for supplies too. Some of their people had become ill with cholera. The sick ones were quarantined in an abandoned homesteader's cabin with no one to care for them. My mother had seen cholera before, so she volunteered to help. Not long after, Papa became sick.

"That's when the army showed up and told us we had to move away from the area. Seems people in previous wagon trains had become ill and died there too. An officer told us the Indians had been calling the entire valley "Water of death" for several years. Indians avoided it altogether.

"He also told of an old rumor. People, years ago, who used water from the homesteader's well became sick. No one knew for certain if the well was poison, but when the army bivouacked in the area. They barricaded it. People kept ignoring the barricade, so they declared the entire area off-limits to everyone—including thirsty travelers.

"The army then moved us to another valley about five miles away. The stream through it was small, but with enough water for us and our animals. They wouldn't let our sick people stay at the homestead. They set up tents for them about a mile from the army bivouac area. Mama and I stayed at this so-called infirmary because Papa was one of the ill. Mama worked there full-time caring for all the sick."

"Did your father recover?"

"No. Papa died, but Mama stayed until all her other patients either died or recovered and left. It was during this time the Army would bring us into town for supplies. I met Hesed as I was wandering the streets looking about. An Indian girl approached me and asked me in perfect English if I needed help or directions. She was about my age and friendly, so we started talking. That was the beginning of the best friendship of my life.

"Mama became ill while cleaning up the infirmary. Hesed and I cared for her as best we could." She paused as if to gather her emotions.

"I'm sorry," I said. "You must have been close."

"We were. I am certain she died of cholera—the same thing Papa and the wagon train people died from."

"How long ago was this?"

"Nine years. I was sixteen. I moved into the upstairs of the barbershop with Hesed. She shared everything with me until I found a job working for the dry goods store. Hesed was the reason I got the job; she talked the proprietor into giving me a chance. She is the most generous person I know."

"I know that to be true. Do you know what her name means?"

"No, I don't. She has never told me. I've never heard it before, so I assume it's a Cherokee name."

"It's not Cherokee. It's not meant to be a name at all. It is a Greek version of an ancient Hebrew word. A rough interpretation is something like loving or merciful kindness, but it's more than that. It denotes a hierarchy, where a superior one is giving mercy to one of a lower position, like a king being kind to his subjects, or as God giving grace and loving mercy to the ancient Hebrews. All through their history, the Israelites used it to convey God's love for people, never for peoples' love toward God.

"Isn't it ironic? The word 'Hesed' is now being used as a name for an Indian woman? For a person who is viewed by most whites as an inferior being and who is living and breathing the very meaning of the word to anyone who needs it—Indian, Negro, or White? Makes one wonder who the superior being is and who the inferior is, doesn't it?"

"Perhaps now," Ciara said, "you can understand why I think so highly of her. And why I am so concerned about the future of these people."

"I also have a better understanding of the principles you champion in your editorials—all peoples are equals, no matter their skin color, heritage, or circumstances."

"I believe when we become a state, and when other new states consume the entire Indian Territory, we must all accept each other into full and equal citizenship and status. Then, we can become truly free. I believe we must include all nationalities and races, as well as both the Negros and the American Indians. We need to look at each other not as problems but as opportunities to serve and help one another."

"A radical concept, Ciara, a major change in our national culture."

"Yes, it is, and I believe the way to begin is by giving these people the best preparation we can for them to become equal and contributing citizens. We can start today with simple acts of respecting and educating them."

"Your editorials state so clearly and repeatedly—if I may say so."

"Mr. Grayhawk, this town and region have a golden opportunity to set the idea into motion when, in a few years, we become the state of Kansas. If we can adopt these principles as a state, we'll prove to the nation it can be done. It will take a while, but I believe it can happen and will be better for everyone. There are others who believe so too. Calls reverberate in every state in the Union for freedom for all."

"Calls for the status quo are also common, Ciara. Some people feel so strongly about it there has been, and will be more, armed conflict to maintain it."

"I know. I've heard of incidents in several states and here in the territories too. I hope and pray we can avoid widespread conflict, but we must change. I don't see any future for any of us if we can't . . . or won't. As for me, I'll do what I can to convince others that we must prepare everyone, white, Indian, and Negro, for a new and different world. Their survival, and our own, depends on it. It is getting late, so I must go. I still have newspaper work to do before tomorrow."

***

Daylight was beginning to seep through my bedroom window when I woke. I had not slept well all night, thoughts of Hesed's disappointment at my not knowing if I met her father continued to haunt me. But the real reason I couldn't sleep was not because I had disappointed her. It was the memory of why I did what I did—my reason for leaving North Carolina and my Indian friends during the summer of '38 and then not returning to them. I expected Ciara or Hesed to ask me about it. Whatever my answer, I would never mention Keevah as my reason.

I could not forget the chance encounter in a tavern in North Carolina with Ol' Smitty, the former muleskinner who befriended me at the canal diggings when I was in Ohio.

"I'm headin' south for the winter," the old man told me. "Ohio winters are gettin' to my joints real fierce-like anymore. Just as I was leavin', the diggin's a few weeks ago, that Norwegian blacksmith you was askin' about showed up. He said he was leavin' too—headin' for St. Louie. Rumors were the army and lots of freighters needed blacksmiths and farriers, and they were payin' top wages. He was takin' his family and was thinkin' bout settlin' down in those parts. I know it's been a lot of years since you was askin' bout him, but I thought you might like to know."

Ol' Smitty's story put me in a quandary. Should I conduct my business here and return to my Indian wife and daughter, or should I go find Keevah and my son? My situation reminded me of the well-known paradox known as Buridan's Ass, which I remembered from

Aberdeen Grammar School. The hungry and thirsty ass could not decide to go to a haystack and eat or go to a bucket of water and drink. Unable to decide between two equally favorable options, he died of thirst and starvation.

I reasoned I could avoid becoming that ass; I could always return to my wife, but I may not always know where to find Keevah and my son. Against the resounding voice in my gut, I bought more supplies, reshod my horse, and made the wrong decision.

※

My planned three-week trip to St. Louis turned into three months after waiting in Kentucky for a ferry to be rebuilt. An earlier flood had swept away or destroyed every ferry and boat capable of ferrying a horse and rider across the Mississippi River.

When I reached St. Louis, neither the army nor any of the numerous freight companies knew anything about a Norwegian or his family. I expanded my search up and down the Mississippi and Missouri rivers until I found a small freight company in St. Joseph, Missouri. The owner remembered him.

He told me there must have been a flood of blacksmiths looking for work last spring. That Norwegian was one of the few good ones at his trade. The man kept him on as long as he could, but there wasn't much freighting work in winter, and he had no need to be shoeing mules. The blacksmith took his family back to Ohio last October; said he wanted to get there before snow started flying.

The man said the blacksmith was a restless sort anyhow, the sort who wouldn't stay long wherever he went.

※

When Hesed brought my breakfast, I was already up and in my chair. She sat in the other chair, facing me.

"Grayhawk, I don't mean to pry, but I can't stop worrying about your wife and daughter. Were they . . .?"

I took a deep breath, tried to marshal emerging emotions, and began my answer, knowing I could never mention Keevah's name, even if I had to lie.

"I spent far too much time searching for the blacksmith as I traveled through Ohio and Kentucky on my way back to them. When I did get home, our village was ashes, and everyone was gone. Nobody would tell me anything except the army had rounded up all the Indians and started moving them out west to the Indian Territories. The few whites who took over the land burned the village and put up their own buildings not more than a quarter mile away.

"I went to Fort Smith, where the soldiers who escorted the Cherokees were stationed. The army couldn't or wouldn't tell me anything about where they had been. So, I started searching among the Indians in the territory."

"And . . . did you find . . .?"

"I found one woman who knew them during the first few weeks of the march; she remembered them because she was struck by my wife's name, Ahyoka."

"Ahyoka, I know the name," Hesed said softly. "It means, 'she brought happiness.'"

"Our daughter's name was Ester; she was four years old when I left them to meet the men in North Carolina. The woman told me she looked for Ahyoka after the army released them in the Territories. She found three others who were in the group with Ahyoka. They told her our daughter, Ester, died from exhaustion one evening after the day's march. Ahyoka refused to let anyone tell the army; she said she would tell them in the morning.

"When morning broke, they found Ahyoka holding Ester in her arms. Both were dead. Every person in the group knew Ahyoka was exhausted from carrying Ester, but they all believed she had died from a broken heart. They were right; I know how she loved that child.

"After I found my wife and daughter had died on the trail, I followed every route they might have taken, searching for someone who could tell me where they were buried—or even if they were buried . . ."

"Have you—"

"None of them even knew where they were. They couldn't stay long enough to bury anyone. The Army always took care of that to keep the march moving."

"I know," Hesed whispered.

"Hesed, I'm sorry to bring up your loss again."

"Now I understand," she said softly, "how you knew about my story." Her dark eyes glistened with tears. "We both lost part of ourselves on that trail. I am so sorry, Grayhawk."

"I continued searching for months . . . lost my way: I couldn't deal with the pain of losing them and of what I had done. The devil alcohol got me. One day, I woke up with a splitting headache. I was on a barge taking pigs down the Mississippi river to New Orleans. If I walked on, signed on, or was shanghaied, I don't know even to this day.

"Anyway, I did as I was told; I slopped the hogs and shoveled the pens all the way down the river. In New Orleans, they paid me and let me go.

"Hesed, it's to my eternal shame, but the first thing I did was find a den of alcohol. I don't remember much after that. A lot of time passed. I do remember one night I wish I could forget. It happened in a bar. I was half sober because I had spent the last of my money. I was begging anyone to buy me a drink.

"This man approached me. I knew him—a liar and a cheat, but he always had money. He offered me a drink; I took it. Then he said he would take the scrimshaw I wore around my neck for payment. I kept it in a bag even back then, but in a moment of drunkenness, I must have shown it to someone. Somehow, he knew what I had."

Hesed's dark eyes became impenetrable as every expression faded from her face. She riveted her gaze on me, alert to my every word. I paused for a moment, puzzled by her intensity. Something I said had triggered this change from casual conversation to silent interrogation. She was in her Indian mode, with no explanation why. It was useless to ask.

"I wouldn't give it to him, so he grabbed and jerked hard enough to pull me to the floor. He had his knife in his hand before I realized what was happening. He cut the buffalo-hide strap from around my neck. Before I could get up, he was out the door.

"I chased him despite the other men yelling he'd kill me. He was gone. I spent most of the night searching every sleazy bar and joint I could find. I would rather die than lose my scrimshaw. When I saw him, he was leading another man from a bar around to an alley. I followed close to them in the dark. In the light of a side window, the thief showed my scrimshaw and named a price.

"'That's mine,' I yelled. 'You stole that from me.'"

"The thief cursed and pulled out a pocket pistol. The other man fled. I couldn't tell you what I did next—it's all a blank. Askira's training and my reflexes must have taken over. Several men who had been watching later told me I kicked the pistol away and broke the man's knife-arm when he tried to stab me. I don't know what else I did. All I remember was staring down at the man lying in front of me, shocked at what I saw. He lay still, his head facing one side at an awkward angle—his neck broken.

"That's when the deputies came. I spent the next three weeks in a filthy New Orleans jail cell with a window too much like Doctor Kendrick's treatment room. The sheriff told me to count the days—twenty-one days. Then I'd hang—in three weeks—when the circuit judge arrived. 'Just to keep it legal,' he said."

I paused to focus on Hesed dark eyes, resembling those of a doe now. "Yes, Hesed, I have sunk as low as a man can go. And, I have killed a man—in anger."

"Because of a stolen scrimshaw?"

I focused on a spot on the far wall of my room, near the ceiling.

"It was more than a scrimshaw, it . . ."

"Go on," she whispered.

Her voice and manner were gentle, but I sensed urgency in her probing.

"Hesed, I loved Ahyoka, my Cherokee wife. But, long before her, I loved another woman. We never married. She gave me the scrimshaw. We were just children when she gave it to me, but it has always been special to me—it always will be for as long as I live."

Hesed's complexion couldn't hide the growing paleness of her face. She appeared stunned, unable to speak.

"I fathered a son with her. A son I have never seen—my son, whom I have been trying to find for years. He would be a man now, my only living family."

"I am late," Hesed whispered. "I must go; I have chores to do. You are alive, so later, you will tell me how you got out of jail, won't you?"

"I will, Hesed, but please don't say anything about my scrimshaw or the woman who gave it to me. Don't tell anyone—not even Ciara. It's personal."

Her answer was slow in coming, but I never doubted her.

"I—I won't."

"They took my scrimshaw and Bible from me while I was in jail; those were the only things I owned. Those three weeks were the longest the scrimshaw has been out of my touch . . . ever."

"Thank you for sharing with me."

She left me puzzled. What could I have said to trigger such interest in my story? And why was her usual graceful departure so awkward and deliberate—when it was clear she wanted to run?

I could make no sense of her ungainly leaving, but I knew I had to tell her the full story of how I escaped those Louisiana gallows. I began recalling the details in my mind so I could try to make sense of it to her.

They said I sat in that reeking jail cell for twenty days. I don't know; I didn't keep track of the times the odd window at the top of the wall traded its mocking hints of day for night. It didn't matter. I had done with my bare hands what they said, and I would hang for it. But I knew it was not my worst. I'd left Keevah with child, my son, whom I'd never seen. And I'd left Ahyoka and my daughter, Ester, defenseless and alone at the very time they needed me.

From the coal mine in Scotland to Keevah in Boston to the Tennessee mountains, every family I had was either ripped from me, or I'd abandoned them. Now, I had no one, not even the McDowell sisters, who had never liked me. Even so, they were better than no family at all. And, Father McDowell, I'll never know how much he sacrificed to give me a new beginning in America—only for me to hang as a drunken murderer.

Very shortly, I would die—alone, with no family to care. That grieved me more than the dying.

When Hesed came with my evening meal, I shared how I'd hit bottom in that jail cell. She sat motionless, without expression, but I sensed a tension between us. The same urgency I saw in her earlier was still nudging. She wanted to know something about me I wasn't telling. She never spoke her questions—but bored into my soul with those intense eyes as if dissecting my every word.

"When they came to take me from my cell, I thought I would soon die. Instead, they took me to a room with nothing but a small table and three straight-backed chairs. Two well-dressed gentlemen sat at the table on which my scrimshaw and Bible bag lay. "Neither the sheriff nor any deputies were there. The jailer didn't enter; he just shut the door and left. The businessmen rose and told me to sit, which I did. The men remained standing.

"They told me I was not the type of customer they wanted hanging around their establishments. They were interceding because they believed what I did was in self-defense, and they didn't like the sheriff's view of justice; it was giving their entire city a bad reputation.

"They told me the sheriff didn't agree with them. He argued I ought to hang. As it turned out, they convinced him otherwise. From several veiled hints, I gathered their means of persuasion included blackmail. The sheriff said he would consider my release an escape. If he ever caught me in New Orleans again, I would never leave alive; he would make certain of it.

"The men told me they would give me a horse and supplies, and I was to get out of Louisiana and never come back. If they ever saw me again, they would turn me in and never say another word in my defense. I picked up my scrimshaw and Bible before they escorted me out a back door straight to a nearby livery. They gave me a rundown nag, a worn-out saddle, and a bag of dried bread and salted fish. Before I could say a word, they told me to go. I left and never looked back."

I stopped telling my story and focused on Hesed's reaction. She showed neither approval nor disapproval of me because of my less-than-gallant way of escaping death on the gallows. Instead, she reminded me of a hunting hound, casting for the trail, impatient to find the spoor of her suspected game.

"Where did you go?"

"I wandered west to Texas, looking for but never finding anyone who knew the Norwegian blacksmith, or his son. I assumed my son took the name of the blacksmith.

"I got tired of working whatever odd jobs I could find, and I got tired of being hungry, so I volunteered with General Winfield Scott's army at the Mexican border. I heard the Texans were having troubles with Mexicans and were fighting the Mexican Army. Mexico refused to accept Texas's independence. General Scott was recruiting volunteers to join his regular army troops to stop Mexico. My age didn't seem to be an issue—nor did my lack of skill with a musket. The army wanted men to back up and support the young men on the front lines.

"In less than two months, we sailed south to Vera Cruz, Mexico, and right into a war. We captured Vera Cruz from the Mexicans easily enough and moved inland, where we fought many skirmishes and one big battle at Cerro Gordo. I got a bellyful of shooting and killing there. The carnage was every bit as bad as what I'd seen aboard those French warships.

"I ended up in a field hospital at the city of Puebla while General Scott moved on to Mexico City. The Army established a garrison at Puebla to protect their supply line from Vera Cruz and the Citadel, which served as a hospital for hundreds of sick and wounded soldiers. My wound healed quickly, so I spent the rest of the war helping surgeons with the injured.

"To retake Puebla, the Mexicans laid siege on us for a good month, but we fought off every attempt. About the middle of October, after General Scott's army captured Mexico City, the Mexican army surrendered. Not long after, we began our trek back to Vera Cruz to board ships to take us back to Texas. Most of us volunteers mustered out of the Army sometime in mid-November."

Hesed left the room to get a pitcher of water and two clean glasses. After filling both with water, she sat and again questioned me.

"I see how you learned about army field hospitals. What did you do next?"

CHAPTER 14

I told her how ten of us bought good horses, civilian clothing, and supplies. With what was left of our army pay, we started out for Santa Fe. We figured we could make it easily by Christmas. We did, but three of our group who had suffered more serious injuries in Mexico decided to stay and heal in Santa Fe. The rest planned to follow the mountain branch of the Santa Fe Trail north and spend the rest of the winter at Bent's Fort.

I was hesitant about taking the mountain branch at this time of year, but a lot of freight went over that trail with numerous horses and mules. Bent's Fort was not a military fort but a large trading post and the last place for traders or explorers to stock up with supplies before continuing on the trail or going west into the mountains. My interest in the fort was its freight business. That meant a lot of work for blacksmiths and farriers. One of them might be the blacksmith or his son—my son.

The weather was pleasant in Santa Fe, and we were all in high spirits as we prepared for the trip. Two days after Christmas, seven of us set out for Bent's Fort on horseback with two pack mules loaded with supplies. Everyone told us the mountain branch of the Santa Fe Trail was the fastest way to get there.

Santa Fe Trail, Mexico 1847

Six days later, we were at Willow Springs Station and ready to start over the pass.

"So, this is what the Mexicans call *Raton*?" I heard one lad from southern Louisiana scoff. "Means mouse in Spanish. This will be easy."

"Don't bet on it," another said. "Old man Paco at the station says it's hard and dangerous, even in summer."

Old Paco was right. The higher up the mountain we went, the steeper and rockier the trail became. Snow from recent storms packed into crevasses and in sheltered areas between boulders and under trees. Distant mountain peaks were white. Winter was not holding back in these mountains. I hoped we could get over the pass without further snowfall.

Footing for the horses and mules became more treacherous, and our progress slowed the higher we went. At times, snow drifts hid visible clues of the trail. When we strayed from the path, ice-covered rocks and items discarded by previous travelers became perils for our animals.

Late on the afternoon of our first day, one of our sure-footed mules tripped over a snow-covered piece of a broken wagon wheel and went down. Even after removing his heavy pack, we were unable to get him on his feet. After clearing away snow, we saw his right foreleg was broken. We had no other choice but to shoot him where he lay and leave the carcass for the bears or wolves.

Coming darkness forced us to camp within a hundred yards of the carcass. Snow began falling as we finished setting up camp. Before we finished dividing the supplies from the fallen mule's pack, new snow was coating the sides of our tents. Following our military habits, we each pulled a two-hour guard shift with one other man throughout the night.

One of our men, Jacob Endicott, whom we all called Endy, had been a lieutenant in the regular army. After Mexico surrendered, many officers like him mustered out of the army along with hundreds of volunteers. He still carried his military-issue Colt Walker revolver. The new type of handgun was more powerful than anything else we had, and it carried six rounds. All our other guns were smoothbore muzzle-loading percussion muskets and one percussion rifle. The rifle, though muzzle-loading like the muskets, fired its round farther and with greater accuracy.

The new revolver was always with the man on guard duty. He would in turn pass it on to his replacement. None of us knew if bears in these mountains would be hibernating or not. Wolves could still be about, so with the dead mule close by, we were taking no chances. Having six rapid shots instead of one might save a life from any large predator.

Snow fell all night. We arose early, ate a breakfast of cold tortillas, and attempted to break camp. Snow continued to fall as the wind began to swirl and deposit drifts of the white stuff on the lee side of every tree and boulder. Before we could complete packing our gear, the wind picked up, making it impossible for us to see beyond a few feet.

Accepting that we were bound to this place until the storm passed, we tried with varying degrees of success to re-erect our used army-issue two-man pup tents. Leaky as they were, they still provided some protection from the biting wind. Before dark, the wind let up, and two of us ventured out to feed and care for the horses and mule.

When we broke camp the next morning, the sky was clear. We tried to move on, but the new snow made it impossible to tell where the trail went. After hours of tedious effort, we found ourselves less than four hundred yards from our last camp. We could go no further. We cleared snow to set up camp, and everyone set about gathering firewood.

Because we were on horseback and not pulling wagons, we figured it would take us less time than the usual 12 days to cross the pass. Once over the mountains, we reckoned it would take us another two weeks to reach Bent's Fort. We provisioned enough reserve food for us and the animals for ten extra days. We should arrive at Bent's Fort with supplies to spare. But we had already consumed an amount equal to a quarter of our reserves. We cut rations by a third to each man. The horses and mule would need full rations for energy and to keep from freezing, at least until we got out of the mountains.

Two days later, clear skies and a bright sun began to melt enough snow to allow us to follow the trail. We made slow but steady time. Each of us had packed a few pan-fried biscuits in our pockets. We ate these throughout the day as we picked our way without stopping. Before the sun dropped behind the last peak to our west, we made camp. Our animals were exhausted. Plunging through deep drifts was hard on them, even though we alternated lead horses to break a path for the following animals.

Endy, the former army lieutenant whose powerful revolver our guards carried, spoke up as we ate our meal of fried salt pork and pan bread.

"I know horses—used them my entire life, civilian and army, and I will tell you we can't continue to push them like we've done today.

We need to start later in the day, rest at midday, and stop earlier. We take care of them; they'll take care of us."

Several men joined me in muttering agreement.

"It means we will make less distance each day while we're in deep snow, and it will take more time to get to Bent's Fort. We need to go on half rations . . . as a precaution until we get off this mountain." We all agreed.

Progress for the next three days was slow. We reckoned we were within a day's ride from the summit when we stopped and set up camp. Our guards hollered to tell us snow began falling after we crawled into our tents. Soon after, swirling gusts began driving snow through every opening in our war-torn canvas shelters.

We ventured out to check and re-tie any loosened tent-ropes as well as we could. By the time we finished, the falling snow reduced our visibility to a few yards. Every man, including those on guard, crawled into his tent and tied the entry flaps tight to reduce snow from blowing in. The freezing wind blew hard all night and well into the next day.

Several men tried to venture out in dropping temperatures to care for the animals. One attempt to get food to them was successful. Almost blinded by the wind-blown snow, the two men found their way back to camp by the sound of our firing a weapon every few minutes. We decided then the animals weren't worth losing someone's life. They might get hungry, but they would survive without our help.

It was two days before we could dig out and scavenge enough dry wood for a huge fire to warm ourselves. While surrounding the fire and eating our first hot meal in three days, two men said they were going back to Santa Fe.

They argued we were not even at the top of the pass yet, and Bent's Fort was farther still. We could leave them their share of rations. They planned to stay there until the snow settled down enough to follow the trail and then head back down. We could not convince them otherwise. They stayed; we moved on.

I hoped they made it. I never heard anything more about them.

It took us two more exhausting and slow-going days to cross over the top. Another hour of slogging through deep drifts found us at a spot sheltered by large boulders and surrounded by a thick stand of scrub trees the Mexicans call *piñons*. We set up camp as light snow began sifting down from a darkening sky.

Our troubles soon began. We were all gathering firewood when one of the men ran back into camp, yelling at the top of his lungs. Another man, Williams, had slipped and fallen and had cut his thigh with his camp axe. We all rushed to the bloody scene. A tourniquet slowed the bleeding, but we had to carry him back to camp. Another man and I worked to stop the bleeding while others returned to gathering enough firewood for warmth and cooking.

It was a bad wound. It required a surgeon's care. We had no surgeon. Our military experiences taught us to do what we could with what we had. Remembering what I'd seen done on the French warships and at the army field hospital at Puebla. I cut enough of the man's leg tissue away to find the cut artery. With a red-hot tip of my army-issue knife, we cauterized the artery and several small bleeders. Our patient had passed out by this time. We closed the wound and sewed it with the heavy thread we had brought along to mend our tents.

When we finished, our shirts and pants were stiff with frozen blood. The other men had the large coffee pot steaming with hot water. Stripping our bloody clothes off and washing our bodies with snow and hot water while standing in the freezing mountain snowstorm was sheer torture.

Even with men holding blankets to shield us from the breeze, the inescapable cold ravaged our bodies. Shivering uncontrollably, we struggled into dry clothing, crawled into our tent, and pulled blankets over our heads. I thanked God for Paco, the old Mexican caretaker at Willow Springs Station, who convinced us to buy more blankets before starting up Raton Pass.

I must have been in my cocoon for hours before I crawled out. With a blanket wrapped around me, I joined the men around the fire. Endy was talking.

"Williams can't ride, and someone needs to stay with him. I'll take Grayhawk, and we'll go to Bent's Fort for help. We'll take my mare and the Roman-nosed bay, along with the pack mule."

"Those are our best horses," one man exclaimed.

"I know. With good horses, the two of us can make faster time, but we will need extra rations. The rest of you stay here."

"If you take our extra rations, what are we going to eat before you come back?"

Endy shrugged his shoulders and raised an eyebrow. "You have provisions and horses; you will not starve."

The thought of eating his horse made the man swallow hard, but he nodded he understood.

The men divided the rations and equipment without further comment. Endy gave his Colt Walker revolver and ammunition to the man taking leadership of the camp. It was a powerful gun, but it was also heavy. We didn't need extra weight, and we had already planned on taking the longer-range percussion rifle in case we had to hunt for meat. Increasing wind and snow soon drove us all into our tents for the night.

After two more days of heavy snowfall, Endy and I left at sunup. New snow made it difficult to travel, but we needed to move on for the injured man's sake. Often, one of us had to dismount to probe drifts and determine if we were about to venture over hard ground or sink into snow above our heads. We did get better at judging where to go to find the trail based on open areas between the irregular tree spacing.

Several times, we almost lost a horse because we urged it to go where it didn't want to. We soon learned to trust our animals and let them pick their way at their steady but safer pace.

Three more days, taking frequent breaks to rest the horses and mule, allowed us to keep going until dusk settled in like a chilling blanket over the mountains. Each evening before dark, we made camp, built a fire to heat our meal, melt enough snow for our animals, and fill our canteens. After tethering and feeding the horses and mule, we crawled into our pup tent and pulled blankets around us. Sleeping with the canteens next to our bodies kept them from freezing during the night.

The fourth day found us plodding under a dark and lowering sky—more snow clouds. According to old Paco's descriptions, we were far short of where we should be. The drifts were not as deep as they had been near the top, but struggling through drifts was still hard on the horses. And, hard for us when we had to walk to pick up the trail. We stopped and made camp when the freshening breeze contained a few flakes of new snow.

Knowing we were in for a storm during the night, we tethered the horses in a stand of scrub *piñons* and set up our camp a couple hundred feet away in an area sheltered by three taller pines. Within minutes after we had crawled under our blankets for the night, the wind began beating the sides of our tent. Soon, snow was blowing sideways. We tied the flaps of the tent closed as tight as we could. Wind-blown flakes still wafted in and settled on the blankets around our heads as if to drive home the point winter, not us, ruled in these mountains. We hunkered down for the coming blizzard.

After digging our way out of the tent two mornings later, we found drifts up to our waists in places. Three men, one injured, waited up on the mountain for us, so we saddled the horses, packed the mule, and started down the trail again. It took another three days of strenuous trudging and riding before we reached the valley where old Paco said we should have been two weeks ago. Snow was not so deep here, and the animals had much easier going. Though exhausted from the long day, we made a late camp with high spirits and hopes we would not let our companions down.

Those high spirits plummeted the next morning when we arose to find our mule gone. His broken tether rope and the multitude of tracks in the snow told the story. Endy's horse, a well-muscled sorrel mare, had deep scratch marks on her back and shoulder as well as bite marks on her neck above her withers. Her skin around the bites twitched as she turned her head to see the cause of her pain.

"These are puma tracks." Endy pointed the rifle at some clear tracks. "One large one and a couple smaller ones—maybe last year's cubs."

"What are pumas?"

"Mountain lions. They are almost always alone, even when hunting. Three of them together means a female with twins. Our animals were easy game for them. Looks like one of the cubs tried to take down my horse."

"It couldn't?"

"Not easy for it, but I think something else drew it away. The mule's tether rope is broken. He must have panicked, broken the rope and run. That triggered the cats' instinct to chase. He wouldn't have a chance against a grown puma, not to mention one with two nearly grown cubs. Come on; I'm sure we'll find him."

It was easy to follow the tracks to the partly eaten carcass. We stopped at a distance to look for any sign of big cats. Nothing was visible. I felt relieved because we had one single-shot, muzzle-loading rifle—not adequate for three pumas.

"Keep an eye out." Endy released the cocked hammer on the rifle and walked to the carcass. He leaned the rifle next to the mule's opened belly and stooped over to unfasten the halter from its head.

I was scanning through the trees when I saw a tawny flash out the corner of my eye. I whipped around to see the puma flying over Endy. My friend's sheepskin hood was in the animal's mouth. Twisting in mid-air like a playful housecat, its forelegs groped for a hold on the man. Endy screamed in pain as several of the puma's claws found flesh and slammed him backwards. Even as he fell, he slapped both hands on his head.

Hollering at the top of my lungs, I started running toward them. The puma's leap carried it past the fallen man. In an instant, it turned and bounded into the thick stand of *piñons*.

Endy lay on his back in the snow. His large fur-lined head gear lay many feet away. Both his hands clasped his bare head. Blood was already oozing between his fingers. I knelt beside him and pulled one hand away to see what the cat had done.

"You're bleeding badly. We've got to stop it."

"She tried to bite me, got my hat when I ducked, hit my head with her claws, felt like a mule kicked me."

"We have to stop the bleeding." I stripped the heavy scarf from my neck.

Then, the big cat screamed. The sound, though far back in the trees, sent chills down my back. I'd never heard anything like it.

"That's her victory scream after she makes a kill," Endy said.

"Sounds like the devil himself. Will she come back?"

"Not with two of us here. You did the right thing when you yelled and ran toward us."

"Let's get your scarf. It'll take two to bandage this."

I opened his coat enough to pull the scarf from his neck. After moving his hands away, I examined the wounds. Two jagged gouges ran from his forehead to the top of his head. Ragged flaps of his scalp, torn loose by the cat's claws, lay attached to the sides of the bleeding gouges.

"This may hurt. I need to move parts of skin back into the scratches."

He winced in silent consent as I worked at the bloody task. His hair was long enough to hold back from the open wounds as I pushed and pulled scalp pieces back into place. After I did what I could, I wrapped one scarf into a big roll and pressed it over the wounds.

"This will absorb blood like a bandage and keep the skin in place. Now, I'm going to wrap the other scarf under your chin and over your head to secure the bandage. It needs to be tight to stop the bleeding. You won't be able to move your jaw. You ready?"

He never moved all during the time I wrapped and tied the scarf. I knew it hurt. I recovered his sheepskin hood, pressed it down over the bulky scarves, and cleaned what blood I could from our hands and from his face and neck. As I did so, I noticed holes and tears in the leather. The puma had bitten through it when Endy ducked. Had its teeth found his head, the injuries would be much worse.

"We were lucky," I said as I fingered one of the holes.

Endy's response was a grunt and a grimace.

"Can you walk? We need to get out of here. That she-puma is going to hang around. She's not going to give up this meal ticket without a fight. She has those cubs too. She'd fight a grizzly to protect them."

"Help me up. I'm not going down easy."

I helped him to his knees, where he took a moment to regain his bearings. I was surprised at how much blood stained the snow where his head had lain.

With my help, he stood and took a few wobbly steps.

"Take it slow; you'll be alright."

"She knocked me down good. You better carry the rifle. Let me stand here a minute."

We made a slow trip back to camp. He wasted no time in brushing most of the snow off a nearby boulder and sitting on it. I studied his face as I broke dead limbs off the *piñons*. He looked pale. I didn't like it—I had seen men die of shock.

"You building up the fire again?"

"Yes. We're staying here until I'm sure you're able to travel. We both need to warm up and eat something hot."

"I'll be alright to go."

"You took quite a blow and left a lot of blood back there. I'll decide when we leave—no arguing."

He explored my face for a few moments before lowering his gaze to his feet. When he did look up, he nodded.

"I picked the right man," he murmured.

I warmed up the last of our beef jerky and fried enough pan bread to last us several days. Endy nibbled at the food while I packed up the camp and readied the horses. The injured horse could not carry a man in the saddle because of her wounds, nor did we have anything to treat them with.

I tried the packsaddle the mule had carried. It was better, but not a good fit for the horse. Nevertheless, we had to use it. Those supplies were essential if we were to survive in this wilderness. Using the injured horse as our pack animal meant only one man could ride at a time—the other would have to walk. We took turns. Endy's rides became longer each time. I did not want him exhausted.

He rode most of the time for the next two days. When we stopped for the night of the second day, the sorrel stood spread-legged with her head hanging. I removed the pack and checked her bite wounds.

"Endy, you better come look at this."

I watched as he examined the swelling around the punctures. A couple of puffy holes near her withers, close to where the packsaddle rested, were seeping a bloody and foul-smelling discharge.

"Cat Fever," he said. "She's a real trooper to go this long without complaining. I should have paid more attention to her. She's a good horse."

"What could you have done?"

He shook his head. "Not much. Horses don't handle these kinds of injuries well. Big cat bites are bad, and we don't have anything to treat her."

"We can't leave her here."

"No, we can't. And she can't travel. Look at her. She's one sick pony, and it'll get worse. This will kill her . . . no matter what we do."

"How long?"

"Days. We can't let her suffer. We need to put her down." He stepped away from her and said, "Let's make camp down the trail. Put the pack on your horse. We'll both have to walk."

After I placed the packsaddle and camp gear on my horse, Endy picked up the rifle.

"Take the horse a hundred yards down the trail and wait for me."

I reached out and grasped the rifle forestock. "I'll do it."

Without a word, he dropped his gaze to his feet. I expected him to agree.

After a moment, he looked up and locked his eyes onto mine. His grip on the rifle tightened. He slowly shook his head.

"She's my horse."

I started walking, leading the healthy horse with me. When the shot echoed between the mountains on the sides of the narrow valley, I stopped and waited.

Endy caught up, looked at me for a second, then gestured down the trail. We walked in silence. It was almost dark before we stopped. We ate a few pieces of cold, left-over pan bread and made camp for the night.

The next morning, we packed our one horse with the supplies we thought were essential, leaving everything else on the ground. We walked in silence for a long while before we stopped to rest.

"You holding up?"

"I'll be okay. Need a break."

"You lost a lot of blood back there. Scalp wounds bleed."

"Hurts too. We'll be out of this valley and onto the prairie in a day or two. First chance we get to shoot a deer or a pronghorn, we'd better take it; ever seen a pronghorn antelope?"

"No, I haven't."

"You'll be amazed, but we won't see one until we get on the prairie. They're smaller than deer but faster. They'll be watching us; they're curious, but they like to keep their distance. We'll need to keep a sharp eye out to see one before it spots us and moves out of rifle range."

"I'll be watching."

"We'll have a better chance at a deer while we're still in these mountains—maybe in the foothills. Keep an eye out. We'll never make the fort without meat."

Two days later, while I stalked a small herd of deer, Endy held our horse and rested on a fallen stump near a clump of *piñons*. After trailing for hours, I managed to get close enough to take aim at a yearling.

The frigid air sharpened the echoes of the rifle shot. All but one of the herd bounded into a thick clump of *piñons*.

Carrying the small deer over my back, I tramped through the snow until I could holler to Endy. He met me halfway with the horse. We spent the rest of the day butchering and smoking the meat over a *piñon* and sagebrush fire. I was disappointed at how little meat we ended up with.

Our hungry horse spent the day pawing snow to find sparse grass. Endy told me to tether him away from the *piñon* trees and sagebrush. He said eating those could make him sick. What little grass he found may have been the most he'd eaten since we left the mountain.

With the day's rest, Endy claimed to feel better. Confident in our ability to make Bent's Fort, we left early the next day with our supply of half-smoked meat. That day, we made it out of mountain country and into rolling hills of prairie. Instead of steep hills, trees, and boulders, we faced either patches of shallow wind-blown snow or drifts over our heads.

We had a harder time with the cold here than up on the mountain. The prairie wind never stopped blowing. It stole heat from our bodies right through the fur-lined clothing the old timers in Santa Fe said we needed. The Roman-nosed bay was one tough horse. Though half-starved, he continued carrying Endy through the cold without complaint and only with dead grasses and weeds he could find under the snow for nourishment.

One week later, chilled to the bone from the biting wind, exhausted, and with miles to go, we sat huddled in our blankets before a too-small fire, trying to dry our socks and warm our frost-bitten feet.

"I can't make it, Lanny. You'll have to go ahead."

"Not a chance. You're coming with me."

"Can't. Don't have strength. You need to go. Tell the rescue party where I am."

"I'm not leaving you. You'll never live through a night alone without a fire. We're going together. You'll make it."

"I might not make it anyway. That puma might have taken me out—like she did my horse."

"You are not a horse, and you're going with me. We leave everything except blankets and food, and you ride the horse. Now eat."

After three more days of trudging in snow and body-numbing cold, I was exhausted. It was a struggle to think. At times, I would lose my focus and stray from the snow-covered trail.

Endy fared worse. I wrapped every blanket we had around him, but he often shivered uncontrollably. Other times, his fever peaked till he begged me to loosen the blanket ties. Often, I could make no sense of his garbled mumbling.

Early afternoon, I lost my way. We stopped next to a thicket of scrub brush. I hoped the brush would protect us from the unrelenting wind. I helped my half-frozen companion off the horse and set him close to the brush. He was alive but helpless. He didn't even try to speak.

With hands numb from the cold, I scavenged as much firewood as I could from the scrub and sagebrush and tried to build a fire. It was frustrating. Even using tinder of tiny twigs and sagebrush tops, I could not get a vigorous fire. The frozen twigs and branches would smolder and smoke before yielding little flame and heat. Placing more twigs and branches on the weak flames increased the smoke and my fears before they too began their feeble burn.

All the food we had were some pieces of pan bread I fried several days ago and two frozen strips of half-smoked venison. As I tried to warm the venison and take the frost out of the panbread, I thought of God. My long-ago passion to serve as a minister still nudged from deep within me. But now, that seemed to have been the dream of a total stranger. My many failures to serve as I wanted and my situation here—alone and lost in this desolate frozen prairie—was my reality now. And worse, I was failing again.

This time, I would fail my companions, Endy, whose life depended on me. He would never survive the hardship of another day like this one. And the men I had left on the mountain, they would freeze or starve if no rescuers knew they were there. I would keep trying, plodding till I died, but I knew I could never reach the fort. It was too far and too cold.

Endy and I told each other weeks ago of our belief in God, but we never prayed together. I knew my reluctance to pray with anyone was due to my shame of failing my God, of failing in so many ways, in failing my families, in failing those I had loved, and in failing to share His story with men I'd known—ones who needed to know.

I yearned to pray, but could I dare approach God now? Could I expect Him to listen to me? Would He even want to? I had no right to lift my voice to Him. My broken life and failures were offensive—even to me.

To close out the world, I shut my eyes and hung my head. I wanted to ask for forgiveness, for Him to rescue us. I couldn't. I didn't deserve either. For the sakes of Endy and the men I'd left behind, I wanted to cry out and plead for the only hope they had—God's mercy. I tried—all I could muster was a broken whisper, "Jesus . . .". Every other word hid from me within the frozen fog sapping my brain.

We didn't see or hear the Indians until they rode their horses into our frozen camp. With signs and broken English, their leader said they had seen smoke from our pitiful campfire. They were a Cheyenne hunting party on their way to a traditional winter hunting ground. Their people, wintering near the fort, depended on the deer and wapiti elk meat the hunters would bring back.

They built up our fire, fed us a hot meal, and sent a man back to tell the fort proprietors to send a rescue party. After wrapping a heavy buffalo robe around us, the hunting party moved on, leaving one man to keep our fire going. That buffalo hide saved us more than the food and fire did, for it stopped the merciless wind from stealing life from our bodies.

Three evenings later, dressed in dry and warm clothing, I sat by Endy's bed, feeding him warm gravy and bits of meat from a thick venison stew. His frostbitten hands, wrapped in bulky bandages, lay useless by his sides. Groups of at least a half-dozen mountain men crowded into our tiny room each time we told and retold the story of our trip and of the men stranded on Raton Pass. In the absence of a doctor, some fur trappers wintering at the fort used their mountain-grown and sworn-by remedies to treat the infection in Endy's wounds. Whatever they did brought his fever down.

Twenty days later, all our companions, including injured Williams, were safe for the winter. To those of us who had crossed the mountain, Bent's Fort was a roughhewn piece of heaven.

Henrysville, Indian Territory of the United States, 1850

Hesed didn't try to hide her sigh of relief, nor did she veer from her mission to find out more about me.

"And you kept your scrimshaw and Bible with you all that time?"

"I did. Regular army soldiers had stricter rules and discipline than we volunteers did. I had to conceal my scrimshaw from officers several times during training, but after we boarded the boats to Vera Cruz, about anything was allowed. The army was more lenient with volunteers because they wanted bodies to fight the Mexicans.

"I left Bent's Fort in the spring of '48, alone, to travel north. It was a long shot, but I figured to search among the Oregon Trail travelers all the way back to Independence, Missouri, for my son. The Cheyenne let me through, but I found most of the plains Indians were not pleased to see me. They were of no help.

"Frustrated after a year of failures to find anything, and after several narrow escapes from hostile Indians who wanted my horse, my gun, and—"

"And your scalp?"

"That too; I headed back south. I went back to searching eastward along the Santa Fe Trail and throughout the Indian Territories, hoping it might still be possible to find something about Ahyoka and Ester. A year later, I arrived here, at your town of Henrysville, the same way I left Bent's Fort—alone."

Hesed stared at me. Her Indian eyes shared nothing—not a single emotion or hidden thought.

"Then, you found me lying in the dirt in your street."

"I'm glad we did," she said. "You certainly knew how to get our attention, and I know one little Indian boy who will be forever grateful to you."

I didn't tell Hesed of those long months where I relived the mistakes, misfortunes, and griefs of losing every person I considered family. During those years wandering the frontier, I queried every person I met about the Norwegian blacksmith and any young man they may have known by the same last name—my son. No one could tell me anything. It was a search fueled by determination, with fading hope of success.

Chapter 15

"Your Bible and scrimshaw must mean a great deal to you," Hesed said. "Those Indians would trade about anything for a scrimshaw."

I nodded.

"I've seen your Bible, the first time by accident, if you remember. May I see your scrimshaw? We don't see any here in the Territories."

I hesitated, then thought it could do no harm. I slid my treasure out of its leather pouch and handed it to her. As she reached to take it, her hand quivered for a second. As her gaze took in the details of the carving, her face blanched. Even her copper complexion could not hide the effect of what she saw. In a moment, she regained her outward composure but couldn't squelch the tremor in her voice.

"A girl gave this to you when you were both young. Right?"

"Yes. Hesed . . . what is it?" Her hands were shaking.

"Hesed, look at me."

She refused.

"You know something about this scrimshaw, don't you!"

She focused on the object in her hand, ignoring my glare.

After a long moment, she looked up, drew a deep breath, and hugged the scrimshaw to her breast. Her eyes narrowed under those level brows and searched deep as they locked onto mine. She stood and shifted her stance to face me square on. Her jaw clenched as her lips pressed together. Then she spoke.

"Grayhawk, what is your given name—your Scottish family name?"

My gut dropped. I reached for the scrimshaw.

"Give me that."

She surrendered it as if it were burning her fingers. But she didn't back off.

"Your name?"

In a moment, her expression relaxed. Her voice softened to a coaxing plea.

"Before you became Indian . . . before you married Ahyoka . . . and why Grayhawk?"

I hesitated, not sure if I should say any more about my past. Hesed clearly knew something about my scrimshaw. What she knew could lead me to my son or even to Keevah. Answering her might be worth it, but . . .

"Please, Grayhawk," she whispered. "Please?"

"Ahyoka's family name was Whitehawk. Her mother and father and both pairs of grandparents had hawk in their names. I don't know if it was clan tradition or coincidence. It didn't matter. It was important to me to be part of her family—to belong, so Ahyoka and I combined the first three letters of my family name with a 'y' and added 'hawk' to form Grayhawk. That's who I've been ever since. I ignored my adopted name. It was no longer important."

"And your given and family name?"

I paused, uncertain if I should say more. Her level brows, when raised in question with an encouraging nod of her head and a hint of a smile, didn't seem so demanding.

"Landsdale Grahame," I confessed softly.

Even as her hands darted to her mouth, I saw color drain from her face.

"Oh, dear God. Oh, my dear God."

"Hesed, you know something! What is it? Tell me. You could help me find my son—my family. Hesed, please. Tell me!"

"I'm sorry, Grayhawk." She backed toward the door and clasped her hands in front of her mouth. Tears began welling in her eyes. "I can't tell you now. Believe me, I can't. I am so sorry. I must go."

When the front door slammed, I knew she was running.

I tried rising. Pain put me down before my broken leg touched the floor. My own body held me prisoner again with the goal of my quest so near but still beyond reach. I pleaded to unhearing walls that Hesed not forsake me, not now, not when I was this close.

Early evening, a young Indian girl wearing a flour-sack dress and hand-me-down moccasins, much too large for her, brought me my meal. I knew right away it came from the hotel kitchen.

"Where is Hesed?" I asked.

"Hesed with Ciara. Baby come. She help. I bring food morning and night."

"How is Ciara doing?"

"Ciara do good. Baby take time, you know."

"Yes, I know."

"Hesed say Bearstriker come tomorrow, help you walk. Hesed say she sorry. I go now." She left without a further word.

I wondered if Hesed was sorry for refusing to tell me what I wanted to know or if she was sorry Bearstriker was coming to start me walking. The first possibility already stung, and the other could be excruciating.

***

I was right about the sting, and it wouldn't go away, but Bearstriker came to heal, not to hurt. He laced and relaced the stiff boot to his satisfaction and then helped me stand and put weight on my broken leg. I felt discomfort but no pain.

"We'll have you take a few steps tomorrow. If all goes well, you will be walking across the room in a week. A few more steps each day and in a month, you can walk as much as you want. After another month—if all goes well—you'll be walking without the boot, perhaps with a smaller one. I will be here every day for the first two weeks to make sure the boot is right. Don't try to walk without me."

The Indian girl showed up late with my evening meal. She must have been waiting for Bearstriker to leave.

"Baby come. He boy. Ciara good. Hesed sorry she not come. She stay help Ciara. She say you understand."

"Yes, I understand. Thank you for helping me. What is your name?"

"Me . . .? Mary Yellowbird my name."

"Mary? As in the Bible Mary?"

"Yes!" Her eyes flew wide as a smile filled her face. "She love Jesus, wash his feet. Ciara say you go big preacher school, teach people Bible. We have church, no more preacher. You preach us when you better? You teach us Jesus and Bible?"

Her questions caught me off guard. I stammered as I tried to tell this young girl I couldn't preach. I couldn't tell her what she wanted to know. I lied.

"Mary, how old are you?" Anything to change her focus.

"I twelve soon."

"And how old are you right now?" Her long braids seemed like an attempt to grow up too soon.

She glanced out the window, hung her head, and dropped her gaze to the floor.

"I ten now," she whispered.

My heart sank as I watched her shoulders droop. For the first time since I met her, she refused to make eye contact with me.

"Ten is a fine age, Mary, and you speak English well for a ten-year-old. Where did you learn to speak English better than many adults?"

"I hear grownups." She kept her gaze on the floor, but her back straightened, and her shoulders crept upward. "And I hear Hesed. I like hear Hesed. She help me with hard words. I speak Cherokee and English too."

"I speak Cherokee, Mary. Would you like us to speak Cherokee with each other?"

"No!" Her focus darted to my eyes before dropping to the floor again.

I remained silent as innocent eyes crept upward to lock on mine. Her softened voice explained. "I want speak English. I learn. I want you preach English in church." She paused, her child's brow pinched, and her lips pursed into a silent oh . . . "Maybe you preach Cherokee for some. I go now."

Before my eyes, this child matured well beyond her wishful age of twelve.

"I so happy go church." She skipped to the door and departed, a soon-to-be-twelve ten-year-old with her smile and bounce renewed. And she left me with my conundrum.

She brought my meals for the next two days. Her simple delight in serving with every kindness she could think of overpowered my intentions to tell her I couldn't preach. I couldn't force myself to kill her hope of learning and worshipping in church again.

On the second day, after Mary had been gone for a short time and I had finished my evening meal, I heard her unique knock on my door, even though it was open—her way of announcing her presence.

"Come in, Mary."

She bounced into my room with the zeal of a week-old fawn on a warm spring day. I welcomed seeing her again. I missed conversations with Hesed and Ciara. Bearstriker was not so much a conversationalist as he was a healer. Most of the information passed between us concerned my injury and recovery. Anyone to talk to was welcome.

"Mr. Grayhawk, you hear? I have idea."

I chuckled. "I will hear, and I will listen since you're going to tell me anyway."

"You have time leg get better."

"I have too much time and too much boredom. Broken bones heal slowly."

"Ah-hah!" Her triumphant grin flashed for a moment before being replaced by the earnest face of a child on a mission. "I help bakery every morning. Work and deliver finish after lunch. I come here every day. You teach me speak English. I want speak English like Hesed. You teach me? Every afternoon, you teach me? Please?"

"Umm . . . Mary . . . listen to me . . ." I hesitated, then muzzled my response. Ciara's words about preparing these people for their coming new world echoed in my head. This young girl, speaking her broken English, would survive well if her world of today never changed—but tomorrow?

"Please," she whispered.

The image of a body wrapped in a canvas shroud for burial at sea thrust itself into my consciousness—*Luc,* the young French sailor I avoided sharing the full truth of Jesus with because I was afraid of what men might do to me. And I remembered my resolve, made as lashes tore flesh from my back, to tell him everything straight. I also remembered my late resolve was worthless. It was just that—too late.

"Mary."

Those big, expectant eyes focused on mine.

"Yes, I will teach you every afternoon. I will be happy to teach you."

Squeals preceded her words. "I work hard, Mr. Grayhawk. I want speak English like Hesed."

"Yes, Mary, you must work hard, for there is much to learn."

"I work hard. Make you proud. Tomorrow afternoon?"

"Yes, Tomorrow afternoon."

"I go now." She bounced to the doorway.

"Mary."

She stopped in her tracks and fixed questioning eyes on me.

"I am already proud of you."

Her eyes widened as her jaw dropped. An instant later, those eyelids squeezed tight as a grin took over her face. It was still broadening as she flitted from sight.

She brought breakfast the next morning, again prepared by the hotel kitchen. I preferred Hesed's cooking.

"Hesed say she bring dinner tonight. You teach me this afternoon?"

"Yes. I will teach you this afternoon and every afternoon. I will see you then."

"Mr. Grayhawk, what you do horse? You no ride," she shrugged a shoulder and gestured to my thigh-high boot. "Broke leg."

"I think I'll keep him for a while. After my leg heals, I'll ride him again."

"You not like he pull wagon for you?"

"No. I don't think so. It would break his spirit if I put him in traces. He likes his freedom."

"Hmm . . . like Indian pony?"

"Yes, Mary, just like an Indian pony."

She focused dark eyes on me for a long, silent moment.

"You good man, Mr. Grayhawk," she murmured. Then, she was gone.

Mary kept her word about being on time and working hard. Our first lesson went well, considering all the English she knew came from hearing other Indians speak. Except for Hesed, none of them knew much about the English language. Mary could neither read nor write, but she was intelligent and determined. My heart told me I had made the right decision.

Based on my assessment of her, I sent her out for pen and paper on which I intended to prepare lesson plans. Teaching her would be a challenge. I welcomed it. This young Indian girl had crystalized for me the reason for my being here—to help Mary and others like her, prepare for their future. A future bound to be different in ways we could not fathom.

An hour after Mary left, I was sitting in my chair formulating teaching strategies when I heard Hesed and Ciara talking as they entered the house. In a moment, Ciara tottered into my room carrying a blanket-wrapped bundle, which I assumed was her baby. Her expression was a mixture of pride and delight, which I understood, and a manner of apprehension, which puzzled me.

"Congratulations," I said, "how is our new mother, our new mama?"

As I spoke, Hesed slipped into the room, taking a place in the background by the door.

"Our new mama is fine," Ciara said in a trembling whisper. She continued standing in awkward silence.

My heart sank. Something was wrong. She was scared.

Suddenly, she stepped forward and placed the bundle in my lap. She continued holding it until I had it secured in my arms. Then, she stepped back as if to conceal her shaky breathing from me.

I didn't know what to say. Ciara kept her gaze on the bundle and tightened her lips to conceal their quivering. On impulse, I bowed my head over the baby. For the first time in many years, I prayed. In silent conversation, I asked God to somehow make this child healthy and whole.

When I looked up, Ciara stepped forward. "Hesed told me you showed her your scrimshaw," her voice quavered. "Would you show me?"

I scrutinized her face. Why in the world, at a time like this, would she want to see a scrimshaw?

"Please." Her whispered plea sounded frail and nervous—frightened.

I freed a hand from the bundle, slid the scrimshaw from its pouch, and handed it to her. She lifted it near her face to examine it. One hand darted to her mouth to muffle a gasp; I heard it anyway. Tears filled her eyes before she whirled and put her back to me.

Hesed stepped close to her. I was sure the two of them were scrutinizing the scrimshaw. After long moments, Hesed's gaze locked onto Ciara's eyes. With a smile, she gave her confirming nod.

Ciara turned and handed the scrimshaw back to me. She knelt on both knees and started unwrapping the bundle. She lifted a corner of the blanket from the baby's face and beamed up at me with an enormous smile and tear-filled eyes.

"I want you to hold him. He is a perfect little boy," her voice now strong and clear. "His name is Landsdale Ferguson Franklin. We are going to call him Lanny. He is your grandson."

"What?"

"He is your grandson, named Landsdale after you, and Ferguson after Mama. I am your daughter."

"Ciara, I don't have a daughter. I have only a son. I've never seen him. I don't even know his name."

"You were misled about a son."

"Keevah's housekeeper told me herself."

"I know. Mama told them I was a boy. She was afraid if they knew I was a girl, they would try to take me from her. She knew her father well. She wanted to keep me safe—with her. She never told them the truth."

"I have been searching all these years for a son."

"Mama had only one child, my Papa. I am that son, but as you see, I am a girl." All tension was gone from her voice and manner—replaced by sheer joy. "And this little guy is your grandson."

I looked long at the sleeping baby in my lap. A deep burden lifted from my heart and soul. Meaning for life returned.

"Y—you told me your mother died . . ."

"Yes, Papa, I am so sorry." She rested her hand on my arm, much as I remembered Keevah did when we consoled each other on the *Muireann*.

"Mama died the way she lived, giving of herself, caring for others. A few months after her husband, the man I thought was my father, died, Mama told me everything—about you and Bo, her family, the scrimshaw—everything. She gave me her half of the scrimshaw. Hesed has known the entire story for years; I've shared everything with her. She put the pieces together from all you told us and from what you showed her. We were just now checking to see if your half matched mine. They match perfectly.

"Look!" She pulled her half from her apron pocket and reclaimed mine from my hand. She placed the two pieces together, much as Keevah would have done. Despite the contrast of my stained and worn half against the clean ivory of hers, our scrimshaw halves made a perfect ship, the *Muireann.* I stopped myself mid-gasp. Even Ciara's movements were like Keevah's when she used to do that. I knew I would see Keevah in this daughter of mine for the rest of my life. And now, I could thank my God for it.

"Mama's youngest brother, my uncle Kevin, is still alive. The other two ran the shipping business into the ground. Both were lost at sea in the last ship they had—trying to smuggle slaves from the Caribbean Islands. Uncle Kevin and I still write to each other. He will be here in a few weeks.

"Oh, Papa, Mama loved you so much. When my stepfather was alive, she never mentioned you. After he died, she told me everything—so many incredible stories. She never forgot."

"Nor did I, Ciara . . . nor did I. I've missed so much life, so much love."

"Oh, my Papa, the life you missed is not important, it's the miracle of the life you have now that matters—the life we now have together. We are family, Papa. We are family."

Epilogue

A hush settled throughout the small group of people when I rose from my front-row seat beside Ciara. Using a stout cane for balance, I made my way to the front of the little church. With caution, I worked myself into position to sit in the straight-backed chair provided for me. Encased in a thigh-high boot, my foot and knee were impossible to flex in any direction. It took me a few moments to extend my mending leg under the small table placed there for my lectern. Not a sound came from those watching and waiting.

Once settled, I looked around the room, rough-sawn exterior siding being its only walls, and into the eyes of those present. Most of them were Indians of all ages, with a smattering of whites here and there. A multitude of expressions greeted me. Some showed eagerness; some revealed anxiety for my health, and others displayed relief I had accomplished my journey without falling and embarrassing them or myself.

Two soldiers, a grizzled sergeant and a young private, sat in the back. Each wore clean uniforms, with hats in hand, in respect of where they were, rare behavior for the Army in Henrysville, or anywhere in the Territories for that matter. Their countenances gave them away; they were pleased to be among people of kindred spirit, never mind one's skin color.

As my gaze drifted from face to face, I felt a connection with each one, something I had not experienced for many years. Some I knew well: Enoli, the old Cherokee who had fashioned and fitted me with the boot that enabled me to walk, Jack the barber, and the Cherokee healer, Jeremiah Bearstriker, whose frequent visits had brought us closer as I healed. Young Mary, her face beaming, had packed an entire bench with her family. Each offered confidence and nods of encouragement.

A tall Negro minister and his petite wife sat on the third bench to my left. On their right, their young son sat next to his father. On their left, a married daughter and her husband sat close to each other. Appearing rather distinguished now, Elijah and Anna had been thrilled to hear about me as their wagon train stopped near Henrysville for supplies. They told me a young Indian woman recognized their names as she was proofreading an article for the local newspaper. She rode out to invite them to her patient's first worship service.

I smiled to myself; Hesed could heal in many ways.

Dressed in traditional Cherokee attire, Hesed slid down the wooden bench into the seat I had vacated next to Ciara. Her white doeskin dress, plaited sash, and beaded moccasins would make any Cherokee princess proud. And she was deserving of such. The previous evening, she told me the young Cherokee man who moved in unison with her had asked her to marry him. Hesed persuaded me this very morning to conduct the ceremony here in this church. I agreed. Her persistence would have left me no choice had I tried to decline, which I did not.

Ciara's husband sat close by her side and held their infant son, my grandson, Landsdale Ferguson Franklin, in his arms. He and Hesed's young man had returned a week ago from testifying about conditions in the Territory before a U.S. Congressional committee.

Kevin, the youngest of Keevah's three older brothers, sat on the bench behind Ciara. He had arrived from St. Louis two days ago to see his niece and new grandnephew. Though years had added maturity to his face, his demeanor reflected the same determined courage he possessed many years ago in standing up to his brothers and forcing them to sell me into impressment aboard a French ship, thereby saving my life and making this day possible. Ciara, her emerald Keevah's eyes glistening with tears of pride and love, focused with fierce anticipation for my coming words.

Perhaps to gain reassurance from the memory of her mother, I took a second to touch my half of our broken scrimshaw, still hanging around my neck, beneath my shirt. Ciara's hand stole from her lap to her chest. With eyes focused on mine, she tapped the tips of her fingers on a pendant she wore under her dress—the other half of our scrimshaw.

I dropped my gaze and opened Keevah's gift, the sweat and bloodstained Bible I had persisted in carrying yet had failed to open for so many years. After blinking a few times to clear my vision, I silently read the scripture I would share from, a message that for years, had burned within my heart and soul.

"Restore to me the joy of your salvation,

and grant to me a willing spirit, to sustain me."

Psalm 51:12 NIV

I looked up again into the small group before me. Their journeys, some as tangled as mine, had led each of them to this place at this hour. I aimed to know each soul in this room, town, and region. I realized now God had been letting me taste their pain, His mercy, and above all, His grace, preparing me to share His comfort with these hurting people. As I scanned each face, I sensed joy in their eyes. A joy that, despite their earthly hardships, I knew to be eternal.

My gaze settled on my daughter, my son-in-law, and my grandson. The broken scrimshaw of my life was again whole. I had lost my Keevah for the duration of my time on this earth, but in this tiny village and once abandoned church building, I had found true family, a family that included my own flesh and blood. Moreover, I had returned home—to the arms and to the house of my Lord.

HISTORICAL NOTE

On May 30, 1854, the United States Congress passed the Kansas-Nebraska Act, which created the Kansas and Nebraska Territories. The southern border of the Kansas Territory was set at the 37th parallel. As a result, the Indian Territory was reduced to the area now known as the state of Oklahoma. The Bureau of Indian Affairs had previously negotiated treaties with numerous Indian tribes to cede their Kansas Territory lands to the U. S. Government in exchange for reservations on lands elsewhere.

The path to Kansas statehood was a long and bloody struggle between those wanting a free state and others who wanted slavery. Three years of violence between the anti and pro-slavery forces earned the territory the nickname "Bleeding Kansas"—a presage to the American Civil War.

From 1855 through 1859, four constitutions, the second one allowing slavery, were prepared and submitted to the U.S. Congress for statehood approval. None of the first three were approved. A fourth constitution, after ratification by vote of the residents of the Territory, was approved by Congress. Kansas was admitted to the United States as the 34th state, a free state, on January 29, 1861.

Made in the USA
Monee, IL
29 August 2024

64809159R10148